# To Kiss the Purple Moon

## J.P. HICKMAN

To Kiss the Purple Moon
J.P. Hickman

Copyright © 2015 J.P. Hickman
ISBN: 978-0-473-33528-1

Cover design and Interior Formatting by Integrity Formatting
Cover photo by J.P. Hickman
Edited by L.J. Donaldson

# Dedication

*To my beautiful mother,*
*Avril Valerie Hickman*
*flying free with her most precious Jonathan Livingston Seagull*

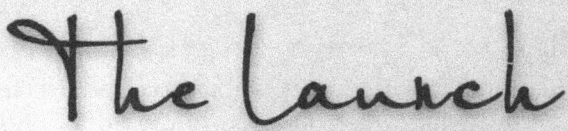

# The Launch

The sun was still a while from waking up, stretching out and peeping over the horizon this early morning, but already the beach was starting to come alive.

It was like this every holiday season. The small coastal town swelling from a laid back local population of around ten thousand to a bustling, viby seventy thousand as the city slickers invaded the beaches, and then as the day went on, the restaurants and pubs.

They had worked the whole year for this four-week period, and now that they had landed, pockets chock-a-block with hard earned cash, it was as if they were fun possessed. They were going and determined, to have fun, and lots of it, spending hard doing so.

This was the time of the year to let it all hang out. And believe me some of them let it all hang out. A kaleidoscope of shapes and sizes. Some that were chocolate to the eyes as the bulges, bumps, boobs and bums winked at you as they walked passed. Perfectly flat, bronzed tummies idly soaking up the golden rays, as they lay on brand new brightly-coloured beach towels.

Then there were the other hangouts: the beer bellies that must have cost a fortune to create. Admittedly, they were more like Brussel sprouts than chocolate to the eyes, but they managed to grab your gaze just as effectively as the 'pleasurables' did. The robust, rounded masses seemed each to have their own personality and greatness, and you just couldn't help wondering what it must be like to carry that load around all day.

The annual gathering was one of those weird human traits. Yesterday dressed up to the nines strutting around the city streets, shopping centres and offices, blindly walking past each other without even being aware who or what was around you. Now not even twenty four hours later, a large sample from the various towns and cities arrive on the beach and strip down in front of each other to half naked, or more.

No one cares and no one minds—quite the contrary they all love it! It's like they have all been drawn to this one place, with common understanding and purpose. Instinct? Habit? Dunno man it seemed to be more than that, it was as though they knew they were all going to be there. Not as individuals but as a cloud of the most beautiful energy. To love, live and play together, even if it was only for four weeks, and even if it cost all their hard-earned cash. They didn't seem to care. They just wanted to be part of it and be together.

They craved this refuelling period, had looked forward to it for the past year. Not even questioning or wondering what the fuel was or where it came from.

They just knew they had to take their fair share on board so that they could make it through the next eleven months.

The locals loved it too! Gosh man, why wouldn't they? Time to get the bank balance into the black again as they reaped the rewards of maintaining and preparing the town for the influx. Beautiful bodies to party with, beer bellies to top up. And most of all feel the buzz that goes around. What was it hey? It was almost tangible. It gave you goose bumps and seemed to go right through you as you were lifted from your local slumber to this crazy, rampant high.

He had been woken up that morning by the skipper banging on the window of the rental and barking out "Oi butthead! Are you going fishing today?" Of course he was, time to make some money. You needed a bit, especially when all the stock from the city was down. They just loved a piece of the coastal boys. Dunno why? Maybe it was something they could talk about and tell their mates about when they got back home, or maybe it was that they knew they could go all out, have a good time, no inhibitions, and then disappear back to the concrete jungle with memories and no baggage to deal with that might taint the reputation. There seemed to be this mystique around the beach boys, and they loved it. For these four weeks they were like pigs in a strawberry patch.

Bouncing outta bed so fast it seemed like his body had reached the door, but when he got there, his brain had been left behind. "Pissed again last night I bet!" said Mike. "Wine women and song hey? You just can't help yourself can you?" Jay's brain caught up with his body and he looked at Mike through his puppy dog blue eyes and just smiled. He knew that Mike would give his left ball to be in his position. He wasn't being scolded. It was just Mike's way of showing his approval, with a tinge of jealousy thrown in. "Better put some pants on before you go any further, you're not climbing into my car in your undies boy," barked Mike.

With the brain now back in place, but not yet quite up to speed, Jay rushed back inside as though the president was now waiting for him, grabbed the first pair of board shorts he could find and half stumbled, half fell his way back out to the car while trying to put them on at the same time as walking. "Looks like it's gonna be a good day weather wise," Mike said in a slightly calmer manner. "How's the ocean looking?" asked Jay, as he by nature looked up for any movement in the clouds, the first sign of any wind to come. "You should know, you were the one prostituting yourself on the beach the whole night," replied Mike. Jay laughed and thought, "Shit man ol' Mike really has a way with words." And then he started wondering how the heck Mike actually knew that he had spent most of the night loving it up on the beach?

And as bubbles of his most recent escapade started entering his brain, his mind drifted as he remembered the warmth, the softness of her skin, and the gentle rush of the ocean in the background. "Oh yes the ocean!" he spoke out aloud as his brain went from left field to right. "There was a bit of a swell running, but nothing too big, and outside, hmmm looked pretty flat hey."

Mike turned the corner to his house and the boat came into view. "Damn you stink of booze man, I could get drunk on the fumes," he muttered. "I didn't have that much to drink hey, couple of beers, and oh yeh one or two tequilas, hmmm and sucked on a brandy when the beer ran out, but that was over the whole night," justified Jay.

Mike glanced across at him, without saying a word, slowly shaking his head. His frown and half closed right eye sort of saying, "So tell me arsehole, how does the whole night mitigate the volume of alcohol consumed?"

Mike pulled into the driveway and they both got out. By now, there was an anticipation in the air. There always was, you just never knew what kinda day it was going to be. So many variables out there in the deep blue. The current, the swell, the surf, the water clarity and colour, what were you going to catch, and how much?

Not saying another word they both headed off in different directions. Preparing and loading the boat was now routine and second nature. Very simply Jay did it all, fuel, rods, reels, bait, tackle etc, while Mike went into the house and organised the sandwiches and coffee for the day.

It didn't matter what Jay was doing, to him, it had to be done right. He wasn't perfect, but he was a bit of a perfectionist. Most probably why Mike enjoyed having him on board. Preparing the boat for going out to sea, going out and being at sea, you needed to have your wits about you. The ocean does not forgive easily without some kind of consequence and there is no local store out there, to pop into to pick up something you forgot behind.

Jay lit up a smoke as he waited for Mike to reappear. Mike seemed to know exactly how long it took to load up and then always, as the boss needed to do, kept the slaves waiting a while just to prove a point.

Walking from the house back towards the boat with

seeming purpose and authority, Mike looked towards Jay, "when ya gonna give that shit up?" he huffed. Which was ironic since he himself had, after smoking his whole life, only just given up three months before.

Jay didn't answer, there was no point. Both hopped into the beat up ol' Landrover, Mike coerced it into life and they wandered off down the road, boat in tow, towards the slipway. Not much was said on the way down, it didn't need to be. They understood each other and were comfortable in each other's company. Funny that because by character they were poles apart. Jay sort of loving, kind and gentle—well on balance anyway, while Mike was brash, demanding and in general full of shit. He seemed to be a bit bitter about life in general, like it owed him something. And of course anyone that had made anything of his or her life was an arsehole. But that was Mike, love him or loath him, that was Mike and he did not actually give a damn what anyone thought of him. Which Jay actually admired.

Jay opened the door and skipped out of the 'Landy,' simultaneously undoing the shackles holding the boat to the trailer and guiding Mike as he reversed the boat down the slipway and into the river. And with both of them working in tandem, and the boat floated, Jay hopped on board fired up both motors, and idled down the lagoon towards the ocean, warming both motors and coming to a gentle nudge onto the beach, while Mike drove the 'Landy' around and onto the beach to meet him.

There was now, depending on the tide, a couple hundred-meter pull across to the ocean. It was a bit of an art to get it all done with the least amount of exertion and without frustrating the hell out of each other, but they had it pretty well waxed. Pull out the winch line, winch the boat up onto the first big air filled rubber "sausage" time the placement of the second sausage and then, just like the roman slaves moved mountains of rock, gently reverse the 'Landy,' pulling and rolling the boat towards the ocean edge. Mike was in control of the vehicle and winch while Jay handled the boat and rollers. It was Mike's time to show the world who was in charge, as he sat in the 'Landy,' steering wheel in one hand winch control in the other, while Jay broke out in an early morning sweat as he worked the rollers from the back of the boat as they popped out, back to the front. It suited them both, Mike was in his fifties and although lean and wiry from the years of fishing, he had done his hard physical apprenticeship, while Jay, in his early twenties, loved the excursion, the challenge of getting this eighteen foot of boat across the beach and into the water.

The early risers, locals included, but in particular the townies down on holiday loved watching it all. So different to their daily grind back in the city. Same planet, but so different they could have been on the moon. You could see those close by were intrigued, even impressed and were dying to be part of it all. But they knew to keep their distance, this was a bit out of their comfort zone and the combination of surf, sand, sweat, cables, motors and boat was a potentially lethal combination.

Now came the tricky bit, the last couple of meters where the boat had to be pushed in by hand. Misplace and let it fall off the rollers and the wrath of Mike would be unleashed. Admittedly, more bark than bite, but no one needed a noise to break the beauty of this magnificent morning, especially with an audience. Jay uncoupled the winch cable from the boat, fed the remaining cable back onto the winch then stripped down to his undies, throwing his pants into the front boat hatch to keep dry, as Mike drove the 'Landy' out from in front of the boat, hopped out, and then together they rolled the boat into the shore break.

Jay loved this part of it all. Alone, warm salt water rolling in under eighteen foot of fibreglass, while he manipulated it by holding onto the back of the two outboard motors and simply directing the nose into the surf. Rising and falling with the boat as the water heaved her up and down. It was impressive to watch and, yeh, took a reasonable amount of skill and experience to prevent being sandwiched between the boat and the beach, cut open by the props or drenched.

He stared out to sea, his favourite place in the world. The sun had now just risen above the horizon and it was the most beautiful, gentle, golden yellow you could imagine. The fireball reaching out and tinging the sky in a waft of golden oranges, pinks and blues, in the way only nature can do. He could taste the delicious salt in the sea spray, smell the myriad of ocean delights, feel the contrast of the enveloping liquid around his legs and squeaky clean sea sand beneath his feet. His whole being became light as it was flooded with the juices of nature that fed deep into his soul and he was at total peace. The boat had now become one, and moved with the energy of the ocean, and so did he.

Mike parked the 'Landy' at the top of the beach, just at the foot of the mighty dunes and then sauntered down towards the boat. He never hurried back, he was still proving to the audience who was in charge, and how powerful he actually was. Jay let the shore break bring the boat back up the beach a far as possible, Mike timed the surge, and without even getting a foot wet jumped over the transom and walked up to the controls. With both the motors still hitched up, and their props staring eagerly up at Jay as he stood behind them, he pushed forward on them as he worked with the ocean to 'refloat' the boat and move her into deeper water.

This is where it could all go horribly wrong, they were working at opposite ends of the boat, Mike wasn't looking at Jay or what he was doing, he was looking towards the ocean and waves that were coming towards him. Mike was the one that was going to fire the 150 horse power into life while Jay was the one standing in and around the horses, waiting to open the gates to let them go. There would be blood and bone and lots of it sprayed all over the place if the timing was out. Not much was said at this point, there was too much noise, so they used all their other senses to intuit what the other was doing; it sometimes seemed that they communicated through a sixth sense. Stuff just happened in harmony, without any sign of a signal or command being given.

Jay got the boat to water deep enough for the motors, Mike flicked the ignition switches and the motors cracked and brayed into life, ready to bolt the hell outta there at the first opportunity. Jay vaulted up on board between both the motors, spun around and unhitched both of them in a flash, dropping them below the water, which gurgled and grunted through the exhaust outlets. Mike engaged both motors, and held back just long enough for Jay to walk up to the front of the boat and stand alongside him before he cracked the whip. The boat reared up out of the water, the motors neighed and snorted in excitement as they powered forward, the boat coming down gently onto the plane, striding out into the most perfect silky gallop.

Mike was now on stage for the whole beach to see. The launch had, so far, gone like clockwork; he had proved his ability on the beach, and it was now time to show off in the ocean. The craft slid up and over the rolling, white, broken surf and up towards the big backline. Nature's mesmerising wall of emerald green and blue billowing towards them had Mike transfixed. Powerless to react, to let go of the mighty volume of energy before him until the very last second when self preservation kicked in. Milliseconds before catastrophe, he throttled back hard and went into a sharp180 degree turn. With the thunderous might of the ocean breathing down on their tail, he opened her up again, galloping back towards the beach.

The spectators' breath taken, either in awe, or just wishing they were on board as Mike pulled back on the reigns just before overshooting the shore break, slowed, but kept the craft on the plane, put her into a broad sweeping turn aiming her back out to sea. Then he repeated the whole ride over and over again until the ocean relented and opened her arms to allow them in.

The break had come on about the third circle and Mike let her go. Boat and motors air borne over the broken wave. Then, as though on ice, we shot out over clean water to the back line zone, throttling back as we were lifted effortlessly by two to three meters of the newly forming swell. Then, we were out.

Jay now lost in his own bubble thought, "Wow, what just happened man? It's taken over an hour from jumping outta bed to this "here and now," and it's all just been an emptiness of peace and perfection." What he didn't realise or comprehend it at this stage, was that it happens to everyone, not the same journey, but the same buzz and high from life, when circumstance and situation allows a rush of a thousand beautiful energies to enter through all your possible senses and membranes.

Mike manoeuvred the boat up to and between the shark nets as Jay untied the hatches, took the bait box out and moved to the back of the boat. It was a half hour journey out to the fishing grounds and even though the motors had, and would persist to break the natural sounds of the ocean, Jay could lose himself again, in the sights, smells, motions, temperatures and textures that flooded his whole being.

The frozen squid had softened a bit as he sliced through their bodies to remove the guts, throwing it into the "kaleidoscope" wash created by the motors. The bait had to be sliced and ready to go by the time they got to Mike's chosen spot in the ocean. Not for any reason apart from that that was the way Jay operated.

Mike slowed the boat as he got to the fishing grounds, Jay unlocked and dropped the depth sounder and prepared the anchor and rods while Mike searched for the hidden pinnacles deep down below. "Hmmm what would the ocean produce today?" Jay wondered. "Get ready!" commanded Mike, "there's some decent sign of fish down there; we'll take a drift over it and see if it's worth throwing the pick." Jay picked up his rod and stabilised himself with his knee on the gunnel. Mike, taking the drift and breeze into account positioned the boat, took the motors outta gear and switched them off.

The whole mood instantly changed as the mechanical bark of the motors was replaced with the sound of the caressing wash of the ocean against the boat. "Ok go!" Mike said in a tone that suggested he was commanding the launching of the space shuttle. Jay threw his rig over the side, controlling the reel deftly with one hand while allowing the one kilogram of lead to take the stream of a dozen baited hooks down into the deep blue as quickly as possible. Mike swivelled around on his chair watching Jay's every move, if there was fish on the feed he did not want to miss out. The sinker hit the bottom; Jay took up the slack and almost instantly heaved the big rod back, winding furiously at the same time. His rod doubled over as it took up the strain of a big one. They were here! "Must be Geelbek," said Mike unable to contain his excitement. Then realising the rush of energy had allowed his mouth to lose control, he tried to make amends by giving further instruction "Don't lose the bloody thing now, we need the money." And just in case Jay didn't know by now, continued with, "this boat cost a fortune to run!"

"Yeh, feels like a Geelbek" confirmed Jay, his whole body tuned into counteracting every evasive manoeuvre the fish made to stay alive. Just over halfway up the fish succumbed to the change in pressure, its air bladder blew up and the fight became a whole lot easier. Mike gaffed the fish on board; it was Geelbek. They both knew this was a "shoal fish" and where there was one, there were plenty more. This was going to be a good payday!

# The First Encounter

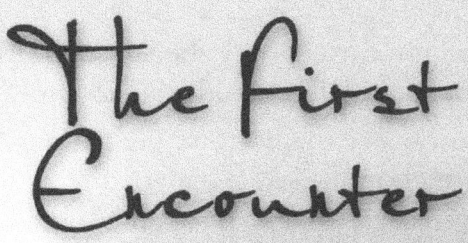

With the first fish on board, Mike didn't hesitate; they didn't want to drift too far off. There are no road signs out there and if you lost the spot, you may not be able to find it again. He started up the one motor, swung the boat around and headed slowly back up to where he believed the fish were. With the depth sounder ticking away Jay got ready to throw the anchor. "Got them," Mike mumbled, implying that there never really was a chance of him not finding the spot again. He continued idling up ahead of the fish sign, anticipating where the current would allow the boat to sit once the anchor had hooked up. "Ok now!" he barked, and Jay let the anchor go.

As it plunged down into the watery depths he kept control through the rope so that the chain attached to the grapple did not fowl the whole system up. This would render the anchor useless and they would drag the whole lot right through the shoal of fish. And hmmm if that did happen, Mike would lose his rag.

The anchor hit the bottom; Jay fed out enough rope to let the anchor lie down, then tied it up to the bollard on the nose of the boat. The anchor dragged for a while and then grabbed. "Phew, so far so good" thought Jay. They waited for the boat to settle and then in what seemed to be an orchestrated action, they picked up their rods, threw their traces over board and down they went. Both sinkers reaching the sea floor together; they tightened up the loose line, and waited, every nerve alive and ready to react to whatever attacked from below.

But, nothing! Not a touch. "Shit" spewed Mike. "You should have let it go earlier." Jay didn't respond, he knew he had dropped it according to instruction and it was futile debating it anyway. Mike was always right! "I'll let out some more rope," said Jay as he fixed his rod in the holder. Two meters, ten meters then . . ."I'm in!" barked Mike. Jay tied off the rope and before he could make it back to his rod it was straining in the holder. "Me too. Wahooo!"

For the next couple of hours they loaded the boat with fish. It was physical, but fun. Their backs bent, muscles straining. The sun beating down on their backs, they were in heaven. One of those days where it all comes together. The elements, the ocean, the fish, all playing their part. Even when Mike's next fish was taken by a shark and after wrestling with it for a while when he lost his whole trace, he couldn't stop his cynical, jovial banter. "Bloody shark, the taxman, just has to take his piece of my pie." Which was ironic in itself given that he hadn't actually paid a cent of tax in his life.

"Where's that bloody coffee? I take you out, put you

on the fish and you can't even pour me a cup of coffee. No damn fucking respect you youngsters." Jay put down his rod and poured the coffee. "Wanna sandwich?" asked Mike. Shit man they were only apricot jam sandwiches, but always perfectly made on the freshest bread. Mike knew that Jay hadn't eaten, and more than likely wouldn't eat again for a while after they got off the boat. He knew that Jay had been waiting for this sandwich. "Thanks man," Jay replied reaching out and taking one. They both sat there in silence eating and drinking. Soaking in the luxury of being in this very special place. The luxury of being surrounded by the fruits of Mother Nature, the Garden of Eden for the soul. An endless bounty of the most perfect energies to feed off of, rejuvenate and grow the spirit.

It could have been minutes; it could have been hours, neither one of them cared. They just sat there enjoying the moment in time, in paradise. Then one of the fish thrashed around in the hatch triggering Mike into action. "Oi time to gut these fish, we gotta get back and get these fish to the buyer before the day runs out," he said in sort of a half polite manner. He knew that this was a bugger of a task, he knew how proficient Jay was at getting it done and did not want to rock the boat. He knew that if Jay felt like it, he would slow up and Mike would be forced to get stuck in too. "Another sandwich?" bartered Mike. Yeh, that would be good," Jay smiled. He could read Mike like a book.

"Ok when ya finished eating we'll pull the anchor, then if you can start gutting the fish we'll drift for a while and I will see if I can pick up a couple of reds for the pan." Another one of Mike's coercive tactics to avoid picking up a knife, knowing that Jay would not say no to the potential of taking a fish home for diner. But it worked for both of them so Jay just got stuck in to the task at hand. He sort of enjoyed it anyway. The fish they had caught was food from the Creator. It needed to be treated with dignity and respect. It was the transfer of energy from one being to another. There was no margin for waste. Even the guts of the fish themselves created a feeding frenzy. Sea birds squawked and jostled for the best pieces as they were thrown overboard, the little 'Cuda' birds backing their agility to flit in and out, taking prime cuts from right under the powerful beaks of the slow and deliberate gulls. Small fish appeared out of thin water to get their fair share too.

"How's that one?" said Mike as he pulled a nice fat, red Englishman on board. Jay knew what was coming next. "Ok that one's mine, now I'll see if I can get you something." Mike just could not help himself. Jay put down the knife, washed his hands overboard and started reaching for his rod. "Ok, ok man we'll share it if that's all I get, shit man you are such an arsehole, just carry on gutting the fish, don't you want to get paid?" Mike said in a totally non-threatening voice.

Then "Dorado!" shouted Mike out aloud. The word spoken at a level of excitement that switched Jay automatically back into action. They were big game fish that were attracted to floating objects, especially if there was activity around those objects. But you had to be quick, they didn't stick around too long, but when they were feeding they would eat just about anything, so Jay just took his existing rig and threw it overboard, allowing the hooks to sit about a meter underwater. It was almost a surreal kind of fishing. You saw the fish, you saw it coming up and taking your bait, then, mayhem. They fought like crazy and gave one of the best aerial displays that is only second to that of marlin and sailfish. Mike had already winched his line back up off the bottom and it wasn't long before he was hooked up too. Jay's fish relented, and came alongside beaten and tired.

It was one of the most beautiful fish you could get from the ocean. Sort of like the magnificent colours and unique shape of the tropical fish you would see in the tank of a foyer in a hotel, only, the fish was a huge amount bigger. A big blunt and rounded forehead, tapering into a sleek and powerful body. A white underbelly moving through to bold yellows, emerald greens and majestic royal blues. The fish never really adhering to any particular fashion, with the range of displays changing with its mood and condition.

Jay had grown to love the look and vibrancy of the Dorado. He reluctantly gaffed it and brought it on board. It's funny how he had changed as he had fished through the years. In the beginning, everything and anything was just a fish. Now after years on the water, something had changed within him, and he couldn't work it out. Some fish looked like they were food and were meant to be taken, while others, like the Dorado, seemed to "ask you questions" when they came on board. And although they were very, very tasty, it just did not seem right to remove them from the ocean for your wealth and pleasure.

Two Dorado, a couple of reds and a hatch full of Geelbek, Mike called time, started up the motors, kicked them into gear, and pointing the nose of the boat towards the towers on the distant hill, started cruising back towards the beach. Masterfully timing his run to planned perfection ensuring that Jay had gutted the last of the fish, washed them and put them back in the hatch just as they got to the shark nets.

Mike was now faced with another routine quandary. The beach was still packed to capacity. A holiday season special. He knew that he was again forced to be polite and friendly to the lifeguards on duty. It was now up to them to dictate where he would beach the boat. Close to the lagoon, or however many hundreds of meters further down the beach they liked. They knew ol' Mike well. They knew that he was a person as full of shit as you could get. Harmless, but full of shit, generally impatient and who had already let the pro lifeguards know what he thought about them and their profession on more than one occasion. Mike knew how hard they had to train to stay in shape, to be able to tackle the unrelenting waves, rip tides and currents. He knew how they had on many occasions forgone all self-preservation to rescue tired and almost lost souls from the jaws of a watery grave. Their sacrifice, diligence and commitment to protect the thousands of people they never even knew. But he always only reminded them of how lucky they were to spend hours on the beach, and get paid for doing so. How they spent all their time perving at the boobs, bellybuttons and bums rather than keeping their eyes on the swimmers. So yeh, it was more envy than anything else and the lifeguards knew it, they knew he didn't actually mean everything he said, but still, they loved winding him up. And now again it was their time to remind Mike that they too had power to dictate and command, if and when they wanted to.

But every now and again everyone seemed to be on the same wavelength, and this was one of those days. Most probably, and even most obviously, because everyone had been flooded with the same incredible juices of nature the whole day, and they just couldn't help gorging themselves on them. Now they were just too satisfied to let it all change. Subconsciously they wanted it to go on forever.

"Mike to tower, Mike to tower, come in please." They had heard him, they couldn't not have, they had seen him coming in from miles away, stop and circle just outside back line while he called. But as humans will be humans, and even though everyone was having a good day, they just could not resist dictating, at least for a couple of minutes of Mike's day. He knew it too. "Fucking arseholes, bloody lifeguards supposed to be a professional service and they can't even pick up the radio. What if it was an emergency? Too bloody busy perving, I bet! Wankers!" he spat.

"Is that you Mike?" They just knew they had given him enough time to rant. Clicking instantly back to his friendly mode, knowing that they still had him by the 'short and curlys.' "Yeh Mike here, how's it going today?" The lifeguards not finished with him yet and putting the screws on replied. "Hey, it's pretty packed down on the beach, dunno where it will be best for you to come in?" "We got a full load on board, even got a fish here for you blokes, I was hoping to come in as close to the lagoon as possible." Shit man butter would not have melted in his mouth. There was a long silence as the lifeguards weighed up Mike, the hard arse vs Mike, the fisherman. They knew there was almost no chance they would get a fish either. Mike always conveniently forgot about it until he was well off the beach and it was too late to turn around. "Come in Mike." "Yeh receiving" "Ok wait until we go down and clear the beach and then I will call you to come in. Come in straight in front of the lagoon." "Message received. Standing by," he replied. The siren wailed signalling to bathers to get out of the water, while two volunteer lifeguards were ordered to run down and clear a path for the boat to beach. "Come in Mike." "Yeh receiving" "Ok you can come in now. Come in on the flag and keep a look out for bathers and beach goers." "Thanks a million! Over and out." Mike switched off the radio. "Fucking wankers," he muttered.

Jay couldn't help smiling and chuckling to himself. "Mike will be Mike and will always be Mike," he thought, and continued, "wonder what could have switched him, or has he always been like this from birth? Then answered himself, "naah surely you can't be born bitter and twisted?"

Reality, time and motion kicked Jay back outta dream world as Mike suddenly opened up the horses and powered the boat towards the shore. They were now both back into sixth sense mode, no time, no space, no silence to be able to communicate through normal portals. Liven all the senses you have and suck in the signals available including the ones you can't see, taste, smell, feel or hear. Don't try comprehending it all, just do it. Become empty, alive and at one with creation.

The timing and selection had to, once again, be perfect. Read the water, choose your flat between two waves and hold steady pace between them. Too slow you get caught, turned sideways and flipped. Too fast, overshoot, breach and flip. Then the last dash for the beach. Hold back, hold back, hold back, giving yourself as much water as possible, wait for it to run up the beach and then bolt. You wanted to be left high and dry.

Bugger it up and you land up half in and half out of the ocean. The boat would then be at the mercy of the relentless shore break, pushing her from side to side and flooding the deck with water. Naah, this had to be done right, especially with the full house watching and waiting.

After so many launches and beaching's under his belt, Jay had worked out how to pull both monster motors up into the hitched position at once, just after the boat hit the beach. This was a feat that everyone watching admired. Mike of course claimed credit for it; after all, who do you think trained Jay?

With Mike now gunning it for the beach Jay walked back towards the motors, and facing out to sea, steadied himself with his thighs against the motors, leaning out over and holding onto the back of them. As Mike hit the beach the momentum surging Jay backwards and assisted by the kick of the skegs hitting the beach, both motors eased up and locked in place. Roaring, hissing and spitting water and sand until Mike shut them both down.

What a rush, and now again, what a contrast. Wet and wild, hair-raising and deafening, to instantly, high and dry, motionless and silent. Isolated in perfect nature, to surrounded by a throng of humanity.

Mike jumped off and strode casually towards where the 'Landy' was parked, while Jay sat there for a moment as the sounds of the beach drifted slowly back into his consciousness, inquisitive onlookers coming in for a closer look. He stood up, untied the hatch and took off the cover for everyone to have a look at the bounty. He allowed a couple of exuberant kids to jump on board and get a closer look. It was part of the unique holiday experience and vibe that he enjoyed. The bubbliness, the different characters, the banter, the questions, the praise and admiration.

But this time there was something strangely different. There was a warmth, a connection, a silent powerful buzz. He jumped down onto the beach, it always seemed a lot more solid than when he had left it early in the day. Sort of like the feeling you get after you get off of a trampoline. Like the force of gravity had doubled. His body was bronzed by hours in the sun, glistening with a feint touch of perspiration, his long, dark hair bleached at the tips, muscles pumped and honed. The white lines of dried salt giving his skin texture.

What was it, what could he feel? Slowly he turned around and there it unmistakably was. She was looking straight at him. They stared directly into each other's eyes for what seemed like forever. Jay was confused. Who was she? Did he know her? Everything and everyone around him was a blur. It was as though she was standing on a stage commanding the performance and attention; the supporting actors were peripheral and were just taking up space around her. He could feel his body getting hot. A blast of the most delicious energy reaching deep into his inner most parts and without intention or knowing why he started moving towards her. Drawn to and wanting to bathe in more of what ever it was she had.

Then suddenly, he was brutally ripped away. "Hey, what the hell are ya doing boy, get the eff'ing winch out and hooked up, your day hasn't finished yet!" shouted Mike out the window of the 'Landy.' And without hesitation Jay got back to work reversing this morning's proceedings, getting the boat rolled up over the beach and back into the lagoon. He didn't have time to think until just before Mike drove off back around to the slipway leaving him with an envious, "Can't you concentrate on anything except pussy for just one day?" "Crikey man, give it a rest!"

The boat now waiting patiently on the edge of the lagoon rocked as Jay leapt onboard and ignited both motors. He turned the boat upstream towards the slipway and at last had another chance to look around for her. He could already feel she wasn't there anymore, but refused to trust his instincts as he scoured the crowd and beach for her. But he was right, she was gone.

# The Bartering

The fish buyers were already at the slipway when Jay
cruised up towards it. He clicked the boat motors outta
gear and shut them both down. The boat sighed as she
nudged and rested herself up and onto the banks of the
lagoon. Jay strolled to the back of the boat and lifted up
both motors. He knew what was coming next, that
inexplicable and frustrating human trait of bartering. No
one ever seemed to be able to just agree up front on a
fair price for goods and services. They had to squeeze
for every extra cent. It didn't seem to matter exactly how
much they could actually squeeze, but it was more a kind
of show of power in their own individual, private world.

Money in hand gave them this power and they could
not resist the urge to impose it. And even though the
word had already got out over the boat radio waves that
the Geelbek salmon had been feeding well all along the
coast that day, the buyer asked Jay in an unknowingly

expectant voice "How'd ya go today?" "Not too bad hey, got a full hatch of Geelbek." "Pheeew! Dunno if we will be able to take it all, hey," whistled the buyer. "Still got a freezer full from what we picked up earlier today from the other boats," he continued. Jay knew this was bullshit; the buyers supplied a city of more than five million just sixty kilometres north, and they wouldn't even be able to make it to the city before selling out to their customers along the road back home. "Yeh well, speak to Mike," Jay said nodding at the Land Rover now turning in and winding its way down towards them.

Mike was ready for them. He idled the 'Landy' to the front of the trailer. Jay automatically lifting it up, and as Mike nursed the 'Landy' forward he dropped it onto the hitch, locking it in place. The jolt triggering Mike to put the 'Landy' into reverse and then positioned it on the slipway in front of where Jay had now positioned the boat. No one spoke as Jay pulled out the winch cable, hooked it up to the boat and then worked in unity with Mike, easing her up out of the water and onto her bed of cushioned tubular steel. A concert of silent energies being transferred backwards and forwards between man and man, between man and machine, wire ropes, steel, fibreglass, the water and the earth beneath. All working in harmony to achieve success without incident. One transgression, one diversion of energy to the incorrect destination and there could be a finger lying on the ground, a hole in the boat or similar accompanied by the associated pain and or fury.

With the curtains closing, Mike now looked across at the buyers. This is where his full-of-shitness worked in his favour. "Hope you got full pockets of money, 'cause if you haven't Marty wants the lot," he said in a rehearsed matter of fact manner. He knew that you never sold or bought half a load, it was all or nothing, an unwritten law of commercial fishing and fish buyer pride. It was a sign of weakness, vulnerability and failure not to be able to afford the lot. The buyer tried again, "Shit! Dunno hey Mike, freezers are still full up from earlier today. Battling to get rid of it all," he persisted. Mike didn't say anything, but not breaking eye contact with the buyer, reached for his phone. "How much ya got?" asked the buyer before Mike was even able to touch a button. "Got about a ton, Marty wants the lot for seven bucks a kilo." "Seven bucks, shit man I'm only getting 7.50 and I still gotta get it to where it's going." Another lie, the fish were retailing for twenty so the wholesale price was around ten or twelve bucks. Mike started dialling some number that didn't exist and put the phone to his ear. "Ok man, I'll take it, for fuck sakes. You're a hard bastard. I got a family to feed as well you know," the buyer said in the most despairing voice he could conjure up.

And with the deal done and dusted, the two slaves, Jay and the buyer's sidekick loaded the fish from the boat into the vehicle's massive chilly box, while Prince Mike and the buyer counted out and exchanged the cash. You knew that the buyers had got the best part of the bargain, the middle men always do, and now that the deal was done and the pain of letting go of the hard cash was over, the buyer beamed a huge smile as he waved goodbye and accelerated up the slipway and out of sight.

Mike had buried the cash in the 'Landy' and walked over to where Jay was finishing cleaning up and washing everything down. "Fucking arseholes, they just never give up trying to screw you," he said. Mike had dropped his guard for an instant and Jay saw the weariness and

hurt in his face. He wondered again what had turned
Mike from this seemingly inherently compassionate
spirit into the hard arse he now portrayed and lived.
"Yeh, well business is business," said Jay, trying to let
Mike know that he should not take it personally.
"Fucking arseholes," he mumbled again. And then
sensing he was being advised by Jay, retook control of
his emotions "You still busy? Thought you would have
finished up by now? Gotta get moving man. Fuck I bet
you still got that bit of fluff you saw on the beach earlier
today on your brain."

Jay didn't have an immediate comeback. He knew,
even though he would never admit it to Mike that he
couldn't actually get her out of his mind. But now that
Mike had brought it up, even though by pure
coincidence, Jay did start to wonder how much of an
effect she had, had on him. Jay was a bit of a player.
Loved parties, music, loved living and loving life, having
fun and he loved women. But, "gosh never felt like that
before!" he thought. His mind continued on, "Shit, man!
I felt her before I saw her and when I saw her, phew!
The heat man the heat. What was that?"

They didn't say much more, if anything, on the way
back to Mike's house. They just enjoyed the ride and
each other company. Mike reversed the boat back into
her spot in his garden, Jay unhitched the trailer, then
unloaded all the tackle and stuff, packed it away in the
outside room and then waited around for Mike to go in
and come back out of his house.

This was the ritual of paying the slaves. Mike with his
paymaster façade strides out, shoulders back, chest out,
his whole understanding and acceptance hurting like hell
knowing that he has got no choice but to let go of the

dosh. Looking straight at Jay, "Fuck, this boat costs a fortune to run" and then waited for a response. Jay lit up a smoke. "I had to give that shit up you know, couldn't afford it anymore." This game of poverty Mike incessantly played at this point in a day's fishing normally got to Jay, but for some reason, today; he didn't actually give a shit.

With Jay not playing the game Mike continued. "Ok, you got four hundred and seventy kgees, at two bucks that's nine forty I owe you," he said looking away and thrusting the cash out towards Jay as though it was too hard for him to actually witness the visually departing of it for too long. "Thanks Mike that was a really cool day." "Yeh, well don't go and piss it all up against a wall now. And don't go whoring around tonight either. I want to get going early bells tomorrow and go have another crack while they're still out there." "No worries," said Jay as he wandered off back down the road. Mike let him go a distance then yelled out, "What about your fish for dinner, don't you want it? Got too much money now or something? Jay jogged back. "Shit! Sorry man, I forgot all about it." Mike handed him the fish, looked into his eyes and said, "She really did get inside your head, hey?" "Was it that obvious" thought Jay, but then dismissed the possibility thinking "Naah not that obvious, just that Mike and him had always been able to read each other without talking anyway." "Just been a long, hard, fun day," said Jay breaking into a broad smile. "Thanks for the fish, and the day out on the big blue, I'll catch ya tomorrow morning."

Off he went for the second time. Mike stood there watching him go. He didn't know why, he just did. It wasn't concern, admiration or anything else he could put his finger on. It was just like a wondering, a wondering as to what had got inside of Jay today. Without even knowing it, Jay felt Mike's eyes on him, turned smiled and gave Mike a thumbs up, then continued on home. Mike shook his head involuntarily for no apparent reason, turned and walked towards his house.

# The Demanding Request

When Jay got back to his place, the sun was well down behind the horizon; it wasn't dark yet, the sky just that magnificent, majestic blue with streaks of bright, pinky, orange as the sun bid farewell for the day. Jay looked up towards it and instinctively thanked the Creator for the magnificence. "Hmmm," he thought, "What are we doing down here? So much beauty, so much fun, so much delicious life to live, love and experience, but all the shit you have to go through as well? Where are we actually headed? Is there even a final destination?" Jay loved having conversations with himself. He wondered who he was actually talking to in his head. It was weird because sometimes he would be asking questions and then other times answering them, or at least receiving the answers. "Is there more than one of me inside there somewhere?" he asked himself, smiling at the thought. "Gees—two of me, that would freak ol' Mike out," he spoke out softly as his smile broadened.

Jay hadn't opened the door yet; the changing sky had had him transfixed and had sent his mind into space. Then, the phone rang, jolting him back to the here and now. He hurriedly lifted up the pot plant, got the key, opened up and jogged through to pick up the phone. "Jay, hello." "Hey what's up? I heard you guys smashed it today?" "Hey El, yeh got about a ton hey . . . so yeh good day out . . . what about you . . . how was the surf today?" "Shit man, mind blowing, seriously, couldn't get out the water, just wave after wave after wave." El sneaked in a quick breath not allowing Jay to respond yet, and continued, "and then the talent on the beach . . . fuck seriously man you slipped up today!" he blurted out.

It was one of those conundrums Jay had, had to get used to. If the weather was lining up for a good beach day, he would be out on the water fishing, and in a way, miss out. He didn't mind too much though. He had weighed it all up before; the pros, no nine to five boring ol' job, and going fishing allowed him to be regularly isolated from the hustle and bustle of humanity for hours on end on the beautiful ocean. Both reasons far outweighed the cons of missing out on a surf or two and a bit of perving the talent on the beach. He knew as well, that most of the real holiday action happened at night anyway, so all in all the sacrifice was worth it.

Jay wasn't really concentrating on the conversation and didn't respond to El's excited enthusiasm of the day gone by and his insinuated potential for scoring with the holiday 'hotties' later on, so El persisted. "So where we gonna go tonight?" He didn't ask if Jay was keen to even go out or not. That was a given in holiday season, and a pocket full of cash to go with it made it a forgone conclusion. "Dunno hey, I'm a bit worn out and looks like I got an early start tomorrow," replied Jay. "Fuck ooooff," said El in a drawn out exaggerated 'you gotta be kidding me' kinda voice. "Seriously," said Jay trying to sound as convincing as he could, and at the same time feeling strangely uncomfortable that he was actually even contemplating missing a night out and not really understanding why. Jay continued before El tried to persuade him otherwise. "Just got back 5 minutes ago, still got a fish to fillet, then clean up and stuff, so yeh, might give it a miss tonight, hey." "Whatever! Don't be a pussy man, I've already done the spade work. Shit man, all you have to do is rock up and you will get laid tonight. I've already told them that you will be coming along." "Who's them?" asked Jay. "Two of the most delicious pieces you have seen man. I pointed you out to them when you came in this arvo, and the one has the real hots for you already."

Jay was always a bit dubious of El's predetermined picks. There was always at least one hot babe amongst his selection, but they had already been earmarked for his attention and even though it hadn't always worked out as he had planned, there had been times when Jay had been saddled for the night with the 'hotties' not so hot best friend, just to suit the satisfaction of El's desires.

"Think I'll give it a miss, man," repeated Jay, "wanna be fresh for tomorrow. "Could be another big day out to sea and I want to smack it if it is." And before El could respond, just to beef up his declination with some facts of life, added in a slightly sarcastic manner, "haven't all got the luxury of a prepaid five day a week job like you know. I gotta take advantage of the fish running with the weather lining up while I can."

El was still buzzing from his day on the beach and his anticipation of the night to come and didn't want to be brought down by Jay's seemingly ungrateful response. "Ok, bro, but don't say I didn't think of you first. I'll give Steph a ring; I know he'll be keen." "Sweet, I'll catch up with you tomorrow then," replied Jay, relieved at El's submission. "You really are a girl," said El. "I can't believe it, but anyway, your loss, catch ya later."

Jay put the phone down, thankful that he had got away with it so lightly, but also sort of confused as to why he had turned El's night out down. Pre-organised stock ready and waiting was always a really good way to round off a solid day out to sea.

Jay went back through to the kitchen, picked up the fish, sharpened the filleting knife and deftly separated the pure white flesh from the bone. He thought back on the day, the sunrise, the launch, the fishing, then with his brain on autopilot, the girl he saw on the beach jumped back into his head. The thought from his head was converted into a rush of ice-warm goose bumps, which washed across his arms and shoulders. He lingered in the moment and the juices for as long as the energy exuded would allow, before it left his body and continued on with its infinitive journey. Snapping back to the here and now, he packed the fish away in the freezer and headed off towards the shower. The warm, gentle, steamy water allowing him to drift off again. "Who was she?" he thought. He wracked his brain. "School days? Uni days? Previous holiday seasons? Some party or night out? A friend of a friend?" The self-questioning went on and on, but he couldn't recall any previous encounter.

He got out the shower, dried off, threw on some

shorts, grabbed a 6-pack from the fridge, went through to the front porch overlooking the garden and lit up a smoke. "Wonder if she will be there tomorrow?" he asked himself. "What should I do if she is?" Jay knew he didn't have the answers and was getting frustrated with himself for letting her have such an affect and impact on his private time, so he consciously let her leave his thoughts, emptied his mind and let it fill with the delectable energies of nature and the evening available all around him.

Half-a-dozen empty beer bottles later the night was halfway through and he still hadn't moved from where he was sitting staring up at the stars. He was glad he hadn't gone out; he didn't feel like he had missed out on anything. Quite the contrary, he had loved the time alone just soaking up the feel, sights and sounds of a crystal clear night. Lost and beautifully alone, unconsciously meditating with the universe, creation and Creator.

# The Ridicule

Jay was already waiting by the boat when Mike came out the house. Mike was looking down, fumbling through his pockets for the car keys, still expecting to have to go and drag Jay out of bed, so was startled when Jay wished him good morning. "What the fuck, you nearly gave me a heart attack, you idiot," said Mike. Jay accepting Mike's greeting as a compliment cheekily returned fire, "can't sit around the whole day waiting for the old folk to get going. Shit, man, the fish will be half way across the ocean if I have to wait for you to get started." "You're full of shit!" said Mike. Jay laughed 'cause he knew he was being full of it. Mike was normally up at sparrows fart and always had to use every technique available to get Jay up and out of bed.

But although Jay was always full of fun and generally at peace with what was going on in the world, today he just seemed to be that much more energetic and alive.

And having the jump on Mike, he continued with his jovial onslaught. "So what happened Mike? You get stuck on the nest this morning, or did you get on the piss last night?" Mike was still on the defensive, and could only respond with. "Hey, why haven't you packed the boat yet?" "Because you got the keys to the backroom." "Well here they are, get it sorted, I'm gonna get the coffee and sandwiches ready. Shit you have fucked up my whole routine this morning, why couldn't you just wait for me to come pick you up?" grumbled Mike. Jay smiled to himself. Only Mike could legitimately crap on a person for helping him out and believe he was still right. One last bullet ensued. "Any cheese to go with the bread and jam today, hey Mike?" "Fuck off, and get busy! We're late already," came the predicted response.

By the time Mike came back out he had composed himself, regained his position of dominance, and as they both climbed into the 'Landy' just couldn't wait to get 'it' out. "Ya know what?" he asked, and before Jay could respond, "you just can't wait to see her again can you?" Jay stayed silent pretending that he did not know or care what Mike was referring to. "Ha I knew it!" Mike said with a raucous, victorious laugh. "I just knew it, from the moment I saw your reaction to her on the beach right through to this miraculous waiting for me this morning, I just knew it. She has got you!" Mike burst out laughing again. Jay didn't understand why Mike found this so funny until, "Hook line and sinker, she has got you," concluded Mike with another outburst of laughter. "The mighty and the free to prostitute himself has been felled and chained, Waaahahaha," he continued in self indulgent delight.

Another human trait that Jay had recognised amongst

beings on this earth . . . if others can't have your
freedom, they just can't wait until, and will rejoice when,
yours is supposedly taken away. Jay knew it was too late.
Mike could read him like a book, but he tried anyway.
"Whada ya mean? I don't even know her," he retorted
in hopeless defence. "So you didn't even manage to
hook up with her last night?" Mike probed. "Why would
I? Like I said, I don't even know her. Anyway I didn't go
out last night." "Hahaha that makes it even worse. You
didn't go out last night because of her. You're a gonna,
boy hahaha. The king Casanova's been dethroned . . .
hahaha." Mike spent the rest of the journey whistling
happily away, every now and then glancing at Jay,
laughing and shaking his head.

Jay stopped even noticing or paying any attention to
Mike. His mind was once again in deep discussion with
itself. "Who is she man?" "Dunno hey, just can't think."
"Why am I feeling this, how can she have such an
instantaneous effect on me?" "I know hey, it's sort of
scary." "Well not scary, but weird man." "Nice weird
though." "Yeh and that I suppose is what can make it
scary." "Wonder if she'll be there today?" Dunno, do
you hope she is?" "Hmmm let's see what the universe
delivers . . ." Mike's voice abruptly ended his monologue
"Ok forget about your 'freedom slayer' right now boy,
we wanna get this boat in the water without incident."

Jay breathed a silent sigh of relief as the slipway
appeared and he could jump out of the 'Landy' and get
on with getting the boat into the lagoon, across the
beach and out to sea. He didn't really think about or care
how it worked, but he knew that his senses would plug
into the myriad of sights, sounds, smells, tastes and
touches being emitted from everything and everywhere

around him, and that, if he opened himself up to them, he could work in harmony with them filling his being with peace, perfection and understanding. And that is what he needed right now, some peace, perfection and in particular, understanding.

Out at sea, you very rarely had two big catch days one after the other, which today, Jay was strangely happy about. It meant that Mike was thankfully too busy hunting the fish, trying to fill the boat like the day before, and seemed to forget the whole 'babe on the beach' topic. But as the day's fishing drew to a close, Mike made it very clear that he was not going to let this one go that easily. "Ok boy, that's good enough for today, time to hit the beach and get back to your loved one."

The thought of her had flitted in and out of Jay's head the whole day, but he had managed to keep his mind under control, focusing and enjoying the moment, the here and now. But now, thanks to Mike, that was well and truly blown out the water. He wasn't sure how, but Mike's words had sent a surge of volcanic adrenalin surging throughout his body, and without thinking, thought, "Shit, I hope I see her there again today." For the first time he realised that he actually wanted more of her, and was excited by the prospect.

"Tell ya what," said Mike in a strangely father-like tone, "it's still a bit early so we'll pull anchor, then throw out a trap stick and take a drift for a Dorado or something while I help you gut the fish." After all the flak Mike had given him about the girl on the beach, Jay desperately wanted to come back with something like, "help me gut the fish, shit you are getting soft in your old age," but he knew he could bank that one for later once the job was done, and that a comment like that right now would be like shooting himself in the foot. So he just nodded and went about getting prepared to lift the anchor.

Once they had started the drift, they didn't say much, if anything at all, just went about the business of cleaning the fish and enjoying the luxury of the watery wonderland that they were at present part of. All done, Mike fired up both motors and with a sense of satisfaction, pride and power opened them up. The boat responded by surging out and on top of the water, both surfaces rushing, sliding, gliding and bubbling away together seemingly revelling in each other's contact and company.

Jay stood up front with Mike; the beautiful, warm salt air rushing passed his face, again at perfect peace, as he got lost in riding the ocean back towards the beach. Mike throttled back about three hundred meters off the beach. "Ok boy, keep your eyes peeled for those shark nets, don't wanna fuckup a good day's fishing getting the props tangled in that lot." "There's the buoy over there to the right," pointed Jay. Mike headed over towards it and worked his way around the first set of nets. "There's the second set," said Jay. "Ok now when we hit the beach stay focused on the job and not on your piece of pussy, hey," said Mike laughing out loud. Jay instinctively took a long, quiet deep breath to try and compensate for the excess of adrenalin that had just been shot into his blood as Mike's words had revived the pictured her waiting on the beach. "Shit man," he thought, "what's happening to me?"

He walked to the back of the boat to prepare for the beaching while Mike continued on with his banter and bartering with the lifesavers for permission to and where to beach. Mike turned around, "You ready back there?" "Yep all good." Mike waited for the next set of waves to move under the boat and through towards their ultimate destination and then picked the back of one to come in on, opened up, the nose lifting high and then coming down softly onto the plane. It was all in slow motion for Jay as his being seemed to be in a few places at the same time.

Everything was a focused blur for him as the boat hit the beach, the motors lifting in slow motion, silently roaring and spitting out a whirlwind of sand and water before Mike shut them both down. Then a seemingly endless stillness before the beach crowd started to motion expectantly towards the boat. Jay couldn't work out how much time had actually passed before he managed to click back into the here and now, but Mike had already jumped out of the boat onto the beach and was half the way up to fetch the 'Landy.' "Phew he is actually gonna give me some space," Jay thought. His hands and mouth working instinctively to accommodate all the questions and fish-show time, but his mind and eyes were concentrated on searching out only one thing.

A rush of warm energy ran up his spine and into the back of his skull and without knowing why he turned around and stared straight into her eyes. She was standing about fifty meters away. He started to move towards her then stopped himself before he even took the first step. They hadn't taken their eyes off of each other and Jay's heart was pounding so hard he could feel it in his throat. He obviously didn't know it, but he would learn later, so was hers. It was as though they were through their eyes feeding each other with the most beautiful juice from a distance, and neither of them could get enough. Neither of them knew exactly what was happening or what the other was feeling or going to do next, so they each just stood there, soaking it all up, uncomprehending . . .

Jay heard the sound of the 'Landy' firing up and dragged his eyes towards it, just to make sure he didn't overstep the preparedness Mike had come accustomed to. He started to close the fish hatch off from all the curious and eager onlookers and move towards climbing off the boat and onto the beach, and as he looked back towards her, she was looking towards and talking to some other bloke. "Shit," thought Jay as the bubble burst, "she's with someone. Fuck! Just my luck." Mike was halfway to the boat, but Jay couldn't stop looking towards them, his brain alight and on fire with a myriad of questions and answers. "Who is he?" "Dunno hey, boyfriend? Husband?" "Naah can't be man, looks a bit old." "Yeh but some girls like older guys." "But they just don't look like a couple." "Funny asshole, what does a couple look like?" "Hmmm good question, but not like that." "Then who is he?" "Family?" "Father?" "Naah, not old enough." Jay forced a quick glance back towards the oncoming 'Landy' now just twenty meters away. "Shit! Gotta get busy, shit!"

As he walked towards the front of the boat to hook it up to the winch he glanced back towards her. She was looking straight back at him and realising he would be 'unavailable' for the immediate future, she inconspicuously raised her hand to just in line with her shoulder and gave him a wave. It was like Jay had grabbed onto a bare 220 volt wire, his entire body bristled sending his skin into a delicious shiver, standing his hair on end. He just managed to respond before she turned and walked off with the guy she was with. Mike gave the horn a blast to get Jay's attention and focus. Jay looked at Mike who was wearing the broadest smile ever and lip read what he was saying, "Get a fuckin' move on," and then back to the big broad smile. He walked towards the 'Landy,' undid and started pulling out the winch rope, allowing him to turn around and look again back at her walking away. "Yaaay, they not hand in hand, must be family," Jay comforted himself silently.

They got the boat up the beach and back into the lagoon and Mike headed the 'Landy' back off the beach to get around to the slipway. But not before throwing out another full-of-shit comment, "Gees, what's wrong with you boy. Shit, man, I would have had a date by now. You get a wave, hahaha, and you choked up. Hahaha one wave and he chokes hahaha you've lost your touch man, hahaha."

Mike drove off and Jay was only too happy to see him go, not for any other reason but that his mind was hitting overload, and Mike's words were not easing the load. "Shit," he thought, "I've heard of love at first sight, but this is ridiculous!" This can't be . . ." Jay's thought process was interrupted by El's voice, "Hey Jay, how's it going brother?" Jay turned around and saw El coming towards him with two girls 'attached' one more intimately than the other. Both were very good lookers, genuine 'hotties.' Skin bronzed by the sun, hair beautifully wild and bleached by the sun, wearing tight shorts and bikini tops. "Hey El, yeh not bad hey, not as good as yesterday, but good enough. How's it going with you guys?" "Real good, well it is now. Shit this morning I was a bit under the weather, hey." Jay laughed and El continued, "Looong night," he said smiling and looking

44

towards one of the girls, winking and then reaching in for a prolonged kiss. She giggled, bumped him with her shoulder and then kissed him again. "Yeh, so like I said, this morning was a bit of a rough one, but we're ready to go again tonight. Let me introduce you. This is Jane, who is deeply in love with me," El said beaming from ear to ear, "and this is Glenda who is deeply in love with you," he continued and beamed even wider. Glenda slightly embarrassed by the comment looked down at the sand then back up at Jay. "Hi," said Jay, "good to meet you both, and Glenda don't worry about him, he's a farm boy and never really had any tact," Jay smiled. "Ok stop the bullshit," said El, "What time can we pick you up?" Jay just knew this was going to be awkward. "Hey not for me tonight, I'm buggered." "Fuck off!" came the reply "What the fuck is wrong with you?" said El looking across at Glenda and then back at Jay, asking him with his eyes, "are you blind?"

Jay didn't really know how or what to reply, something had happened to him over the past two days and he couldn't quite work it out himself, so how could he explain it to anyone else or expect them to understand? "Where ya all going?" asked Jay in an attempt to ease any discomfort. But El was not prepared to let it go. "Oh so that's the thing hey? We not good enough for you now?" said El grabbing the two girls one under each arm. "It all depends on what we are doing?" "Aaah, funny man," exclaimed Jay, "just thought I could catch up with you there and then you won't have to come pick me up." "Bullshit," replied El, "then you can just make some excuse for not coming when I see you again." "No, seriously, I'll meet you there, but I had better get going, hey. Mike will freak if he gets to the slipway before me." "Ok, we'll be at the "Deep n Liquid Blue" from about nine." "Sweet I'll catch you guys there later."

And with the night out uncomfortably organised, Jay hopped on the boat ignited both motors and set course for the other end of the lagoon. Feeling El's eyes on him he turned to see what he 'wanted.' El didn't say anything, just had a confused look on his face, shook his head sending out the message "You gotta be kidding me, seriously, you gotta be kidding me!"

Loading and cleaning the boat and the banter with the buyers getting the fish sold seemed a welcome distraction to Jay as it allowed him to unload his mind, and at the same time keep Mike from continuing with his persistent ridicule. But it wasn't long before they were on the road back home, and of course Mike would just not let it go. "Sooo slipped up again, hey? Why didn't you get her number or something? Oh yeh, that's right she had the big bloke standing next to her." "No," replied Jay defensively, "didn't need to. I'm going out with El tonight, he's already hooked me up," he continued pretending to be excited about it all. "Yeh right!" exclaimed Mike and persisted, "I wasn't born yesterday, that chick on the beach blew you away man, you don't even know how or why, but she's got you!" "How the heck does he know that" thought Jay, "Damn! He knows me too well man."

Jay realising he was on a hiding to nothing relented. "Yeh, dunno hey Mike, will just have to see what happens. I'm not too fussed one way or the other," he lied. He knew that no matter what happened he would puzzle on and on about the effect she had, had on him for a very long time, and would always yearn for and want to seek out that energy she had emitted and allowed him to absorb, bathe and soak in.

With Jay acknowledging defeat, Mike lost interest in the tormenting and adopted a fatherly tone. "Don't talk shit to me man, you two had a very obvious connection. Even watching it from a distance, it was blatant. Seriously. So go for it man. Nothing ventured, nothing gained." "Yeh, I'll check it out if I get the chance, but dunno how long she's down for, and not sure who that dude is that was with her." "You'll see her again, she'll make sure of it and that guy must be an uncle or something, she wouldn't have waved to you like that if it was her boyfriend." "What the heck," thought Jay, "Mike must have bloody eyes like an eagle? How did he see her wave?" But he liked what Mike was saying, and also knew that Mike had been down a long, windy and bumpy road himself. He was street wise, and in general knew what he was talking about in the worldly matters of life, love and living.

It had been two long and satisfying days out at sea, and with the forecast still lining up for the next day, both of them relaxed and enjoyed each other's company in pleasant silence as they continued on. Then, reaching Mike's place, parking up, unloading the boat and with everything sorted, Jay concluded "Well, that's it hey Mike, another day another dollar." "Yeh that's it for today. We can only wait and see what tomorrow will deliver." Jay turned and started heading for home leaving Mike with, "Catch ya early tomorrow then." Mike waited for a while then shouted back "Hey Jay, take it easy tonight. Tell you what, if you at the boat before me tomorrow I'll have cheese on the sandwiches for you." Jay smiled. "Deal," he said and gave a thumbs up.

*To Kiss the Purple Moon*

"Thanks for another good day out Mike. Catch ya tomorrow morning."

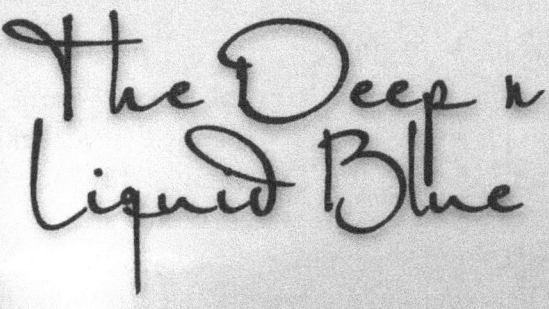

# The Deep n Liquid Blue

Jay got to his place, and hopped straight into the shower. It was already six thirty and he knew that there was no way he could renege on his assurance to El to meet up at the club that night. He knew as well that he needed to be distracted. He actually wanted to be distracted, allow the night to pass by as fast as possible to enable the opportunity to make contact come around as quickly as possible.

Feeling good after the long, steamy shower, Jay dried off, wrapped the towel around his waist and walked over to the fridge to grab a beer. Walking out into the warm evening, he lit up a smoke, took a deep, deliberate drag, looked up and exhaled saying to the blue-black skies, "Please let her be there again tomorrow." Then realising what he had just said, and slightly frustrated with himself, chastised himself. "You're fucked boy, what the heck is wrong with you?"

Jay was usually so in control when it came to the women in his life, a bit of a Casanova, never falling too deep. And now for the first time in his life this one woman had, had such an effect on him in such a short time. It was strange to him, confusing and a little scary. The first beer had slid down without even touching sides so Jay went in to get another, cracked it open and walked back out thinking . . . puzzling out the answers between the opinions in his mind. "How the heck did she do that to me? Who is she?" "Dunno, but it felt sooo good hey?" "Hahaha, shit yeh! That was incredible! That was like perfect sex from a distance and through the air. No, it was like pure, I dunno, perfection, how would you describe it?" Then again he started getting frustrated with himself, "Shit, I'm fucked up man, this is ridiculous!"

Jay loved having these mental discussions and debates with himself, but this was a little different. This time he didn't have the answers, but what he did have, was the longing, the longing to see her again. "Fuck this," he said out loud, "time to rock n roll." He looked at the time; it was coming up for eight. "Still a bit early to go down to the club," he thought, "but best I go get a cheeseburger and eat it down at the beach," and then his mind, still slightly out of control, continued. "Who knows maybe she'll be down there?" "For fucks sake man, let it go, get a life, what is wrong with you?"

Jay agreed with himself, squashed the empty beer tin for good measure and to prove somehow to himself that he was still in control around here, got dressed and drove off into town. The main street was starting to bustle with all the holiday makers coming out for the night, eager to spend their hard earned-cash on all the food and fun on offer from the local businesses. The business people knew they had to take advantage of the holiday season, and with all the sights on offer coupled with the incredible energy exuded by everyone having a good time, they literally loved doing it. This wasn't work to them, this was play, and they made money at the same time, and lots of it.

Jay stopped off and got a burger and chips then drove on down to the beach. The moon wasn't full, but it was well on its way there, so the beach was glowing in pale blue light, the sea shimmering, excited and expectant. It's what Jay loved about the ocean, the different moods, the variety of and constantly changing mind blowing scenic scapes. And the best part, no one could ever take it away, No one could build on it, farm on it, destroy it in any way. Well, not yet anyway and not during his lifetime on earth.

A range of groups of people were down to experience and be part of this mystical time, space and place. They didn't consciously decide to be part of it, they were by nature drawn to it. The memories created by the energies from the delicious sights, sounds and smells of past experiences had drawn them back to fill up with more of the delectable juices on offer. They didn't only bring themselves along but brought those close to them as well, so they too could get their fair share. Lovers walked hand in hand blissfully unaware of anyone else except themselves, as they stopped at will to lock lips, tongues and arms. Kids excitedly ran around exploring every shell, rock, puddle and hideout while their parents took the opportunity to relax and take it all in. Small groups of friends were gathering as they used this wonderland as the most obvious place to meet up, have a drink under the perfect night sky, with the crashing of the surf as background music and to discuss the plan of action for the night, before heading off to the chosen pub, club, restaurant or party.

Jay lost in this world going on around him jumped slightly as his phone went off rudely and abruptly. "Jay here." "Hey brother, we all heading to the club, don't let me down now, hey." "Yeh just down munching a burger at the beach, I'll catch you up there soon." "Fuck they are both looking sooo hot tonight cousin," El whispered excitedly over the phone and continued, "you owe me man." "Yeh, yeh, yeh," replied Jay knowing that more often than not El was the one that had fed off of his 'conquests.'

Jay had always loved music. It filled his mind and soul with the sugar of those that created it, his mind and soul then passing it on to and through his body which moved in fluid and perfect rhythm. Once he was on the dance floor you couldn't get him off. And the women loved it. They couldn't get enough. It wasn't that they specifically wanted Jay, but they wanted to dance and dance with him, or at least with whatever it was he was generating. This ultimately culminating in El moving in on his target sometime during the night, with Jay as his best mate being the perfect excuse to be on the dance floor in the immediate vicinity in the first place. And of course Jay himself normally hooked up with whoever was attracted more intimately to him on the evening.

But tonight was a little different in that they, in effect, were already partnered up for the night. Jay parked his car and walked up into the club. He passed El's car on the way there so he knew they were already inside. Jay paid his ten bucks at the door and went in. It was a huge and immediate contrast from the beach, a complete different time and space to the extent you could have been on a different planet completely. The music was pumping, the women all looking like they had just walked out of a fashion magazine, with the guys mostly very casual but a few making an obvious statement of intent with not a hair out of place. But one thing was common amongst everyone, they were all buzzing, everyone in a happy and bubbly space, ready to love and live this night.

Jay walked up to the bar to get a beer. He wasn't too concerned about looking for El, the club wasn't that big and they would find each other sooner or later. Then beer in hand leaning up against the bar, Jay got into another private discussion with himself. "Wonder if she will be here tonight?" "Then what would ya do boy, you already have a date." "It's not a date man, just some cherries that El has organised." "Yeh, but you are committed now, bit harsh to drop Glenda now." "I'm sure she will get over it." "What the fuck!" Jay said quietly under his breath, "I'm doing it again. Let it go and enjoy the evening, for shit's sake!" "And now I know I'm going crazy," he thought, "I'm bloody talking to myself. Ok . . . time to take control and have a rave, enjoy the evening."

He picked up his beer and downed about half of it in one go, turned and looked around the club for El and the girls. He had just managed to empty his mind of his longing and wanting, and the space was slowly and thankfully being filled by the vibe and music entering through his eyes, ears and nose. Everyone in the club was on a high, a natural high that came from being on holiday, in a good place, relaxing and having a good time with friends, family and like minded beings. The music fed and filled Jay's spirit and this drove his body to start moving without moving, he was dancing just standing still. Well, not entirely still, his shoulders gave him away as to where he was headed as they rocked and motioned in perfect and enticing rhythm.

The delicious aroma of blended perfumes and heat coming from the women drove him deeper into the private paradise buried within himself. This is where he wanted to be right now. This is where he was comfortable and at peace and could let go of all the unanswerable questions that had been plaguing him over the past couple of days.

His beer was finished, which he couldn't quite understand, so he ordered another leaned against the bar and carried on soaking up his fill of this free and beautiful rush going on around him. His movement had started becoming a bit more obvious as the music started taking control of his body. It was as though the roles had been reversed and the music was now playing him like an instrument. Waves of delicious energy feeding in through his ears into his mind and through to his soul, then they in turn passing it back on and into his body, which played the most incredible vibe to those around watching and with it. Women passing by and in the vicinity already being attracted, moving in time and smiling back at Jay. And he of course being Jay, in turn, just incapable of not responding as they wanted him to.

Jay swilled his beer back, he knew that once he was on the floor it would be a while before he was able to drag himself off for another. He was an absolute glutton for music, partying, clubbing and for what it did for him.

By now he was well gone, intoxicated and drugged up by the people, the place and the beat, and he started moving towards the dance floor. He didn't care if he had a partner or not, he could dance alone on the floor if it came to that, he had no inhibition when it came to music and dancing. Music was there to listen to and if the opportunity presented itself, as in a club, to dance to, and he refused to let it go to waste.

The music got louder and louder as he got closer to its centre of gravity, and by the time he hit the floor he was in paradise, a state of natural euphoria, bliss and perfection, free of his body which bound him to earthly matters. His mind, his soul now in charge and dictating to his body, which now moved with the music as one.

There were always girls dancing together with each other, as their partners, if they had come with any, seemed only to be able to give the odd appearance now and again on the floor, and had to be a little bit pissed to do so. So generally there was always plenty of talent to associate and rave with. And they loved a guy that could move and entice them. Jay soon had a group of dancing partners rocking away together, they didn't know each other but no one cared, they had similar spirits and they just loved feeding off of and sharing with each other's presence and energy.

Jay felt a gentle tap on his shoulder; it was Glenda. She smiled and said hi with a little wave. He smiled and moved in to give her a hug and kiss. Still holding her shoulders he moved his mouth close to her ear. "How's it going?" "All good hey, nice club. You guys are so lucky to live down here, the beach, the ocean the night life, such a cool place man." "Yeh I know, I love it hey," he smiled and then continued, "live at the beach and then go into the city for a holiday, if you have to," he said laughing, then asked, "So ya ready to rock the night away?" "I'm ready, I've been watching you and don't know if I will keep up, but I will do my best." "Watching me? Wow you must be desperate," he replied laughing again, giving her a kiss on the cheek. "Where's El and Jane?" "Over there with a couple of your mates." Glenda pointed across to the second bar area. Jay glanced across, and there was El looking back with a huge smile on his face, raising his beer in one hand and pulling Jane in up close with his other arm just for effect. Just sort of showing off his prize to Jay. Jay smiled gave a thumbs up and looked back at Glenda. "Shit you are looking hot tonight," he said to her sort of instinctively and not really expecting the words to come out of his mouth. They were destined for his mind only, but it was funny, times like these when his being was flooded with beautiful energies, sometimes the control of his bodily function and behaviour was not as it should be. But she didn't mind, she loved it, the words entering Glenda's mind allowed a release of warm and delicious heat to permeate throughout her body. She smiled with her lips and the heat wave was returned to him as her eyes sort of said, "it's all yours if you want it." Jay soaked it all up for as long as he could, gave her another quick but sumptuous kiss and said, "Ok, let's get this party rocking" as he pulled away and continued on in his indulgence and overdose of delectable sounds, sights and smells.

Time became meaningless as the moon slowly moved on up and over without anyone in the club even noticing or caring. It was well into the early hours of the morning when El came up onto the dance floor and squeezed one of Jay's shoulders. Jay and Glenda were dancing up close, real close. Jay had his hands on the back of Glenda's hips, with her arms around and pulling his face into her neck. After hours of dancing non-stop, he had now slowed down to a rhythmic sway, breathing in her fragrance and tasting the salt on her skin, drifting in and out of reality.

"Hey Jay," said El giving his shoulder another squeeze this time with a little bit of a shake. Jay reluctantly pulled himself away and turned around. "Hey El, what's up?" "We outta here man." "How come, it's still early isn't it?" El laughed, "Yeh it's early all right, it about three in the morning." "Shit!" said Jay, "I gotta get up in three hours time to go fishing." They all laughed. "Ok catch ya later," Jay said burying his face back into Glenda's neck indicating that she would be going home with him and not with El and Jane. She responded by pulling him in even tighter. El and Jane looked at each other smiled knowingly, shrugged their shoulders and walked off.

Neither of them knew exactly how much time had gone by since El and Jane had gone, but Glenda spoke softly to Jay, "Hey we should go, you never gonna get up tomorrow, I mean this morning," she said smiling. "Yeh I know, hey," and looking into her eyes, "Hmmm maybe best not to sleep at all." Glenda responded by kissing him hard and long. The evening had filled them both and they needed to let it all go again, back out into the universe. They carried on releasing their desires, their mouths locked in embrace, their bodies hard up against each other giving and taking at the same time. The whole club, the people, the music, the place becoming a mist, as though they were alone caught up in some mystical whirlwind of light, colour and sound.

Coming slowly back down to earth, Jay was able to speak, "Ok let's hit the road." He kissed her softly and took her by the hand, off the dance floor and out the club towards the car. The early morning was warm with not a breath of wind. The sudden stillness and perfect quiet broken only by the sound of the ocean in the background. "Gosh! Wow man this is heaven on earth," said Glenda, pulling Jay's arm closer into her. "Yeh, I love it hey," said Jay, letting go of her hand and putting his arm around her.

They felt at ease in each other's company, not expecting anything, but just enjoying each other's time and presence. They got to Jay's house, and went inside. "Shit, I gotta get going in an hour," said Jay looking at the clock on the wall. "Shit, dunno how I'm going to operate on the boat today." "I don't know either, maybe you should book in sick," said Glenda with a questioning naughty kinda smile. "Hmmm that sounds tempting, but Mike would freak." "Oh well, I'll just have to sleep in by myself then," she replied teasingly. Jay looked at her and thought about what he was about to give up and miss out on. "Go have a shower," he smiled, "we still have an hour or so. "Wanna come with me?" she asked. Jay smiled, took out a smoke and walked out to the balcony.

When Glenda came out she was wearing one of his T shirts, he turned and feasted on her with his eyes. The thin cloth forming perfectly over her perky, eager breasts. Her nipples hard and protruding were staring 'wantingly' back at him, calling, aching. Her knickers tantalisingly just hidden from sight. Her long, perfect silky smooth thighs almost coming together just below the shirt. Jay swallowed instinctively wanting to rush up and take her in, eat, drink and indulge in everything she was offering, but something was holding him back. For the first time since he had let go in the beginning of the evening, he was confused, and once again frustrated. He loved being with and loving women, it was part of his life, his makeup, his essence, but now he had a beautiful woman before him and he couldn't move.

"Shit, don't do this to me man," he said, not knowing what else to say, "I have to start getting ready." Glenda said nothing, but her body language didn't hide her disappointment. In that instant Jay felt exactly what she was feeling. The sudden sadness sweeping in through his eyes and into his mind and soul then reactively back out to his body as he instinctively walked towards her, put his arms around her pulling her in close and slipping his hand into her knickers grasping and gently squeezing her tight bum cheeks. She responded instantly, putting her arms around his neck, closing her eyes and kissing him with intent, searching for, finding and playing with his tongue with hers. Jay slid both his hands inside the T shirt and up her sides. The goose bumps erupted as he continued to caress her skin before moving around and gently holding both her breasts. Glenda letting out the gentlest of moans from deep within as he squeezed her nipples. Both their minds had emptied as they continued to taste, feel and feed off of each other.

Although they had both subconsciously accepted their early morning fate of separation, they still didn't want to lose whatever delicious energy they could share and exchange from each other. They continued on, swaying tightly together, only parting to allow the other's hands to explore, squeeze, massage, and enter.

Timeless time passed and the swaying had turned intoinvoluntary thrusts and reactions of pleasure, then

Glenda stopped suddenly, pulled slightly back holding Jay firmly by the shoulders then took a deep breath in, looked upwards and exhaled with a delicious groan of delight, as she pressed her groin even tighter into his hand, her whole body shuddering. Taking another deep breath, gasping for air and swallowing hard she melted back into his body. "Wow! Wow you are beautiful," she managed to say. Jay smiled and started swaying with her again, "You're beautiful too," he whispered back.

Both still lost in the whirlwind of energies screaming in, through and around them, Jay's mind was suddenly set alight as the early morning summer sun broke through the top of the curtain and started heating up his forehead. "Shit," he said "what's the time?" "Dunno and don't care," she said cheekily, but actually being quite serious. Glenda let go slowly and leaned back to look into his eyes, smiling, she continued, "No sorry, I know you gotta get goin,' but to be honest I don't care what the time is." She gave him a little peck on the lips, "can't you do that to me again?" she smiled. "Hmmm . . . I think we did it to each other" he replied and returned the gentle kiss.

Jay pulled slowly away, "I better hop in the shower quickly," he said, and then as he was walking away turned and added with a big grin on his face, "wanna come with me?" Glenda was still in her own pleasure zone, swaying to the music in her mind, softly hugging herself. She looked up and smiled, "Be careful what you ask for because it's milliseconds away from you getting it," she replied.

Jay laughed and walked on into the bathroom. He was only gone for ten minutes, but when he came out Glenda was out like a light, curled up on his bed, with just glimpse of her beautiful bum peeping out from the T shirt. Jay looked skyward smiling and thinking just how unbelievable life was, the vibe, the wonder, the wondering, the trials, tribulations, the questions, the answers, and the perfection. "And that's nor far from perfection," he thought out aloud slowly shaking his head as he took in the delight one last time before covering Glenda up with a light blanket, leaning over, kissing her on the cheek and then heading for the door.

# The Day After the Night Before

Before leaving the house Jay went into the kitchen to grab an energy drink out the fridge, by nature, glancing up at the wall clock as he did so. "Ten to six, fuck, I better move my ass," he whispered to himself, as he started coming back down from his erogenous high. His automated bodily functions changed into second and then third gear as he grabbed the drink, turning and shutting the fridge with a back heel, while walking at pace, grabbing his smokes, lighter and fishing jacket before leaving the house and breaking into a slow jog up to Mike's place.

The sweat was already starting to form on his forehead as he approached the last corner. It was still early, well relatively speaking, but the sun was well on her way up and the air was thick, windless and muggy. The sort of traditional 'calm before the storm.' It could still be a day or two away, or it could be just around the corner. The forecasters with all their fan dangled widgets and gadgets only ever had at most a 30% success rate with regard to their timing. They were pretty good at predicting what was coming, but being able to predict when it was coming was another story.

Rounding the last corner, Jay saw Mike was already standing on the deck of the ski boat, and obviously had his eagle eye on the corner, because as Jay came around Mike stood up, looked down at his watch then back up towards Jay and bellowed, "You've got exactly thirty nine seconds to get here, before the cheese exits the sandwich."

Jay still buzzing, laughed so hard inside himself it made it to the surface instantly and he had to stop for a second, shake his head, look down at the road then back up at Mike with a huge smile on his face. "That is such typical Mike," he thought, "so pleased almost thankful that you made it after he knew you had been out the whole night, but still no expression of conventional gratitude." But Jay also knew that the 'cheese on the sandwich' was Mike's way of showing just how much he appreciated him as a, well, almost a friend.

As Jay got to the boat he just couldn't help himself, "Thought I had to beat you to the boat before I got the cheese?" "Fuck off, I thought you were already here," replied Mike and then knowing that that sounded pretty weak and unconvincing continued, "bloody cats, they were all over the boat when I got out here." "Yeh right," smiled Jay as he caught Mike's eye. Then Mike grabbing the opportunity to change the subject, "Shit look at your eyes, they look like dogs' balls! What time did you get home last night?" "Hmmm don't really know hey, it was pretty early. Pretty early this morning that is," laughed

Jay. "On the piss and whoring again!" said Mike jealously, while at the same time also searching for more detail.

Mike not only loved reliving his misspent youth through Jay, but also loved advising and directing him. He felt really connected and close to Jay, he felt something that some would call love, but Mike would only ever be able to call concern. But that was Mike, and he really enjoyed being the fatherly figure to Jay. "No not on the piss, or whoring, just partying into the night, living life and loving some of it too," replied Jay, smiling inside and out with his self-satisfying clever use of words as he walked towards the backroom to get the rest of the bait and tackle. Mike trying to sound disinterested, but wanting more followed after him and continued with the questioning, "So how much 'loving some of it too' did you have?" "Phew! Dunno hey, wasn't keeping time on it all, must have been a couple of hours though," Jay replied trying to sound as cool, calm, perfectly normal and convincing as possible. "Fuck off!" came the reply. Jay laughed, "seriously man." "Fuck aaahff!" huffed Mike as he turned back out towards the boat.

With the boat loaded they instinctively walked around together checking and double checking the tailboard, boat to trailer fasteners, tow hitch and taillights plug to vehicle and then, both satisfied, almost in perfect and synchronised tandem, opened up the opposite doors of the 'Landy' and jumped in. Jay on a roll, continued on prophetically, unintentionally opening himself up for an attack, "You don't have to be screwing something to be loving it you know?" "Hahaha," laughed Mike out loud triumphantly, "So you didn't even manage to get your end away? Waaahahaha!" "Shit" thought Jay, he's doing it to me again. He wanted to retaliate, but also knew he had to be careful what and how he reacted to Mike's 'interrogation' and rebuttal. He didn't want to have to resort or be tempted into demeaning whoever he had been with just to save face with Mike. "Whatever you would like to believe," said Jay. Now with Mike on a roll, he continued his torment, "so who were you with then? Loving away the whole night with the tart El organised for you, or were you with your mysterious beach babe?" he asked while wiping the tears from his eyes.

Jay experienced a sudden almost fear-like rush, as for the first time that morning he remembered the girl on the beach. The juices, the energies from the music, the vibe, and Glenda that had rushed in through his senses throughout the night and early morning had entered and fuelled his mind lifting his soul into a special place of peace, harmony and perfection. Jay had been in control the whole time and that's how he liked it. But now in an instant with just two words entering his head 'beach babe' the consequence in just milliseconds had resulted in confusion and a dry mouth.

Doing his best, but unsuccessfully pretending to have been unaffected, he croaked in a bewildered way, "Naah, didn't see her hey, I was with El and them." Knowing and understanding Jay so well, Mike picked up on it straight away. "Hah! So you failed in your quest hey?" "No, there is no quest, if I wanted to go out with her I would ask." "Hahaha, yeh right! You took what you could get, because you couldn't get what you want," enforced Mike.

Jay knew that this was going nowhere and no matter what he said, he knew subconsciously that Mike was right, and Mike knew it too. So once again he knew it was best to just diffuse the relentless onslaught by admitting defeat and flying the white flag. "Hmmm, s'pose you right in a way, but still had a rave," and then Jay tried to lower the flag a bit and regain some control of the conversation, "but still had lots of beautiful loving too. Glenda is a really cool person, lots of fun, and sooo hot." It worked, Mike turned and winked at Jay, "Good on you mate, don't be stingy. Share the love and love them all," he said and broke out into a huge beaming smile of self and shared approval.

The slipway seemed to appear long before it was due to, and Jay wondered where the past fifteen minute journey had gone to in seemingly no time at all. "Ok focus now boy, let's do it all again without incident," said Mike as they reversed back down towards the water. Then once again going through the motions that they had honed over the years, they got the boat down into the lagoon and across the beach to the ocean's edge. They peered out at the surf and beyond, intuitively sucking in and absorbing as much of natures signals as possible.

The sights, the motion, height and direction of the water, the colour, the white water, the bumps on the horizon. The clouds and their direction and speed of movement.

The sounds, the angles of the noises in the breeze, the size of the force as the surf broke and pounded into the shallow waters.

The feel, the temperature of the air and the water. The heat of the morning sun. All of it feeding through the body and via the brain, into the mind and soul. The body, mind and soul working in majestic harmony feeding off of life, to live and love and love and live on.

"Pheeew, wind's been on that water overnight hey?" whistled Mike. "Yeh, still not too bad though," answered Jay. "Oh well, we are here now and those half arse forecasters say it's not going to get up above twenty knots today, so we will see."

Through the surf, then winding around the shark nets, Mike pumped it out to fifteen fathoms, about five odd kilometres off shore, and then throttled back. Although this was the distance out to the inner reef, it was well short of his usual first stop fishing ground. Jay sitting at the back of the boat facing the shore still cutting and preparing the bait for the day looked around and asked, "What's up?" "It's not getting any better as we go deeper. Not sure, hey, maybe better just 'scratch' around here for a while and give this wind an hour or so to make up her mind what she wants to do. The current's going in the opposite direction to the wind too, so if she does pick up this ocean is going to stand on her head."

Normally Jay would be a little pissed off fishing the in-shore reefs, the harvest was not as lucrative as out deep, but the 'all nighter' was catching up on him quite fast and so he was more than happy to take the 'wait and see' approach before fully committing to a shit, blustery and wet day deep out at sea.

As the day went on it didn't get any better. Mike had set the anchor on a small pinnacle and the current pushing the boat in one direction with the wind wanting it to go in the other, resulted in her sitting side on into the wind, which was picking up constantly and consistently. The white horses slapping into the side of the boat and sending a spray of saltwater over and onto the deck. Although not pleasant, it wasn't unpleasant for Jay. He loved being in, on and around the ocean no matter what.

As far as the fishing went, it was nothing like the previous two days, but they got a good couple of baskets of the smaller reef fish, which were very easy to sell. And there was always a chance of picking up a 'Couta' or two. The very tasty, pelagic game fish that travelled up and down these inshore waters. It was a bit early in the year for them, but there had been reports of a few around and about so you just never knew, and so you always made sure you had a trap stick out when bottom fishing inside on the inner reefs.

They continued on, pulling in a consistent and reasonable haul of the smaller fish, sitting in verbal silence just enjoying each other's company and the vast array of nature's pleasures being continually fired into every one of their receiving portals. Both of them sitting there, minding their own and nature's business in their heads.

As the flood of energies digested deep within Jay's being, they set his mind alight as he started wondering and conversing with himself from an inner most and indefinable space. "Wonder what it is about fishing that just revs you up?" he asked himself. "Dunno hey, wonder if some how we fill ourselves up with the life blood of the fish we are catching?" "What the fuck?" "You know, like from the moment you hook one up, the vibrations from the fish through the line and into our body as it fights for it life, we are draining its life force as we fight to get it on board." "Hmmm you might be right, hey, it is a huge rush, and you must be getting the rush from somewhere, energy can't be created according to ol' Newt." "Well that sucks; we are like leeches sucking the life out of the fish for our own pleasure."

"Well s'pose someone's gotta do it, else ya might as well curl up and die. If ya don't take it from the fish you will need to take it from something else." "Yeh true, s'pose the trick is just to respect and understand what you are doing and not over do it." "Woaw . . . let's get all philosophical should we?" "Well, why not? It's fun when you have time and space to get a little deep and try and understand it all a bit better." "Yeh, ok then what about getting your 'top up' from other fuelling stations like the sun, the water and the wind. The inanimate sights, sounds and smells of nature, then at least you wouldn't have to kill anything to get it?" "Good point, but in this life on this earth you gotta fuel your body as well, which means ya gotta eat and someone's gotta pick it, catch it and kill it, so yeh you know the circle-of-life kinda stuff. Like I said as long as you respect it all." "True, but still, how's the vibe you get from the, as you call it, inanimate, I'm sure water is one of the most powerful energy sources around hey?" "Yeh go on." "Well think about it, you're dying of thirst and what saves ya? A glass of water. You feeling totally drained and go for a long hot bath or steamy shower and 'voila' you are revived and ready to go. Hot and bothered? Go for a swim and you are instantly refreshed" "True, hey, everyone wants a sea, river or lake view? Why? Subconsciously maybe they know the sights and sounds will come flooding in, pardon the pun hahaha, and fill their being, their spirit to overflowing, oops . . . another pun, hahaha." "And what about surfing? Shit man how do you feel after you come out of a potent session carving up in the zone? It's like you walk up the beach without walking, like gliding across the sand reaching your destination without even realising how you got there. Buzzing like 200kV transmission line." "Yeh, shit man, something veeery special about water, even just sitting here on top of it, surrounded by it in every direction. Like look where it's sent us now, into this perfect space of deep self discussion and debate." "Which I'm sure some would call that bordering on mental hahaha." "Well I . . ."

"Hey, Mr Gigolo" came Mike's voice suddenly and in a very strange, calm and father-like tone, catching Jay a little off guard and bringing him 'back into the boat' with a jolt. "Sorry, what's that Mike? I was miles away." "So when ya gonna get a real job?" replied Mike, still in the very unusual almost concerned kinda tone. "What the fuck. Are you on drugs?" was all that Jay seemed to be able to come up with while still trying to bring his mind back from his self indulgent moonlit deliberations to the what seemed, very bright and sudden glare of the 'here and now.' "What ya telling me?" Jay continued, "That this isn't a real job?" "Ok maybe that came across a bit weird I know, but just wondering, don't ya ever want to go studying or something, you know start a career in some profession like thing?" "Dunno, hey, never really thought about it too much. Having way too much fun doing what I'm doing, and you know what they say, if ya love what ya doing you must be doing something right. Life in this body on this earth is not short, I know, but for shit's sake man, it's fast, so you better enjoy it, 'cause it will be over before it begins." "I know," continued Mike, "but I won't be around forever and then what will you do?"

Jay looked up towards Mike. He was sitting there at the helm his legs up on the gunnel staring out to the horizon and seemed so far away he could have been on a different planet. "What the fuck are you talking about?" asked Jay in an agitated and demanding way, in an attempt to snap Mike out of this ambiguous line of questioning. Jay wasn't used to seeing this side of Mike; he seemed for some reason, vulnerable in some strange and unexplained way.

Mike didn't respond. "Are ya trying to tell me something?" questioned Jay further. Mike turned and looked at Jay straight in the eyes "No!" he said, "just don't want you to get left behind. The fishing isn't like it was a decade ago, and it won't be getting any better any time soon. Especially with all these foreign trawlers coming in and poaching our waters these days. They gonna wipe it out just now. Plus I won't be around for ever you know." "Hey, Mike, you don't have to worry, only the good die young so you still got many, many more years to go," joked Jay in another attempt to snap Mike back to earth.

Mike smiled, "Yeh, I know, but I just want to make sure you are on the right track, you not getting any . . ." The trap stick in an instant bent over double and the Penn real went screaming off. The sights and sounds blasting into their eyes and ears to the brain creating an instantaneous rush of adrenalin surging through their bodies and minds. Their minds reacting commanding back out through the brain actions for the body to fulfil. This all within microseconds as though pre-programmed. "Thank fuck for that," thought Jay in between all the organised and natural chaos, "that was getting a little too deep."

Both had reeled up and placed their bottom sticks on the deck, Jay had gone for the trap stick while Mike was getting a second into the water. The 'Couta' like the Geelbek were a shoal fish, the real big ones travelling in smaller groups, but if there was one, there would be more. But they were hunting and continually on the move, so you had to be quick. They would disappear as quickly as they came. Incessantly predating on other fish and creating mayhem wherever and whenever they visited or passed by a reef.

Jay was bringing the fish in closer after its first screaming run, it seemed like sometimes the fish turned and came back for a look before it went off on a second scorching screamer. As it got closer the long sliver of polished, glinting mirror-like silver could be seen deep below the boat sending another squirt of adrenalin into the veins as it provided confirmation of what Jay wanted to see. "Yep, it's a 'Couta.' A nice one!" said Jay. "Well don't fuck it up," replied Mike, "this will be the cherry on today's catch." "Hmmm that's better," thought Jay, "Mike's back!" "Looks like it over 20kgs," said Jay. "Just take it fuckin' easy man; this could end up being a very good day.

Then, "hey I'm in too!" barked Mike as he leaned back on his stick embedding the hooks and letting the reel screech off as the fish took flight. "My fish is back in under the boat again," said Jay. "Good I will leave mine out where it is until yours is on board." Jay fought his fish up to the boat, reached for the gaff and sank it in the fishes open mouth as it got in range.

With the fish gaffed, he put the rod down and keeping the fish in the water lifted its head up towards the gunnel then slipped his free hand in and around the gills, literally holding the fish by the throat in a vice like grip. Jay removed the gaff, picked up the cosh and gave the fish three short sharp and pin pointed blows to the scull before lifting it out the water and putting it out of the way into the hatch. He made it look really easy, but one slip and there could be 'blood and guts' all over the boat. The fish had a mouth full of greased, razor sharp teeth that had turned many a fishermen's day into a nightmare of pain and suffering.

"Where's your fish now?" asked Jay. "Still way out, get another bait out, still might be another one or two around." With his trap stick back out, Jay picked up the gaff and waited for Mike to bring his fish in close. The 'Couta,' although a perfectly engineered missile airbrushed a beautiful blend of blacks, silvers, blues and greens, unlike the Dorado, seemed to Jay to be one of those fish that were designed and built to be taken for food. They looked like your typical 'fish-eating' fish. He wasn't sure how he had come to this conclusion, but the more years that went by, the more he sort of felt intuitively that fish like 'Couta' were there to be taken while fish like Dorado where there to be looked at and left alone. Not that he had left any Dorado he had caught, business was after all business, and in this particular world and space and point in time he hadn't quite worked out all this confusion, questioning and deliberation stuff that went around and around in his head.

Mike's fish was beaten and he angled it in towards Jay, who deftly and without fuss, dealt with and despatched of it in the same way he had done his. They managed to get another three big fish into the hatch before the shoal had had enough of the reef they were harassing and moved on to a new target of fresh and unsuspecting quarry.

"Time to rock n roll," said Mike, "that's good enough for today, and yeh good enough for the week too!" "Yep, doesn't look like the elements are going to allow us out for the next few days hey," responded Jay. "Wanna gut the fish while we are still on anchor or are you keen to get moving?" questioned Mike. With the previous night now starting to catch up with Jay fast, and him feeling tired and kinda weak, drained of bodily energy and function, he responded. "Naah, tell you what, swing me a couple of those cheese sarmies and we can get moving, hey. I'll get it done on the way back in, don't want you to get your hands dirty." "You bullshitter," replied Mike, "you can't wait to curl up in bed and catch up on some sleep after your last night's whoring."

Jay laughed, reached out and took a sandwich, tentatively encouraging his unwilling stomach to relent and take it in. "Yum! You outdid yourself with these, hey Mike. True love and care man." "Fuck off," came the reply. Jay laughed again. "Shit he will never change, just cannot show any weakness" he thought.

With the rods and tackle safely stowed Mike fired up the motors, put them into gear and opened up, steaming diligently ahead, prying the determined anchor from the floor. As it let go the boat lurched forward in a show of triumph, Mike responded giving her more power as the rope raced through the stainless ring attached to the floating anchor buoy. The anchor chain finally reaching through the ring and hanging the anchor up. "Ok, she's there," shouted Jay as his hands registered the metal chain rattling through the ring. Mike throttled back, turned to face the long length of rope now on the surface and idled back towards it. Jay pulled it in, lifted the anchor and buoy on board, and stowed them safely away and out of trouble. Mike turned for the beach, eased the throttle forward to bring the boat onto the plane before throttling back slightly putting her onto a gentle glide.

And once again timed their run back home perfectly. All the fish been gutted, washed and stowed as he approached the shark nets.

Jay moved up front to accompany and assist Mike with sighting the buoys marking the way through the shark nets. Then throttling back once they had weaved their way through, Mike picked up the microphone and went about the ritual, banter and bargaining with the lifeguards. With the permission to beach granted and after silently confirming with each other that they were both ready, Mike studied the sets of waves coming through, picked his spot between them and opened up towards the lifeguard on the beach who had cleared and was keeping clear their landing spot.

Mike on form after three days in a row sent the boat skidding a good couple of meters up the beach as he intentionally showed off his beaching skills. He let the motors idle for a bit and then gave them a bit of a rev, just for effect, before shutting them both down.

The abrupt silence, the sudden stillness, the immediate solidity of the earth as usual left a bit of a vacuum in Jay's mind, and by the time it had been filled again, Mike was already off the boat and the lifeguard that had flagged them in had moved in close. As had the bustle of the inquisitive holidaymakers.

"Hey, Jay, how'd it go today?" Hey what's up Bob? Yeh went ok hey, couldn't get out deep today so just stuffed around on the inside. Got a good couple red fish and then late in the day picked up a few 'Couta.'" "Sweet, so you buying tonight?" chuckled Bob. "Won't be tonight that for sure. I'm finished hey, done three days in a row and last night was an all-nighter." "Aaah, shaaame," replied Bob sarcastically, a big smile on his face, "I know exactly how your 'all nighters' go and you want me to feel sorry for you?" Jay smiled, "Yeh, I'll catch up sometime hey. Shot for clearing the beach right in front of the lagoon man. Shit! Would not have wanted a long pull up and along the beach today." "Anything for my mate, especially if I'm gonna get a cold one out of it next time I'm at the pub," winked Bob as he turned and walked back up towards the clubhouse.

Jay had opened the hatch for all to see what they wanted to and the predictable wow's, ooh's , aah's, questions and admiration that Jay so loved, filled him up and lifted his spirit. It was like a fuelling station, the beautiful energies exuded by the holidaymakers were there in abundance, and by nature, free to be harvested, absorbed, stored, used and shared.

# The Close Encounter

Jay, lost in his own magnetic field, by instinct, kept note of where Mike was. As much as he wanted to give and receive all of what he could from the crowd, he also had to be aware of the job to be done and the control he had to show so that it could be done safely. He saw the 'Landy' was on its way down towards the boat and so jumped off to prepare to get the crowd back a bit out of the 'danger zone.'

Leaning over holding the hatch open allowing them all one last excited peek at the catch, Jay at that instant, for some as yet unknown reason almost froze as a rush of the most exquisitely warm juices welled up from deep within his core, exploding into his chest before radiating down into his arms and up into his face and brain, flooding into his mind and literally sending his heart racing, stopping him from breathing for what seemed like an eternity.

"I felt that," she said in a quiet, but crystal clear voice. To Jay it was all that filled his ears. It was as though he had had headphones on. There was a metropolis of sights and sounds going on around him, but they were all blurred. All he had heard was those three words.

Jay turned and saw her standing centimetres away from his left shoulder. She hadn't looked up at him, and was peering in at the fish in the hatch, almost as though she didn't want anyone to know that she was talking to him. "Hey," was all that Jay could squeeze out, as his mind raced in a scrambled egg of questions, answers and confusion. "Hey," she replied and touched his shoulder in a brief, intentional but totally natural way. Sort of as though they had known each other forever.

Jay let the lid of the hatch come down slowly, trying to buy time to compose himself and clear his head. The barrage of questions still being deliberated between his ears. "What was that explosive buzz? How did she feel it? Who is she? Who is she with? Should I ask her what her name is?"

The barrage was ongoing and relentless, but his 'mind partner' that he always debated these things with was silent and had for once, no answers, so Jay dug deeper, "C'mon man what do I say?" "Ok, ok, ok! I was thinking man, just say something like, I dunno, what ya up to?"

With Jay fast running out of options and being so compelled to rely on his internal advisor, the words had come out without him even realising he had spoken them. "Hmmm, just wanted to get a little closer," she smiled cheekily, now looking straight into his eyes. Another wave of incredible warmth crashed through and washed throughout his body, but he was now slightly more 'in control' and in a way a little more ready for it this time. "S'pose you felt that too?" he questioned in a familiar and gentle voice with a broad smile on his face. She shyly looked down at her feet then back into his eyes, her silence acknowledging and answering his question.

Just then Jay felt a tap on his shoulder; he turned around and came face to face with Glenda. "Hi ya Casanova," she said with a big smile on her face and before Jay had time to utter a response she threw her arms around his neck, pulled him in close and gave him a long purposeful kiss full on the mouth. Not letting him go she pulled her head back slightly and asked, "How was it out to sea today? Catch much?"

Although due to his 'history' with women on the beach and Jay being well versed in situations similar to this, he was in this instance for some reason only able to maintain a partial form of composure and stammered back unconvincingly "Um yeh not bad, hey . . . Glenda meet . . ." "Antoinette," the girl replied saving Jay from total embarrassment and humiliation. "Oh hi," said Glenda in her normal bubbly voice, but still not letting go of Jay. "You down on holiday too?" "Hmmm, bit of holiday, bit of research, bit of this and that," replied Antoinette. "How about you?" "Yeh, just down on holiday for two weeks."

Jay was sucking all of it in, trying to balance, manage and understand the situation all at the same time while still trying to keep control of his duty on the beach and around the boat. Glenda's arrival had shot an instant dose of reality into his being which had planted his feet firmly back onto the beach. Now in full recovery mode, he had intentionally taken the opportunity while Glenda and Antoinette were exchanging pleasantries to note Mike's e.t.a. and at the same time, like a seasoned warrior scan the beach over Glenda's shoulder for the mystery man associated with Antoinette. Jay saw him standing twenty meters or so off and as their eyes met he gave Jay a wry smile, shook his head slowly from side to side and then looked towards the heavens.

Jay couldn't quite work out if the gestures of the man were those emulated to ask the question as to what the man himself had got himself into, what Jay had got himself into or both. Then the man looked back at Jay gave him another smile, looked at the ground still shaking his head and turned slightly away to look out to sea.

A short blast of the hooter by Mike came to Jay's rescue and he escaped back into working mode. "I gotta get going," he said to Glenda as he slowly unhooked her arms from around his neck and gave her a little good-bye peck on the cheek. Glenda, uninhibited, grabbed his face and planted another prolonged kiss on his lips.

"Catch ya later," she said smiling happily. Jay now trying to keep three people happy at the same time, while hurrying to the front of the boat to hook it up to the winch, turned to Antoinette and said convincingly, and as though it had been prearranged and was perfectly normal, "I'll catch ya on the beach tomorrow then?" "Won't you be fishing?" she replied confirming to Jay that she had provisionally accepted his proposal. "Naah, the wind is already up out there and it's only going to get stronger. The ocean will be a bit like a washing machine." "Ok, see you tomorrow then," she replied.

With the winch in place and the tow to the lagoon in

J.P. HICKMAN

progress Jay looked up at Mike and inconspicuously opened his eyes wide pulled his mouth down and to the side while slightly shrugging his shoulders. Mike knew exactly what Jay was trying to insinuate. "What was that all about? Phew, man how does this happen to me? I'm such an innocent dude." Mike had known Jay for too long now, didn't come close to falling for it, or feeling any kind of sympathy whatsoever. He responded with the most unimpressed, 'fuck auf look' he could muster by screwing his mouth up, half closing his eyes and looking out to the side. Jay knew that that was actually Mike's 'stamp of approval mixed in with a bit of jealousy' look so just shrugged his shoulders and smiled broadly back at him.

With fatigue intertwined with emotion, confusion and concentration catching up on Jay fast, from that point through the loading and washing of the boat and the selling of the fish up to the point where he found himself collapsing back into the passenger seat of the 'Landy' ready to head home, was just a haze of time and motion.

If Jay had said two words throughout that whole 'loading and selling time' it was a lot. One of those times when he wondered how all the work had just happened and got done, seemingly without any thought whatsoever, well none that he could remember anyway. It scared him to an extent, because it was like he couldn't even remember focusing on or performing critical tasks, like securing the boat to the trailer or the trailer to the Landy, ensuring all the gear was stowed and wouldn't bump or blow off on the way back. But it also excited him. It was like time travel, one minute you were on the beach, the next you were travelling up the slipway and the hour that had just past was just a blip in time. Living within a kind of imposed meditation, the soul working with the mind, and through the brain taking over bodily function, engaging autopilot to preserve the limited physical reserve. Time, distance and space having no meaning when you are empty and at one with your whole being. Another one of those mind-blowing debates he had had with himself many a time, but never quite got to the bottom of it all.

Mike started up the 'Landy,' engaged first gear and bumped her forward up the slipway towards the road back home. "Well that was awkward," said Mike with a big smirk on his face and abruptly breaking the vacuum of silence inside Jay's mind. "Fuck you can say that again!" replied Jay. "Well that was awkward," said Mike and burst out into a raucous laugh, "but I tell you what, this time I am impressed! They are both delicious bloody creatures man. Shit, I don't know how you do it, hey?" Jay raised his eyebrows, "Well thankfully the universe has her way of sorting stuff out, Glenda is heading back later today, so phew that shouldn't happen again, well not with them two that is," Jay replied smiling back at Mike. "You know what else I can't understand?" asked Mike and before Jay could reply, continued, "they both know that there is only one of you and two of them, but are quite prepared to continue claiming you for themselves . . . and putting up with your bullshit." "What bullshit? Shit, I'm stuck in the middle here, El organised Glenda and then Antoinette, and well you saw, she just kinda appeared outta nowhere the other day. It's not like I've been chasing after anyone." "Aha! So it's Antoinette hey? When did you find that out?" "She told me on the beach today. Gonna catch up tomorrow." "Hmmm, this one's really got to you, hey?" Mike teased and then continued on, enjoying his game, "so what's the boyfriend's name?" "Funny," said Jay, "he's obviously not her boyfriend." "Never say never," Mike replied with another big smile.

"Whatever!" replied Jay far too drained and burnt out to even consider any form of resistance or retaliation. But still had enough excitement in him to fire another bullet, "I'll tell ya all about it when we get back out to sea after the weather passes. You know, that entire soft, warm, delectable, fragrant mystic that I am going to be forced to endure," he said and burst out laughing. Mike grunted his envious approval, and as Jay had just brought his game to an abrupt end, all he could respond with was, "Fucking wanker."

Mike slowed as they approached the driveway, went slightly passed, stopped and started reversing slowly back, deftly gliding the boat back into her designated spot. Jay had jumped out and was at the back of the boat intentionally filling Mike's review mirror to be able to give him the occasional direction and assurance that all was going according to plan. They then both continued on in silence and common understanding with their self assigned duties to get the day's fishing to a predetermined, clean and efficient end, ready to rock n roll the next time the ocean permitted entry.

Mike came back out the house, back to where Jay was standing leaning against the boat having a smoke. "Another reasonable day considering," said Mike as he reached out to hand Jay his share of the bounty. "Yeh, too true, hey, three good days, can't complain about that, but could do with a day's rest to catch up." "Hmmf dunno how much rest you will be getting." "Hahaha you're full of shit," laughed Jay, "but, hey, thanks Mike,

I'll keep in touch. When do you think we will be out next?" "Hmmm, another two, maybe three days? It's going to blow tomorrow. Then I don't know, maybe it will blow the next day too and then a day to settle." "Cool just give me a shout when you think it's going to happen." Jay started walking off. "Hey Jay," Mike called out. Jay stopped and turned, "What's up?" "Don't forget what I was talking about earlier out to sea, hey?" "Yeh what's that?" "You gotta start thinking about getting a real job some time." Jay looked at Mike, there seemed to be a sort of sadness in his eyes. "What the fuck ever," he replied exasperated, then continued, "you need to get a bit of leg over man, you getting old before your time. Shit, you're starting to sound like my father," Jay said jokingly in an attempt to get some kind of emotion from Mike. But he was undeterred. "No, seriously man, just start thinking about it." Then he smiled and continued, "You might have found the one you were looking for, and you know what comes next hey . . . 'kiddywinkles,' and they cost money."

Jay was relieved to see Mike smile and crack a bit of a joke, but could see in his eyes, and more than anything else, could feel some kind of sadness emanating from Mike. "You really, really do need to get your end away man," Jay responded with a smile and wink trying to lift Mike out of whatever he was feeling right now, then turned and walked on, and looking back continued "Catch ya soon, Mike, give the Pink Palace a go, they got some real classy 'numbers' there. Just mention my name and they will give you the works. On the house." "Yeh, yeh, yeh, you are full of shit," replied Mike with a smile. "Catch you around Jay," and then just because he was Mike finished off with, "And give 'Anty' a squeeze and kiss for me." Jay didn't look around again, just smiled within himself and acknowledged Mike's comment by looking at the ground and slowly shaking his head.

Jay got back home, stripped down and went straight into the shower, the hot steamy water reinvigorating him. His body soaking up the heat, the delectable liquid massage, feeding the consequence through to his mind as he drifted into emptiness once more that day. Continuing his drift out the shower, drying off and getting dressed into his usual casual T-shirt and board shorts, Jay walked through, picked up a beer and his smokes, reached for the tequila bottle, took a slug for good measure and continued out onto the balcony. Now in a perfect space he unfolded the sun stretcher to his preferred inclination, put the beer down next to it in 'easy reach' proximity, then lit up a smoke, took a deep drag and lay back. "Fuck life is sooo beautiful," he said out loud, exhaling.

Jay finished the beer in 4 or 5 large gulps, finished his smoke, dropping the butt into the empty beer can, then lay back and closed his eyes. This is the part he loved getting into. He had recognised and unintentionally practiced it over time, and pretty much had it perfected, well, to an extent anyway. He hadn't worked out what actually caused it or why it happened, but he knew that after he had pushed the physical boundaries of his body to the limit, it would literally shut down and let his mind and soul, his spirit, take control. His body, and in particular his head, would feel warm, almost hot, as he let his mind go and escape into its own world. He was aware of his body, but he was free of it too. Able to, what felt like, drift in and out of it, conversing with himself, asking and answering questions but remembering none.

Every now and again getting jolted back to reality as he tried to focus or concentrate too much on achieving the perfect outer body flight, experience or solution. His only problem was that every time, as he got closer and closer to being able to achieve the perfect experience, he would fall into a deep sleep and that would be the end of it all. It wasn't the end of the world, but was mildly frustrating to say the least, to not be able to master and or understand the technique. But then again Jay was willing to take what he could get, when it came to that kinda stuff. He loved knowing within himself that there was most definitely more to this life than just the physical. And of course loved being able to access just a small part of it.

# The Happy Hornet

The heat and sudden bright light of the sun coming up over the trees and shining down onto Jay's face brought him out of his slumber. Someone had been around during the night and covered him up with a blanket. Jay sat up and looked around for a clue, and there it was, a single rose in a glass vase was positioned next to him. The vase placed on top of a card. Jay opened it up.

*Hey Jay, will be leaving early hours of the morning, didn't want to wake you. Thanks for an amazing evening!! Catch ya around sometime xxx*

*-PS I took the opportunity of one last kiss while you were sleeping. Yum, the response was delicious—would have loved to have known what you were dreaming about. ☺x*

Jay smiled to himself, trying hard to relive the last kiss, but nothing, couldn't 'remember' a thing. "Shit, how does that work?" he wondered to himself, "wasn't like I had died or something." "Well, you were dead to the world," laughed his mind partner back at him, and so the deliberation continued. "You know you could be on to something there, although your body is alive on earth, when it shuts down due to exhaustion, your mind and soul have the opportunity to take a break and escape while it can't go anywhere." "Well how did the body respond to the kiss then?" "Hmmm well the spirit most probably didn't leave completely, sort of just grew out and beyond the body, you know like a cloud, just able to grow and spread out at will then condense back in if and when it feels like it, or when conditions dictate."

Jay got up and went to put the jug on, still buzzing with the space he was in and his self-indulgent conversation. Walking back outside, putting the coffee down, he lit up, took a deep drag and continued. "You know like when you wake up suddenly, from a loud noise or something and it takes a while to orientate yourself? Like you are not altogether there. Well maybe you aren't. Ok, only takes seconds, but still could be the mind and soul just getting fully back into and in control of the body?" "Wheweee we are going deep again this morning, hey brother?" "Well what do you expect after a message like that, just trying to understand how I could miss out on something so delicious." "Well I remember it." "Fuck off, you part of me, you arsehole." "Are you sure?" "Funny!"

Jay finished his coffee, and with the immediate debate now over, started thinking of the day ahead, "Hmmm what we gonna do today then, check out the beach, maybe go for surf?" Then in that instant, "Shit! Antoinette, I'm meeting her down at the beach today." The very thought, causing him to stand up and start moving into the house without even knowing why. Got half way there then turned around and walked back out again. Reached down, picked up and lit another smoke. His heart was beating a little faster which frustrated him 'cause he couldn't understand why or how to control it, but it also excited him as it seemed to be pumping some kind of pleasure drug through his veins, his being buzzing and loving living.

"Shit, I forgot to make a time," Jay said to himself as he turned around and started walking back in again. "Hey, relax brother, get some self control, have some breakfast, take your board down and spend the day on the beach." "Good point, shit! What is wrong with me?" "Dunno man, but get some control, take a deep breath and calm down, you're acting like a kid on Christmas Eve." Jay listened to himself and took a couple of deep, deliberate breaths of air. "Ok, breakfast, board, beach, surf, then take it as it comes," he said trying to convince himself that everything was now under control. He reached for the eggs and then changed his mind, "Naah . . . fuck it! Board, breakfast on the beach, then surf."

"She's got ya stuffed brother," he said to himself as he drove out towards the beach. "No, she hasn't!" "Well explain to me how you're in the car and on your way, but you can't even remember picking up your keys, or even starting up the car and reversing onto the road." "Gees who are you? My mother?" Jay questioned his mind partner, annoyed as he actually knew that he was right this time. Then admitting defeat continued, "So, I like it man, still dunno why she makes me feel like I do when she is around me, but it feels good, so anything wrong with that?" "Nothing, just saying she's got ya, that's all." "No she hasn't," the one half of his mind persisted defiantly, "we just connected, that's all." "Connected, hahaha that's as close to 'got you' as you can get." "Whatever."

Jay turned into the car park over looking the beach, instinctively taking in the ocean conditions and quality of the surf as he did so. The sights, sounds and smells, the energies of the ocean firing straight into his bodily senses, feeding his spirit, which in turn signalled and filled the body with vitality, inspiration and direction.

Jay pulled up next to another one of his local mates, "Hey what's up Bee, anything good coming through?" "Hey Jay, it's a bit blown out, but there is a bit of a right coming off the point every now and again. Bit pot luck where it stands up though, gotta be in the right place at the right time." "That's all good, just something to stuff around will be better than nothing. Go and get wet, live, love and play a bit in the ocean." "Most probably get better when the tide goes out a bit more." "Well that's even better then," smiled Jay, "Because I'm starving so could do with something to munch first. Wanna come for bacon and eggs." "Sounds good man, I'm a bit peckish myself, replied Bee without thinking twice.

They both walked across towards the Happy Hornet, a real family, beachy type restaurant overlooking the main beach point. If you got a window seat, you pretty much had a one hundred and eighty-degree view of the beach and ocean. There was also more than enough visual, audible and nasal stimuli within the restaurant to keep your mind busy for a week. Kids, lovers, families, all buzzing, soaking up and exuding holiday excitement. Bright colours of bikinis, board shorts, T shirts and sarongs. Bronzed bodies glistening with sweet, coconut smelling suntan lotions. Laughter and chatter all creating an invisible haze and myriad of electric juices surging in, around and through everyone there. By perfect nature, lifting their spirits to a preferred plane of subconscious peace and perfection.

"Morning Jay, hiya going Bee," asked the waiter with a broad smile. "You guys coming in for breakfast?" "Hey Bob, we sure are. Flipp'n hungry as a horse man. You gotta seat near the window?" "Follow me," replied Bob as he turned and led them through. "You been catching much fish lately, Jay?" asked Bee. "Did ok over the past 3 days. Can't complain. What you been up to?" "Nothing out of the ordinary, one or two houses to finish up, but they will have to wait till after the holidays now, then there is quite a big contract coming out from the council, and I think I stand a good chance of getting it." "That's cool man," replied Jay.

"Here you go," said Bob with a beaming smile that only Bob seemed to be able to produce, "a bird's eye view of the whole beach, and of course the surf just for you guys." "Beautiful, you're a star!" thanked Jay. "What ya havin,' the usual, or the menu?" asked Bob "Two eggs, toast, bacon and a strong coffee for me please, Bob. What will you have hey Bee?" "Sounds good to me." "Cool, make that a double thanks Bob," Jay said smiling. "Your wish is my command," beamed Bob as he walked off.

"Come right with any holiday cherries?" asked Bee. Jay smiled, "Yeh El organised an evening out. Had an amazing time, bopping and rockin' the night away and then finished off with a bit of a kiss and cuddle." "Hahaha yeh, right! Kiss and a cuddle I can just imagine. And talking about fishing, what's this El tells me that you have fallen hook, line and sinker for some other beach babe?" "El talks shit man," replied Jay, and trying to sound as convincing as possible, "He is always exaggerating; she is just a friend I met coming in from fishin.' Catching up with her later today." "Just met up coming in from fishing? Think I might be siding with El on this one," smiled Bee.

Jay knew he was on a hiding to nothing if he continued with the denial. He also wondered if the whole world had suddenly focused in on Antoinette and him. "Why was it seemingly such a big deal to everyone?" he thought. And then he realised at that moment the effect she had, had on himself. It was so 'out there' it was blatantly evident to everyone that was 'watching.' From the first time that their eyes had met, they had seemed to be what you could call reconnected. It was as though they had known each other forever, been driven apart, lost, searching and now found. Their brief moments together switching time off, creating the most perfect vacuum in space, a warm, psychedelic rush buzzing throughout their innermost eternal parts. Everything feeling so at peace, so right and so comfortable.

"Yeh, dunno hey, we just seem to be . . ." Jay stopped mid sentence, as he noted that Bee was not even listening to him as he stared over Jay's shoulder with his mouth slightly open. Bee glanced back at Jay, almost asking a question with his eyes and then back over Jay's shoulder. Jay instinctively turned in the direction of Bee's gaze and as he glanced across it was like he was seeing a vision more than an actual real live person. Their eyes met and locked onto each other's like an automated weapons homing device. She smiled as they did so and continued on in a joyous bounce towards him.

Jay stood up in slow motion and as she got to him she through her arms around him as though she had been waiting all year to do so, opened her mouth ever so slightly and kissed him full on the lips, holding her embrace for as long as the circumstance would allow, then she reluctantly let go and said, "so Jay meet Marco, Marco, Jay." "Hey man good to meet you," responded Marco as he extended his hand out towards Jay. Jay shaking his hand replied, "likewise, and meet Bee, a good surfing buddy of mine."

After everyone had exchanged pleasantries, Jay continued, "you guys gonna join us for breakfast?" "We have already eaten," replied Antoinette, "but you're not getting away with it that easily, we will join you for a coffee," she continued choosing to sit next to Jay, leaving Marco and Bee no option but to sit together on the other bench. "Just another two coffees please," said Jay to Bob, who had come up not just to take the order, but also to make sure he was in on the local intrigue and action that was going down. "No worries brother, two more coffees coming up," he said to Jay giving him a very open and obvious wink of approval. Jay blushed ever so slightly as he turned to confirm that Antoinette had seen the gesture. He raised his shoulders and eyebrows and shook his head ever so slightly to try and say something like, "don't know what he means by that?" Antoinette responded by taking the opportunity to plant another kiss straight onto Jay's lips. She was sitting right up against him, the heat, the fusion the bond was intense. The persistent feeling, almost knowing that they had been 'here' before, they could taste each other from the past and now longed for and wanted it again.

Bee hadn't taken his eyes off either one of them, and was fascinated and in awe to see his 'lady killer' mate subdued in such a devastating fashion by Antoinette. He sat there still unable to keep his mouth completely closed, not wanting to miss a thing. This was history being made right here before his eyes and not only was the fall of the king Casanova something to be witnessed first hand, but at the same time he was also trying to figure out the cause creating the effect on his buddy. And the cause was beautiful to look at anyway. Absolute candy to his eyes.

With Antoinette unashamedly sitting snug up to Jay she looked across at Bee asking in her bubbly way, "so Bee what do you do apart from surf?" And before he could answer, "let me guess you make honey?" Bee laughed, "Naah, wish I did, I love the stuff, but hmmm I'm just a bit of a wanker, sit around pulling wire the whole day." He paused, as did everyone. "I'm an electrician." The whole table burst out in a mixture of relief and raucous laughter. Jay was not saying much, his mind was perfectly empty, his soul equally at perfection and his body sucking up every ounce of energy being exuded by Antoinette. "What about you?" questioned Bee. "I'm out doing some research," she replied. "Oh yeh tell me more." "Well it's sort of confidential at this stage so can't really say much." "Pheeew the plot thickens," replied Bee with a questioning smile.

Just then Bob moved in with the breakfasts and coffees. "Bacon and eggs for my mates, and coffees for my mates most beautiful mates," he said, smiling at

Antoinette and then again looking at Jay giving him another one of his very obvious winks. "Thanks Bob, looks and smells amazing." "My pleasure bro, just shout out if you need anything more."

Bee continued on with his 'investigation,' "and you Marco, what do you get up to?" "Hmmm what would you call my line of work? I suppose you could say I'm sort of like the researchers right hand man. Secretary, fetcher, carrier, protector and general dogsbody." "Wow a man of many skills," replied Bee, who had now for the first time had a reasonably good look at Marco, and realised that there was quite a bit of meat and muscle to the man. Not someone you would intentionally or for that matter unintentionally want to get on the wrong side of. But Bee was on a roll and the more he asked the less he knew or understood and the more intriguing Antoinette and Marco became. "So where do you both come from, there seems to be some Italian in that voice of yours Marco? And Antoinette, hmmm just cannot figure out where that accent of yours is from?" "You are right with Marco," she replied, "he was born in Italy, but pretty much travelled around the world with my family since his late teens. Me, I'm a bit of a child of the universe. My father's business takes him all over the world, so my mom and I have pretty much followed wherever he has gone. I went from school to school, with a lot of home schooling in between so I think I must have a real mongrel accent. A little bit of everything thrown in and blended together." "Wow, that's so cool man," stated Bee. "Yeh, it was, and still is. Now that I'm older and more independent, I just go around on my own, still working for my dad, but not tied to his or my mom's apron strings anymore. He does however insist that where I go, Marco goes, which is cool because we are really great friends, almost brother and sister." Antoinette smiled and blew a kiss across the table to Marco, who shrugged it off just like a brother would do getting a kiss from his sister. "And heaven help me if anything had to happen with or to Antoinette," Marco added looking up towards Jay in a 'sorry mate but my hands are tied" kinda way. "Oh now I see where the protector part of your position description comes in," smiled Bee.

The conversation although brief had started to register with Jay. He had until now been wallowing in the comfort of Antoinette's presence, but now, as he started to come back down to earth it was back to the, 'more questions than answers syndrome.' "Where is she from? What does she do? When will she be leaving? Where will she be going? Why is her father so protective over her?" He was about to go into mind-blowing overload when, "Surfs up brother," said Bee swallowing his last mouthful and looking with intent at the surf. Jay looked out to the point. There was a bit of an untidy, but rideable 4-foot wave peeling off. "True hey," said Jay, and then looked across at Antoinette rather awkwardly. "What you guys up to today? Gonna stick around on the beach or got something else planned?" "Well I was going to spend the next hour or two with you on the beach, but if surfing is more important to you?" she smiled and punched him on the arm. "No that's cool, I will go surfing later," he said looking across at Bee. Bee opened his eyes wide scrunching his mouth up 'saying' without a word being uttered, "She's got you bad boy!" "No don't be silly," said Antoinette, "we'll have plenty of time to spend together." They both stood up at the same time and she continued, "We have our whole lives ahead of us still," she said smiling and kissing him at the same time. The words sent another ridiculously delicious bolt of juice throughout his entire body. "We'll catch ya later then," said Antoinette, "real good to meet you Bee, I'm sure we'll see you round again too." "Yeh, it's been a pleasure. Looking forward to learning more about what you guys are up to."

Antoinette smiled, turned and gave Jay a small wave before turning and walking out with Marco. Bee sat down again while Jay sort of stuck in time and space just stood there watching them go. Antoinette half turned around again just before the door, somehow knowing Jay was still watching her, smiled and blew him a kiss. Jay smiled and trying to, but unable to maintain his supposed domination and control of his self, blew a kiss back, then looked back at Bee who was staring, mouth now wide open, back at him. "Shit man how do you do it? She is incredible!"

Jay sat back down again; his mind absolutely blank was unable to respond to the question. "But tell ya what, this time I think you have met your match," continued Bee with a broad smile. "Fuck this," replied Jay unintentionally out loud and coming back to the present, a little confused and frustrated with his seemingly lack of self control, "time to go get wet."

They both stood up and moved out towards the cashier. "Hey Bob thanks for the service man, real good feed as usual." "No worries brothers, your full stomachs are my priority! As always good to have you around." And then with a cheeky spring in his voice, "and hey Jay, just love your new acquisition man, you are a legend, take care of that one, she's a keeper." Thanks Bob, you are a legend too," Jay smiled back.

Paying the bill and exiting the Happy Hornet, Bee and Jay were half way up to the car park to grab there boards when Bob's voice broke out and literally silenced the holiday buzz and banter going on all around them. "Hey Jay," he shouted out, " looks like she wants to see ya sooner rather than later." Jay froze as the energy transmitted by Bob's voice seemed to emanate and shudder throughout the whole beach, causing everyone in earshot to stop and turn towards him, including Jay himself. It was as though he was in a dream and everything around him was in slow motion, he wanted to react quicker, but couldn't as there was just too much to take in, flooding his physical senses and overloading his mind. The myriad of holidaymakers staring at Bob and then following his gaze towards Jay creating an infinitive expanse that was just too great to take in in an instant. "She left her jacket behind for you," continued Bob, beaming from ear to ear and holding it out towards Jay like a seasoned prosecutor in the dock for the world to see and witness the evidence. The overload of energies careering into Jay's mind now resulted in it losing a bit of control and it reacted by flooding the body with drugs that mesmerised him, slowing his bodily functions down so as his mind could catch up and start responding in a more deliberate and controlled manner. Being as 'drugged up' as he was, Jay couldn't quite remember the walk back towards Bob, but by the time he reached him, his mind was on top of things again. "Thanks Bob," Jay said in an exaggeratedly loud voice, trying to portray to the whole world that there was nothing actually unusual going on and that they could carry on with their life on the beach. And then continued with, "You do know that I am going to be forced to get you back for that hey Bob?" he said in a discreet whisper, smiling and bumping him with his shoulder as he took the jacket.

Jay turned and started walking back towards and looking straight at Bee, trying as inconspicuously as possible to take in as much as he could through his peripheral senses to establish if he was still in the public spotlight or not. With Bee just standing there staring at him and the holiday makers starting to murmur amongst themselves, smiling and glancing back and forth in his direction he realised he was. But his being was now working as one, and if he was 'on stage' in that moment in time, so be it. His regained composure dissipating through the crowd allowing them to get on with their day and he with his.

"She's got ya boy," reiterated Bee beaming from ear to ear. "Fuck off," Jay responded giving him a friendly but firm punch on the shoulder. "I'm outta here, see ya backline," he said breaking into a trot up to the car.

Board under the arm Jay jogged down to the beach and then timing the incoming shore break, accelerated as he reached the water's edge, and with the board held out in front of him jumped over the small incoming wave, gliding perfectly down the back of it. The feel of the warm water washing over his body was like fluid silk. The water's mystical properties filling him with joy, freedom, power and passion.

He powered effortlessly across the surface, until he got to the mid break, duck diving under the first foamy, loving the bubbly mass surge and wash over his body, sucking all the invisible juices the water exuded into his soul, storing them there for as long as possible, feeding off of them, before having to let them go again, and then lining up for the next opportunity.

Out at the backline Jay sat up on his board and waited for Bee to paddle out. And as he reached him Jay spoke, "Now this is heaven brother. This world, this ocean, so mind bogglingly complex, detailed, magical and mystical, but so comfortable, so giving, so natural and so, well . . . so like 'live and let live.' No demands, no expectations, no scrutiny or complications. Bee looked at Jay smiling and shaking his head, then replied, "too right, brother, and watch this for freedom," as he turned, paddled hard and took off on the first wave of the set coming through, hooting as he shot off down the face.

Jay scanned the rest of the set coming through for the next best peak, made his choice and paddled hard to get into position. Too deep it would slide underneath him, too shallow and it was 'arse over tit,' or over the falls as it was more commonly known. Jay stroked hard as the wave approached, glancing back and adjusting the paddling power accordingly to get the timing just right. As he felt the wave lift him up he gave another couple of solid strokes to stay with it, then felt the surge and power of the magnificent beast underneath him as it picked him up and they joined to become one, and in that instant Jay took off into the standing position and guided the board down the glassy blue-green face.

With the wave breaking and crashing behind him they played a game of 'catch me if ya can' as he glided the board up and down the incredible liquid force, picking up speed then stalling at will to tempt it back in, then accelerating off again. The animal lapping and licking at his heels, laughing and playing, at the same time knowing that it could, at will, shut the game down by running ahead and closing the face off. But neither of them wanted it to end, the inert and the living in unison and in harmony, exchanging life forces, in, out and around each other by the perfect design of Mother Nature herself.

Earthly time and matters became insignificant to Jay and Bee as their spirits were fuelled to overflowing, but after two hours or so in the water their mortal bodies started to wane and that old and familiar instinct kicked back in. Messages from the spirit from lessons learned in the past. "Hey Bee, that's it for me hey, next wave and I'll be going in." "Good idea. Could stay out all day, but I'm buggered, the body's run out of steam." "Sweet, catch ya on the inside then," Jay shouted out turning and paddling for the next wave, and then riding it all the way to the beach.

Back up at the car park, dried off and changed, the boards 'locked and loaded,' Jay lit up a smoke, "Thanks for the morning session man, that was real good." "Too right," replied Bee, catch up for another session sometime before the holidays end." "Yeh, definitely man."

Jay got into his car and started reversing out, "Ok, stay cool man, catch up." "Most definitely, shit man not gonna let you off the hook with who, what, when and how you're getting on with Antoinette," Bee replied with a huge smile, "and besides, it's not just you two I'm interested in, just really keen to find out what Marco and her are all about and up to around these parts, two very interesting and intriguing individuals." "Yep will keep in touch," replied Jay giving Bee a big thumbs up and smile before driving off.

# The Jacket

Jay pulled up into his driveway, his body perfectly relaxed, pumped and fuelled from the surf, his mind loving it, guiding the juices into his soul, growing and nurturing it. Stopping the car, he turned to reach for his towel on the back seat, unconsciously drawing his eyes over Antoinette's jacket as he did so. In that instant, in those absolute microseconds his stomach was filled with what felt like a thousand butterflies, rising up and fluttering throughout his body. Wanting to savour the rush for a long as possible, his mind willingly switched to cruise mode slowing his bodily function down to a crawl. Then as the butterflies gently drifted away back into the universe, his mind inconspicuously started opening up again, reaching full throttle before the body had time to comprehend what it was doing, resulting in Jay grabbing the jacket and sitting bolt upright. "Shit I don't even know where she is staying!' he thought.

"Dumb ass," his mind partner responded. "I know hey," and then trying to act brave, "what the heck, who gives a shit anyway, she's just another cherry on the beach." "Yeh right, like you were just mesmerised by the presence of her jacket asshole." "Whatever, just got a bit of shock man." "Then why are you so worried about not having her address?" "Well because I have her jacket and would like to return it," Jay continued. "Yeh, yeh, yeh," his mind partner persisted, "like you have worried so much in the past about wanting to return other bits and pieces of 'conquestadorial' clothing that was left behind after your escapades."

Jay realising that his mind was spinning in a whirlwind of denial let out an extended and deliberate sigh in an attempt to get rid of it. "Ok man, time for a shower," he said out loud as the remnants of his deep breath dissipated slowly, and for the second time, Jay turned and reached for his towel, picking up Antoinette's jacket at the same time.

Getting out of the car he placed them on the bonnet so as he could unleash his surfboard off the roof racks, then, board under one arm he reached clumsily for the towel and jacket. As he did so a business card fell from the side pocket of the jacket. "Ronnie's Ultimate Holiday Rentals," Jay read to himself out loud, "beach front accommodation to cater for all budgets." "Ronnie," he continued on talking to himself, "shit what a stroke of luck, he will be able to give me Antoinette's address."

Jay unlocked the house, striding through to the front deck, placed the board down and forgetting for the moment about his shower, went straight through to the phone, dialling the number on the card. "Ronnie's Ultimate Rentals, how may I help?" came the answer from the other side. "Hey Vee, it's Jay here, how's it going?" "Hey Jay, good to hear your voice again. Wow what did I do to owe this pleasure?" she replied in a chirpy voice. "Hahaha funny, it hasn't been that long you know," Jay responded and at the same time wracked his brain as to when the last time he and Vee had actually caught up. Vee coming to his rescue, "well if you call a month between catch ups, not that long, then I suppose you are right," she replied.

The last evening they had spent together partying the night away came flooding back to Jay who could now respond with confidence, "A month, shit seems like just the other day, these holiday seasons just speed your whole life up man." "I can just imagine," responded Vee knowingly and ever so sarcastically. So what have you been up to?" Jay took the gap, "Pheeeweee been full on man, spent quite a bit of time out to sea trying to make some dough, done a bit of surfing, bit of partying, and caught up with friends of mine at breakfast this morning. We were going to catch up again later then I forgot to take their address down." "Their address or hers?" questioned Vee, just because she could. "No man it's them, not her, Marco and Antoinette," pleaded Jay trying to sound as innocent as possible. "And what makes you think I will know where they stay?" continued the questioning with a subtle but deliberate emphasis on the word 'they.' "Jeepers what is this? The 3rd degree?" asked Jay in a friendly, non-confrontational manner, knowing that at this moment in time Vee had him at her mercy. "Well you know I can't just give out information like that willy nilly," said Vee in the specifically cheekiest of cheeky tones, "what's in it for me?" she asked. Jay laughed, "Full body massage anytime, anywhere, on demand." "Deal!" exclaimed Vee triumphantly, knowing that Jay had always been true to his word in 'this' regard. "Forty two Bottlenose Dolphin Drive," then continuing without even thinking gave Jay more 'critical' information that he needed without him even knowing it or having to ask for it, "they have booked out the place for three months, so you will have plenty of time to catch up. But just remember the deal. Anytime, anywhere, on demand, and I can promise you I won't be waiting for three months," Vee finished off, starting to sound a little excited. "Hey Vee, you're the best man, and yeh, you ring, I'll be there, massage oil and champagne in hand, you will be queen for the day, and I will be at your beck and call." "Slow down tiger, I still have to concentrate and work for the rest of the day," Vee replied sounding deliciously exhausted just at the thought. Jay laughed, "Catch ya around Vee and hey, thanks a mill. Cheers for now."

A strange kind of undercurrent was running throughout Jay's being as he stripped off his board shorts and got into the shower. Gentle in its pace but powerful in its magnitude and volume. It wasn't exactly excitement, but more a kind of relief mingled in with a hybrid of expectation and anticipation. It seemed to put him at peace, but did not allow him to settle as it drifted him around from the couch to the fridge to the front deck and then back around again until finally, it allowed him to drift out the front door and into the car.

The current got stronger and stronger the closer Jay got to Antoinette's place and almost as though it had now taken him a little out of his depth, his heart rate started to pick up as a bit of anxiety was added into the mix, and once again more questions than answers washed around inside his mind. "Did she leave the jacket there on purpose? If not how would she react seeing him again so soon? What was Marco going to say? Was he being a little over eager?"

The questions filling his mind to capacity not allowing his mind partner any time to respond, and before he knew it, he was there. Jay stopped the car, looked up through the windscreen at the heavens and took a deep breath, then exhaled . . . picked up the jacket, got out the car and walked up the driveway.

Jay knocked on the door and waited. He wasn't sure what kind of reception he was going to get from Marco. He had obviously not done anything to upset him, but during there one and only verbal encounter at breakfast, Marco had made it very clear that he was responsible for protecting Antoinette and would be held accountable in no uncertain terms for anything or anyone she got involved with that was not to her father's liking or approval.

The door opened and it was Antoinette. Jay's heart rate increased involuntarily as the visual effect of her image entering his mind through his eyes instantaneously created and released a wondrous chemical into his blood stream. He gulped silently and spoke at the same time which resulted in a sort of squeak coming out in the word "Hi." He swallowed and continued on quickly, attempting to avoid any obvious sign of lack of control, "How's it going?" Antoinette opened her eyes wide and smiled broadly, seemingly surprised, but very pleased to see him so soon again. "I'm all good," she paused very briefly glancing back over her shoulder and then continued, "even better now that I have seen you." The words ricocheting around in his mind sending another uncontrollable bolt of delicious chemical into his body. He could sense that she knew exactly the effect she had had on him, so he didn't try to hide it. "How do you do that to me?" he asked. She flicked both eyebrows up and down together in a kind of wink, "You get what you give you know."

Their eyes were locked in a passionate and wanting embrace. It was as though they didn't even need to be in physical contact to be with, feel and feed off of each other, so they just continued to send and receive through their eyes, not moving, not wanting to be disturbed. Just pouring out and soaking up as much of each other as they could, while they could, the only way they could right now. Then like a light switch Marco's voice instantly isolated transfer of delight between the two. "Who is it Antoinette?" She tore her eyes away and turned her head back towards where the intervention had come from. "It's Jay."

As she spoke Jay held out her jacket that she had left behind at his place in anticipation of the next question, and before it came, Antoinette answered it. "He's just brought my jacket back; I must have forgotten it behind at the beach this morning." They both waited for a response, and it came in the form of Marco walking up behind Antoinette. "Hey, what's up brother?" said Marco. Jay relieved at the 'welcome' replied, "Not much hey, just thought I better drop off Antoinette's jacket while I had the chance. How you keeping?" he asked not knowing what else to say. "Much the same as when I saw you a couple of hours ago," replied Marco.

Jay couldn't work out if there was a message in the reply or not, but wasn't prepared to submit and retreat just yet, so continued, "What you guys up to today, anything special?" Antoinette didn't give Marco the opportunity to respond one-way or the other. "Nothing special, you got time for a coffee?" Jay glanced at Marco, who was unmoved and seemed prepared to wait for his response. "Always got time for a coffee," he said pretending that that was all he was really interested in. "Cool, come in, I will put the jug on. You guys go through, I will get it sorted."

Jay passed the jacket on to Antoinette as he moved inside, and as she took it from him she gave his hand a little squeeze. Another shot of chemical hit Jay's internal systems and a rush of warmed blood surged throughout his body. He instinctively looked at Marco who was staring straight at him. It was obvious that Marco had seen the gesture and its effect. He pursed his lips to the side and raised his one eyebrow. Jay held his breath, and then Marco half smiled at him and gently shook his head from side to side, seemingly, to Jay, a show of acceptance and understanding of what Antoinette and he felt for each other. Jay exhaled. "Come through," said Marco, who was now on his way to the lounge, still shaking his head.

"How do you like your coffee?" asked Antoinette as she moved towards the kitchen. "Two sugars and milk, thanks," replied Jay. "Sweet like you like your women hey?" she replied looking back towards him smiling. "Shit," thought Jay, "she's doing it to me again," as the overload of chemicals now flowing around his body seemed to teleport him across the floor without him even having to take a step.

Jay was a little relieved when she disappeared into the kitchen, he wasn't used to being out of control of his normal bodily functions and as much as he was loving the rush, he needed to regain his composure.

It was a little strange, because they hardly knew each other, but Jay and Marco seemed more than comfortable together. "So how was the surf?" asked Marco, "it's something I have always wanted to try, it just looks so cool, so much fun, but I've never really had the opportunity." "It was and is amaaaazing!" replied Jay. "Being out and literally in touch with the ocean lifts your soul to a higher place. Earthly time stands still and becomes insignificant. It's as though all your troubles are washed out and rinsed away. I s'pose if you could describe it in one word, that word would be . . . exhilarating! If you are keen we can make a plan some time and I will let you have a go." "Thanks man, but I think I might be a bit too long in the tooth to start something like that now." "Bullshit! Give it a go man, I know what it is; it's the fear of making a bit of an arse of yourself on the beach more than anything else, but I can promise you what, no one actually cares, and if anything, they will secretly admire you for your boldness. So don't sacrifice life's opportunities on behalf of others around you. Conquer your subliminal fears. Live and love living life. No one else is going to do it for you." "Wow quite the philosopher," laughed Marco relaxing back in his seat, "and you know what? When I think about it, you are most probably right. I am a shit scared of making a fool of myself. Maybe I do need to," Marco paused, "how do you beach boys say it? Chill out a bit." "Well this is the perfect place to chill man. Sun, sand, surf, good beer," Jay paused and looked up into her eyes as Antoinette came through with the coffee, "beautiful women." he continued. Antoinette pulled a tongue at him, put the tray down, plonked herself on the couch almost on top of him, through one arm around and forcefully pulled him towards herself and then proceeded to give him a full, hard kiss on the cheek. Jay turned towards her, the heat generated and emanating from the both of them fused their gaze, once again sharing and loving sharing their beings, not knowing, understanding or caring what it was all about or what was happening to themselves when they were together, or for that matter when they were apart.

"You two," said Marco in mild exasperation, "you would swear you are long lost lovers and have just found each other again." "Well maybe we are," bubbled Antoinette still staring at Jay, then before dragging her eyes away back towards Marco, planted a reassuring kiss on Jay's lips as confirmation of her last statement. "Hmmm," said Marco slowly shaking his head and looking at Antoinette with a questioning concern.

Marco had never seen Antoinette like this before. She had always remained, well, almost a recluse. Locked in her persistent studying, research and working. Never before had she shown such open emotion towards anyone. It was going to be something new for Marco to deal with, and manage as best he could. He had been raised with Antoinette's dad being his own. A fair, but hard, deliberate and powerful businessman, that was very used to getting his own way. Antoinette was her dad's angel, and heaven help anyone that upset her in any way. And that was Marco's silent brief, to protect her from harm and distress at all costs. No exceptions, no excuses! Now, Marco could already sense that one way or the other, Jay had the potential to create mayhem in her and thus his life. But, he also knew and loved the fact that this was the first time that he had seen

Antoinette live a little outside of the corporate concrete wall she had built around herself. There was a freedom and happiness emanating from deep within her that was tangible and actually came as a bit of a relief to him. Marco realised that he was going to be walking a tight rope for the next little while. Literally performing a balancing act over the wide chasm between the realities of what was unfolding before him and the slightly claustrophobic perception that Antoinette's dad envisioned for her future.

Marco still gazing across at the both of them couldn't help realising how incredibly comfortable they looked when they were with each other. They looked and felt like they were meant to be together; as a matter of fact it was as though they always had been together.

The peaceful silence gradually grew louder and louder inside Marco's head until it reached a crescendo and not knowing or understanding where 'it' came from he could not prevent himself from blurting out, "So tell me brother. What's your take on this life of ours on earth?" Antoinette frowned, and Marco realised immediately that he was, by default, playing the 'big brother' again.

He shrugged back at Antoinette opening his eyes wide, half apologising and the other half 'asking' her, "Well what do you expect, I can't just switch my 'protective mode' off. I've been your protector my whole life."

Jay was a little taken aback by the question; Marco had instantly burst what had become Antoinette and his 'bubble of perfection.' The question had sent Jay's mind racing, charging his body to instinctively lean forward and causing his response to emanate automatically, and at high speed, "Yeh, well it's quite weird hey, it's kinda funny. I don't know what goes on in everyone else's head, but I know what goes on inside this one," he said tapping his finger on his forehead, "so yeh can't yet figure out or understand what, when, how or why we are down here, but I do know that there is something very special about being human on this earth." Marco breathed a silent, internal sigh of relief as he realised that his question had not offended Jay, which he knew, that if it had, would have freaked Antoinette right out. Jay took a sip of his coffee and then looked towards Antoinette, who was staring back at him expectantly. Jay glowed a smile, relaxed back into his seat and with his mind now free and wanting to flow, he continued. "Well you know? Ants with their tiny, miniscule brains build ridiculously complex networks of nests and anthills, beetles have wing mechanisms that cannot to this day be replicated or engineered by man. They fold and unfold them and fly around at will. Spiders excreting their own sticky silk to trap their prey, the obvious intelligence and compassion of monkeys, dolphins, elephants and the like. What's it all about man?" Antoinette and Marco answered with silence, encouraging Jay to expand on his thoughts, before they offered up an opinion, so Jay continued on, "And then you get us, evolved from monkeys!" he stated in a scientific like seriousness, then, "yeh right, so why are there still monkeys?" he questioned, his exasperated change in mood and tone taking them both a bit by surprise. "Why didn't they all just continue to evolve into being human? And if you want to take the argument even further then, if we are as they say, at the top of the food chain of intelligence and perfection, why hasn't everything strived and succeeded over the so called billions of years, to evolve to be human. Surely that's evolutions ultimate goal, no matter what you are, no matter what you start out as, you attempt to evolve to become the brightest and most powerful star?" The mighty expanse of the universe that they tell us is billions of years old?" he said questionably with a tinge of sarcasm. "How much time does everything want to take or to have to evolve into becoming the head honcho on this earth?"

Antoinette and Marco were now more than a little captivated, Jay was now on a roll and there was no stopping him. "Naah, humans, we are definitely different, and are down here for a very specific reason." "Hmmm but dunno, hey, I think that most of us are a little gullible. We seem to have been conditioned from birth to believe in just about anything that is said by the 'great ones.' You know, those scientists and politicians," Jay said in a low important type voice and then laughed out loud. "They are all full of shit!" he said with a big smile, and then continued rolling on, almost like he had been jet fuelled up to the max and was enjoying and couldn't help burning it all up. "Tell ya what though, some of us humans down here originate from a bit of a different place or space to the rest of us. Like how the heck do some people have the capacity to invent stuff like satellites, stuff that has the ability for us to see and talk to each other from opposite ends of the earth from a tiny little hand held black box. How are they capable of designing and building monster ocean liners, shit when you stop and actually think about it, it's mind boggling. Everything that is used to build them the concrete, the steel, the wiring, the plumbing, and then still fit them out with motors, generators, cabins, restaurants, swimming pools, kitchens blah, blah, blah, it's just crazy man crazy! And not only must the ship float, but must be perfectly balanced on the water as well. And what do we do? We just accept it all as 'technology' or 'engineering.' Hahaha," he laughed out loud. "Naah let me tell ya what. It's not technology or engineering. It's ultra-intelligence. It's superhuman with maybe even a tinge of supernatural thrown in. Maybe they, who 'invent' and design it all know what we don't, and they can't tell us 'cause they know that we have to live through it to get it and to understand it. There can't for some reason be any shortcuts."

Jay paused and took another sip of coffee, waiting for some kind of response, but nothing. It was like Antoinette and Marco were watching a movie or listing to someone reading a story. To them it hadn't come to an end yet, and they were waiting in anticipation for the rest, so Jay continued, "Yeh we have been conditioned to just accept it all without question, sort of autocatalytic perpetuation. You know, the product produced by the reaction of a substance accelerates and enhances conditions for more of the substance to react."

Jay looked across at Marco who was wearing a slightly blank look on his face, his mouth unintentionally slightly open. Sort of like he was cross between astounded and confused, so Jay attempted to explain himself a bit better. "Well let me put it to you like this, our parents were taught to conform, believe and just accept, so from birth, we are taught the same and then obviously follow the same behaviour and understanding about life. Then of course the indoctrination continues right throughout our schooling. But, when you stop and think about it, open your mind and look outside the square, to me, there must be various and significantly varied levels of human intelligence operating around and on this earth. And I don't believe it's all to do with our time spent down here in this particular body either. Physically as humans, yeh a bit more muscle here and there, and a bit more beauty here and there, but in general we all have much the same characteristics. Two arms, two legs etc, etc, etc. But as far as your mind and soul are concerned, hmmm, maybe, even though all of us originated from a similar place, just maybe some of us have been around the universe for a lot, lot, lot longer, and have during that time learnt and understood so much more."

Jay paused for effect and then carried on, "I can just imagine, as soon as a 'super mortal' like me comes even close to uncovering the truth, one of the 'super beings' will be activated." Jay put on a subversive accent and pretended to be on his cell phone, "Hey Bill I just got another mortal here getting a bit too close to the truth, you better send a 'scientist' across to set him straight." All three laughed, Jay picked up his coffee again and sat back indicating to them both that he was now finished with his philosophy for the day. "Weeell" said Marco looking at Antoinette, "he's all yours," then laughed out loud and continued, "gees man I will never be able to look at another scientist in the same way again."

Antoinette was intrigued and not only wanted more of, but now more from Jay. "That's all good," she said, "but where does the soul come from then, and the mind?" "Hmmm, do you really want me to go there?" questioned Jay. Marco nodded inconspicuously while Antoinette was a bit more blatant, "Yes come on man you can't just stop like that!" she exclaimed. Jay paused, he was about to expose himself to not only Antoinette, but to Marco too, and the consequences of the latter might not be that positive. But Antoinette's expectancy overruled and dissipated any of his fears and so he plunged in, boots and all.

"Well think about it. Take us humans for example, both the 'super mortals' and the 'super beings,' it doesn't matter. Down here, we are all just flesh, bone and blood. All made, from the same stuff the earth was made of. But like I said with the ocean liners and satellites, just look at the amazing fetes of invention and engineering some of us are capable of. Cities of row upon row of massive sky scrapers, all fed with millions of kilometres of cables and pipelines supplying telecommunications, electricity, all the water and waste water pumping the lifeblood in and out of the city. The network of freeways, roads and railway lines, The Ocean and jet liners, the harbours and airports, the man made seas, lakes and islands. And we all just accept it and take it for granted. These magnificent 'super beings' that directed the creation of it all, how did they gain such intelligence? We don't even dare to question it!" Jay vented breathless and exasperated.

Then, now relieved of the pressure, smiling and teasing more expectation into his audience, he continued, "Buuut, moving on. What do we use to create all this incredible stuff down here on earth?" Jay paused then answered his own question, "Well we can't get it from anywhere else. We use what's lying around on earth. Extract, cut, melt, mould and manipulate it into what we want it to be."

With Antoinette tucked up against Jay, Marco flicked his eyes from one to the other, searching for the direction as to where this was going. Jay carried on, "So if we, whether we are 'super being' or not, are so brilliant, and yes you gotta admit that relatively speaking we are, then surely you gotta start wondering about what created us and everything we are able to work with to create what we do. Surely there is a higher and mightier power, way beyond the intelligence and capacity of the human, that took the stuff lying around the universe and decided to build a couple of planets, stars and suns, and then for good measure, a couple of bugs, beetles, snakes, lions, tigers and of course humans to inhabit one of the planets?"

Jay looked for a response; Marco was frowning slightly, deep in thought and spoke his mind out loud without realising it. "Hmmm, never really thought about it like that," he said. Jay smiled cheekily, "Yeh I know we are really 'great' beings, but shit man, how can anyone ever believe that we are the be all and end all of intelligence? The top of the brain chain."

Marco laughed out loud, "The top of the brain chain, how do you come up with this stuff?" Jay smiled, "Well here's where it gets really scary. Ok, so the High and Mighty power decides to design and build this universe and all that it contains, including the physical side of us. But how did "They" take the inanimate stuff of the universe and make it into an animate, soulful human being?" "You got me there brother," replied Marco.

Antoinette had now sat up straight and was also paying more attention. This conversation had just turned from interesting to enthralling. "Well obviously I don't know, but I think that maybe, somehow, and by incredible design there has been a piece of the Creator implanted into every one of us." Jay paused, "and that's our soul."

Jay waited for a response from either one of them. "Well c'mon," exclaimed Antoinette, "you can't just finish there, there must be more?" she questioned turning straight towards Jay, lifting her legs onto the couch and crossing her feet. Jay looked across at Marco, who too had an expectant look on his face waiting for more and gestured 'and so' with two open hands.

"Well think about it, your soul, a piece of the Creator is implanted into a human body, and as the body grows, learns and experiences, so does the soul, storing this knowledge and experience in the 'brain part' of the soul, the mind. So the mind and the soul are inextricably linked, they are one. They are the body's spirit. Then when the body dies, well hmmm, like the body, ashes to ashes, dust to dust, returns to the earth, the soul also goes back to where it came from. Back to the Creator, who now becomes even stronger and wiser? Or maybe the spirit gets an opportunity to grow and develop even further by being allowed into another new born body."

Jay turned to Antoinette, "And that's where you get soul mates from, where you have lived and loved in a previous time, space and body and have now found each other again in this life in another body." "Wow that's incredible!" said Antoinette, staring at Jay. "Just a thought," said Jay smiling back at her. "Shit you come up with some weird and wonderful ideas," chuckled Macro, "but have to say, makes me think. Jay smiled, "Yeh just something to ponder on, can't get too deep, life is for living and loving man. We will all find out sooner or later, but in the meantime there are too many fish to catch, music to dance to and waves to surf to have to really worry about all that crap," he said. "I like the living and especially the loving part," Antoinette said looking at Jay. He looked back at her and smiled, then glanced back towards Marco, who again had raised his eyebrows, shaking his head slowly looking sideways at

Antoinette.

"Ok said Jay I had better get going." Antoinette stiffened instinctively and motioned towards him, almost to try and stop him from leaving. But right now three was a bit of a crowd and Jay did not want to overstay Marco's welcome so he continued. "Thanks for the coffee it was delicious, and for the chat, well, for listening to me chat that is," he smiled. "Well whenever you feel like another coffee, or if you just want to chat some more, you know where I stay, you don't have to wait for me to forget my jacket behind for you to come visit again." "Yeh thanks, man," replied Jay trying to sound as composed as possible. "Hey, take my mobile number just in case," said Antoinette.

Jay reached for his phone dialling her number as she read it out so as to give her his without having to call it out. Her phone rang and she answered it before he had the chance to cancel the call, "Hi Jay I'm missing you like crazy and wish you were here with me right now," she said leaning her head coyly to the side and staring at him straight in the eyes. "Your wish is my command he replied," blowing an inconspicuous kiss across towards her.

It all seemed to happen in slow motion to Jay as he dragged his eyes away from Antoinette's, clawing his way back down to earth. Marco took a deep breath and looked towards the heavens. Ok, see ya around Marco. Watch out for those scientists hey hahaha." "Take it easy Jay, thanks for bringing Antoinette's jacket around."

Jay walked with Antoinette towards the door and as he got there he turned facing her. "Catch ya round sometime," he said. She responded by moving in towards him and giving him a hug. He took her shoulders and gave them a squeeze, leaned forward and kissed her on the cheek. As he did so she whispered in his ear, "Love ya." Jay summoned all his restraint, everything he had at his disposal in his mind to stop him from holding her tight and kissing her like he wanted to. "Don't do that to me," he whispered and smiled. "Why not?" she replied with an even more enticing smile.

"Because I'm a 'super mortal' and only have a certain amount of restraint," he said jokingly. "Well I'll have to 'un-restrain' you then," she responded. "Shit I gotta get out here before you drive me over the edge." And even though he managed to control the bulk of the consequences of the exchange, a small residual broke through as he leaned forward and gave her the gentlest of kisses on the lips, "See ya around."

He turned and walked away, and turning for one last wave he read her lips. "Love ya," she mimed. He smiled, turned and walked to his car. "Shit I'm buzzing like a bloody bumble bee!" he thought. "How can she do that to me, it's ridiculous!"

# The Flight

## 11

Jay's mind was completely empty for the first half of the trip back home. The world before him just seemed to pass by as he drove along in a semiconscious blur, his body on autopilot as his spirit soared upwards. Habit steered him towards Mike's place, and as he got closer, familiarity snapped him back to earth. Looking up at the clouds marching across the sky, he could see the winds were still pumping, but he pulled up alongside the boat anyway just to get Mike's take on the coming day's prospects. He walked up to the front door and knocked, but getting no answer, he continued on around through the gate to the front to see if Mike was out in the garden or something, but nothing. Up the steps of the wooden deck to the first floor, Jay scanned up and down the magnificent one hundred and eighty degree beach and sea view that Mike had created for himself, but still not a sign.

Jay stood there for a while, transfixed by nature's abundant beauty poring into his innermost parts, then without intention drifted back down the stairs back to the car. On his way back the drawn curtains somehow caught his attention. It seemed a little strange for this time of the day, but Jay was unconcerned. "Sly bugger he thought. Bet he's got a 'piece' on the side and just not letting on."

Back home Jay found himself at a bit of a loose end, he couldn't quite understand it, or for that matter recognise it, but he seemed to be missing Antoinette already. He could not get her out of his mind, the questions a whirlpool as they washed and surged relentlessly around and around, with no respite. He realised that during their whole time together, he still didn't really know who she was, where she had come from, what she was doing out here or where she would be going when she was finished. It was the latter that sent his spirit into a bit of a dive. The fuel that Antoinette had filled him with had been a first for him, and without realising it, he had soared a bit too high, too fast. Now that his reserves were depleted, he was dropping like a stone, and nothing he tried enabled him to pull the nose up and out of the dive.

He slunk back in the deckchair and downed his beer, threw the tin against the trunk of the tree in despair and reached for another, then lit up a smoke. "This is bullshit," he said out loud exhaling a cloud of smoke, "why can't I just be with her?" Then as he came close to crash landing his co pilot pulled out all the stops. "Pooh, pooh, pooh," his mind partner said in the most sarcastic tone possible, "you poor little thing, I want Antoinette, I want Antoinette. Fuck, grow up man, she's just another girl!'"

It worked, "Shit what am I doing man? Getting depressed and all 'wingy' over a girl?" "Yeh get a life brother. Reality check! Sun, sand, surf, fishing and freedom." "True hey, just lost track for a while there, ok back to normal now," Jay finished off the discussion with himself, taking another deep drag, putting his shoulders back and puffing out his chest pretending to himself that he was now fully back in control.

Continuing to act brave for the rest of the evening Jay sank another six or seven or ten beers, which had the subconsciously predetermined and desired effect of numbing his brain, the portal between his mind and body, until eventually, what was left, led him wandering through to his bedroom where he collapsed face down on his bed.

The next morning Jay managed to open one eye, the other still buried in the pillow. His face felt like it had been flattened on one side and his neck seemed to be locked in a ninety-degree turn. It was obvious that he had not moved a muscle the whole night. The first thing that came to him was an excruciating pain between the eyes that led up his forehead along his brow and into his temples. "Fuuuck," he groaned slowly pushing himself up and pressing his hands onto the bridge of his nose in a feeble but desperate attempt to squeeze the pain away.

Being well versed in this condition, automation kicked in as he staggered through to the kitchen, found and chewed two Disprin, washed them down with about half litre of orange juice and then climbed into the steamiest and hottest shower his skin would tolerate.

Standing on the deck wrapped in a towel, the combination of remedies started to kick in, and with the pain subsiding the energies from the outside world were allowed to re-enter Jay's mind. The sun's warmth and glow, the buzz of the beetles and nattering of birds as they blissfully went about their daily duty of survival and procreation. Now lost in his own small bubble of perfection Jay watched as a small flock of birds appeared from nowhere, swooping in over the fence in natural, articulate formation, conducting a perfect wing tip to wing tip synchronised, aerial manoeuvre before landing as one on the grass in front of him. The visual energy entering and setting his mind in motion. "Shit that's incredible," he thought, "they seem to communicate without even opening their mouths, it's like they are all a single, pliable unit when they want to be, and then after landing, disband on silent command to cover as much ground as possible feeding and fuelling themselves. Amazing!"

Jay couldn't seem to take his eyes off of them as the frenetic feasting of bugs and seeds ravaged on. "Hmmm funny, hey," Jay continued on with 'himselves,' "weird the range of birds you get, some eat seed, some eat fish while others just live off of meat. Imagine giving a canary a piece of steak, a seagull a whole pile of maize, or vulture some fresh fish. None of them would touch it, most probably rather starve to death than not eat their 'food of birth.' So what's that all about?" he finished off asking himself.

He didn't quite know where he was going with the rumblings in his mind, but didn't really care either. There was nothing else he had to do right now and the ways and wonders of the world intrigued him. His previous experience in these unintentional semi meditational states of self-deliberation had sometimes given him a slightly better insight and understanding of 'what it was all about,' and if and when the light did 'come on' an amazing comfort and satisfaction came with it.

He wracked his brain for an answer, but nothing, maybe it was still a bit dull from the night before, or maybe some things just have no answer right now and just need to be accepted and enjoyed. The sight of the birds feeding away did however trigger another response. "Oh well seeing as you are all feasting I might as well go and have a bite to eat as well," he said out loud to the small flock in a manner which insinuated that every one of them was listening and could understand.

Jay turned away and walked back into the kitchen, took a couple slices of bread from the fridge and popped them in the toaster. Then, as he reached out for the kettle, his phone rang, and expecting it to be Mike with some fishing forecast, he answered enthusiastically. "Hey what's up?" "Hey Jay, it's me, how's it going?" The now familiar, rush of delectable juices once again permeated throughout his body as her voice entered into his being. "Hey Antoinette, I'm all good. Just having a toast and coffee. I think I over did the brews last night, maybe sucked one or three too many." "Aaah shame," she said, her concern exaggerated and teasing, "want me to come over and nurse you for a bit?" "That's not fair," Jay responded, "I'm weak and fragile right now and these lightning bolts you send through me when you say stuff like that could be fatal." He paused very briefly for effect and before she could respond continued, "But do it again," he laughed. "I love you," she said. "Aauuwch," he replied, "ok stop now. That is really not fair anymore," he continued on, laughing again. "So what's up?" he asked. "Hmmm nothing much, just phoning to find out if you are busy today or maybe you want to come spend the morning on the beach with us?"

Jay's whole body had in an instant been refuelled, his spirit was gliding, dancing on the winds of her voice. "Yeh that sounds cool! What time are you going down?" "Well, we have got a meeting from nine to ten and then we are going down after that." "That's all good," replied Jay without even hearing, registering or thinking of asking what 'the meeting' was all about. "I just gotta pop around and check out what's on Mike's agenda too. So ten, ten thirty on the beach sounds good." "That's beautiful, can't wait, we'll see you there," she paused then "love you heaps," she said giggling excitedly. "Hmmm love ya too," Jay said without even thinking, then sort of frowned to himself as he realised what he had just said. It had come out in the most natural way, but that was just it, he was very unfamiliar with saying those words as naturally and instinctively as he just had. "Yum, those words sound so delicious, I could eat them," she replied. "You're funny," was all Jay could muster, while trying to stay as composed and balanced as possible, "I'll wait for you guys down on the beach, I'll find us a spot on the other side of the lagoon where the three palms are, just a little bit along from where we come in with the boat." "Ok that will be good, I know where that is, see you later, mwah,' she said finishing off with the sound of a kiss. "See you there," Jay said forcefully restraining himself from sounding a kiss back.

Now well and truly deep within the thermal up draught, Jay continued on his glide upwards and onwards. He seemed to be surrounded, encapsulated by an incredible peace, euphoric since hearing Antoinette's voice. His body, his very being, light, happy and humming from the core all the way to the outer edges. His mind at rest in perfect emptiness, where there was no worries, no 'insurmountables,' no issues. Nothing to consider or fret over, just peace and perfection.

Continuing to enjoy the ride, Jay munched his toast and drank his coffee in flight, steered himself through to the bedroom to get changed, then the bathroom for a quick teeth and facial spruce up, before gliding out to the car. "Hmmm, maybe I should take my board just in case there is a wave," he thought, and went back inside to get it, tied it to the roof racks and caught the breeze on over to Mike's place.

Jay once again parked up next to the boat, if Mike was home there would be an eighty percent chance he was doing something on the boat, trailer, 'Landy' or fishing equipment. He always had to be tinkering with something. But not this time, so Jay as he did the day before, swung on around to the front of the house.

Not really looking for anything unusual, Jay didn't see anything and only noticed that the curtains were still drawn once he had started focusing his search for Mike in the front garden. But even after noticing the drawn curtains, and that that signalled that it seemed pretty obvious that Mike had not returned from his night out, Jay was still unconcerned. It was not unusual for a single man to spend the night out on the town, and if he got lucky, not to get back the next morning.

"Fuckin' ol' bastard," Jay whispered to himself, smiling and shaking his head, "after all the shit he gives me about women and partying my life away, here he is whoring it up for the whole night. The dirty ol' bastard, I'm gonna give him such shit when I see him again," Jay chuckled, and still smiling and being pleased with his 'one over' Mike, got back in the car and headed for the beach.

Although not nearly the crack of dawn, it was still quite early, with the freshness of the new day still hanging sweetly in the air and although the beach goers were arriving, neither the car park nor the beach itself was close to full yet. Jay looked at the clock on the dash, it was eight forty five. "Time for a quick surf," he thought scanning and noting the half decent waves moving through.

Still humming like a bird from the phone call and associated expectation of the day to come, Jay took his board off the racks, grabbed his towel and other 'day on the beach stuff,' and moved on down to the spot by the palms where he had arranged to meet Antoinette and Marco. He put all his stuff down and then walked back up higher onto the sand dunes and sat down looking out to sea.

He settled himself, relaxing into the space and allowed nature's juices to surge in through every portal. His body like a sponge absorbing them willingly until it was saturated and they overflowed into and flooded his mind which was now swimming with delight wanting to play and started pouring some of the liquid excess back into his body, unconsciously and by design putting him at perfect peace, harmony and in unison with the universe, allowing him to meditate. His body now warm and glowing, floating on the sand dune, staring into the distant ocean in a brilliant trance like state, setting his spirit free to travel out and beyond.

Time becoming timeless, thinking becoming thoughtless as his being buzzed and vibrated in absolute tune with everything above, below and around him. He got up without standing and started to walk without walking down towards his board, picking it up and continuing on towards the ocean, the onshore sea breeze dancing on his face. He held the board out in front of him and knew what to expect next, he had been here before. The wind flowed under the board and as it did so he positioned it perfectly for gentle lift off. "Don't even think," he whispered to himself, "just believe." He started to sail along about a meter off the beach, using the board as a boat shaped wing, holding it at bent arms length away from his body, his legs trailing weightlessly behind. Jay waited and searched for extra velocity in the wind gusts and as they came through he used them to gain precious height. When he felt he had gained enough and with his spirit now tingling with joyous freedom and delight he started performing above the beach in wide circles, diving down gently then swooping back up and around again. He looked down at the early morning arrivals making their way down to the beach as they stared and pointed back up at him. They weren't shocked or surprised, and if anything just a little envious that at this stage they weren't able to do the same thing. The kids clasping their mom's and dad's hands in anticipation, mystified and in wonder as their parents confirmed to them that they would be able to do the same thing if they really wanted to.

Jay's mind practiced from past experiences kept his physical from doubt, allowing his spirit the extended airtime and unconfined travel that it craved. Now confident in his ability in flight, Jay dived down, aiming for between the branches of the trees along the picnic area, angling through them like a bird and then with velocity on his side, soared back up towards the clouds.

Levelling out and looking down again, he saw Antoinette and Marco arrive and get out of the car, and he watched in anticipation as they followed the gaze of all the other beach goers up towards his 'aerial wonder.' Not wanting to completely let go of the board Jay just lifted three of his fingers that were overhanging the rail in a small wave to acknowledge that he had seen them. Marco shook his head slowly in pleasurable disbelief. Antoinette smiled and blew him a kiss as he went into a long sweeping turn aiming back out to sea and into the wind again, gaining as much height as he possibly could. Jay then went into a slow, deliberate fish eagle type circular glide, feeding and filling off of the incredible freedom, tranquillity and delight. Prickling and exuding with infinitive brilliance.

From his mesmerising loft in the sky, he could just make out Antoinette and Marco walking up to his spot on the beach, then Antoinette continuing on up to where he had been sitting on the sand dune. As she got there Jay's whole body jolted suddenly, almost violently as he literally came back down to earth. "Hey my beautiful Jay," she said walking up and kissing him gently on the lips, "didn't you see me coming?" Jay now playing physical catch up took a couple of seconds to clear his head and realise where exactly he was on earth, then when he did, smiled with absolute delight as the first thing he saw was the beautiful eyes of Antoinette right in front of him. He reached forward and gently held her face in both hands planting a long, warm, welcoming kiss on her lips, then not letting go, pulled his head back slightly, "Sorry man, I was literally miles away, having the most beautiful day dream." "Well I hope I was in it," she said smiling cheekily back at him. "Hmmm as a matter of fact you were." "Yuuum," she responded with a noticeable cheeky glint in her eyes. "No, not one of those dreams," laughed Jay, standing up and grabbing a tight hold on Antoinette's hand started walking back towards Marco.

"Hey Jay," said Marco looking up towards them as they approached. "Hey brother," said Jay "how's it going?" "Good thanks, good to be out in the sunshine. That meeting stuff around the table is not my idea of fun." "Oh yeh, what was that all about?" asked Jay curiously. "Ah just the usual," replied Marco dismissing the reality of Jay's question, "but you would have been proud of your Antoinette," he smiled, "talk about a man eater." Jay looked at Antoinette still searching for a genuine answer as to what the meeting was about. "Oh nonsense," she said to Marco but not taking her eyes off of and smiling at Jay, "it's just my 'business is business' side of me coming out." "So what business is that," asked Jay refusing to let go. "Not now, business is for the board room and this is the beach," she replied.

Jay flicked his eyebrows up and let it go, he wasn't that interested right now anyway, just so happy that he was with Antoinette and at peace again. "So what's that you are reading?" Jay asked Marco noting the book he had in his hand with his index finger shoved in between the pages marking the spot he had got to. "Oh nothing special, just something to relax and pass the time with. It's one of those futuristic sort of adventure novels. Normally quite good, they always seem to have a bit of twist and sting in the tale that you can't see coming. Keeps you turning the pages till you find out what the intrigue and mystery is all about. Nothing too heavy, just stuff to let you cool off in some other world. Do you do much reading?" "Hmmm, I haven't really read much, dunno maybe it's laziness or maybe it's 'cause once I start I can't seem to stop until I'm finished it, so in a way it drives me crazy. I did read the bible once though," Jay said with a smile "Yeh right," said Marco. "No I'm serious man, I did. Took me about two years to get through it all, but read it, cover to cover."

Both Antoinette and Marco said nothing but were staring wide eyed at Jay. So he explained himself, "Well you'll see when you come to one of our barbeques. The fires going, bit of music in the background, everyone having a good couple drinks and snacks, lots of relaxed fun and banter. Then the meat will go on, everyone will have their fill, the music gets a little louder, everyone starts getting a little more festive and then sooner or later you will get a group of guys around the fire. Normally a little bit pissed by now, and what starts off as a discussion soon turns into a raging debate. Nine times outta ten it will be about one or a combination of three things. Sex, which everyone thinks they are an expert on," Jay paused smiled and carried on, "politics is the second subject that all and sundry have the answers to and then of course religion introduces the third field of everyone's expertise," he finished off, waiting for 'the nod' to proceed further. "So how did that all lead you to reading the bible?" asked Marco. "Well one night I was listening to two of my buddies going hell for leather, pardon the pun," said Jay pausing and grinning, "on some topic in the bible, and each one of them had a very noticeable and distinct version of what the bible actually said about it. Then when I sort of picked up on this once, it wasn't difficult to recognise that it seemed to happen every time religion came up as a topic, and not just at barbeques. So I decided to read it for myself and then I would know, what the bible actually said." "Wow that's amazing!" said Antoinette, so what did it say?" she asked with such innocence it caught Jay by surprise. Their eyes met and that beautiful warm rush filled them both, causing their heart rates to elevate which just accelerated and enhanced the deliciousness being coursed through their veins.

Jay laughed, "Well you will just have to read it for yourself to get the answer to that question," he said and continued on, "pheeeweee man there is heaps of stuff in there. What was good though, is when someone started saying something about, 'the bible says this or the bible says that,' I knew if they were speaking crap or not, and it sort of just gave me the freedom to not even be concerned one way or the other. Didn't even have to bother arguing, because I knew what I had read." "Ok then just tell me what you found really interesting," Antoinette persisted. "Hmmm, I s'pose one thing was, when I was a wee 'pilchard' and my mom sent me off to Sunday school, I had always been taught that the rainbow was a sign, a promise for us from God to say that he would never flood the earth again. But what I read was that it was actually a sign for Him to remember the oath he made with man and the animals of this earth that he would never flood it again."

Both Antoinette and Marco looked at Jay knowing that there was and waiting for more. "Well that said two things to me, well actually three. The first, I had been 'taught,'" Jay said indicating the inverted commas with his fingers, "and believed what I suppose you could say was not the truth, or maybe I should say not the whole truth of what the bible actually said. Then number two,

God is 'human' after all. He forgets and needs to be reminded. And all that says to me is that He must have heaps going on in the various parts of His world, and we are only but a part of it, or maybe it's just a time thing and He needs a bit of a diary or 'post it' kinda note to keep Himself up to speed with what's been going on through the ages."

Marco couldn't help himself and burst out laughing, "A 'post it' note, that is the first and most probably only time I will ever hear the rainbow being compared to a 'post it' note. You're weird man, hahaha, a 'post it' note." Antoinette was giggling to, "You're funny," she said, "funny beautiful," she continued on then leaning forward and kissing him. Jay smiled, "Oh well maybe I shouldn't tell you my third," he said teasingly. "No c'mon, you can't stop now," said Marco wanting more of and enjoying Jay's interpretation. "Well thirdly, what I understood was that He made the oath with man and the animals, and that was really interesting to me. You know, everyone always wonders if animals have a soul and so on, well surely they must have if God was going to make an oath with them. Well maybe I should say maybe, and not surely, but either way, it did enforce to me of how important, how special, animals on this earth are to Him."

"That's amazing," said Antoinette, "so what else did you discover?" "Yikes there was so much more hey, and it's difficult to remember it all. After I was already halfway through I wished I had written down my summary of discoveries as I was going through it all, but never did, so most probably was never meant to. I seem to remember a part where angels were sent down to mate with humans, but now as I'm talking about it, I'm wondering if I was dreaming it or not." "Oh so that's where you come from," Antoinette said, smiling incredibly lovingly back at him, "you're half angel." "Hahaha no!" he insisted, "I'm unfortunately just a thoroughbred human." "Well you are my angel," she said throwing her arms around and kissing him and then not letting go tucking her face into his neck. "You two," said Marco, "gees there are three of us down here you know." Antoinette looked up and pulled a tongue at him like you would to your brother, telling him to like it or lump it.

Feeling a little weird Jay decided to change the slightly awkward energy, "Hey Marco wanna go try your hand at surfing? There is a perfect little mid break coming through to have a go on." "Marco glanced around at everyone starting to fill up the beach, "Naah, might give it a miss hey, just cool off and read my book." "Ah come on you big 'woosy,'" said Antoinette, "live a little, go and give it a go."

Marco looked at Jay questioningly. And Jay knowing that Marco would actually love to have a go and knew what his actual barrier to 'going for it' was responded, "Yeh c'mon you big 'woosy,'" he reiterated, "they won't bite and like I said to you before, they themselves have the exact inhibition you have and would actually love to be able to break it down and have a go themselves."

It was all the persuasion Marco needed. He got up ready to give it a go and. taking his shirt off, he grew in stature and got even bigger than he already was. "Shit," said Jay, "You're built like a bloody brick shit house man. What the heck food did you grow up on?" Marco laughed and flexed his guns for show, "just about anything and everything he laughed, not much this body turns its nose up to. C'mon then show me how it's done." "Can I come to?" asked Antoinette, already stripping down to her costume and not waiting for an answer. Jay looked at her and although he felt himself staring, he couldn't stop. His mouth dropped ever so slightly open and everything once again turned to slow motion as Antoinette giggling and moving towards him lifted his shirt off then ran her fingers over his stomach, "Mmm my beautiful six pack tum she said, kissing him then grabbing his hand and pulling him towards the water.

Marco just looked at them in dull but content disbelief, picked up the board and trotted up next to them. Jay regaining his composure started giving the first lesson as they walked towards the ocean edge. "Ok, so don't rush it, when you lie down on the board for the first time it will feel very wobbly and unstable, just sort of become one with it and start to feel and become part of the ocean. Paddle around a bit and get your balance, then we will do the wave catching part."

They reached the waters edge and made their way through the shore break. The cool liquid in complete contrast to the heat of the invisible rays of the sun enveloped their bodies, folding perfectly around them as they became part of it. "Ok jump on," said Jay, which Marco did and immediately tilted over and fell off. Antoinette burst out in laughter, "come on Marco you can do it man," she shouted encouragingly splashing water at him. "Yeh, just relax brother like I said, just feel and become part of the ocean."

Marco looked at the ocean and zoned out, not focusing on anything, but rather determined and wanting. He took a deep breath, exhaled then jumped on the board and started paddling around gaining in amateur skill and confidence. "Yaaay," shouted Antoinette and started clapping, laughing, splashing and throwing water into the air in celebration, "go Marco!" Then she turned and jumped into Jay's arms throwing her legs around and kissing him hard. "I love you so much," she said. "Hmmm I love you so much too," he said smiling, happy and in perfect perfection.

The heat of their two bodies coming together melting the water between them as they swayed, swirled and were mesmerised in liquid heaven. The vacuum they were in stopping time, blurring physical existence and consequence. "Hey Jay what's next then? C'mon man focus on your student a bit here," called out Marco paddling in close and splashing them both. "Sorry brother, just giving you some independence out there, it's part of the learning experience," he said smiling and reluctantly letting go of Antoinette. "Ok Marco, paddle a lit bit further out then turn and paddle in on a wave, the key to success is to go from lying down to standing up in a flash, it's called 'taking off.' Don't mess around just use those guns of yours and go for it. Start your first wave or two by going from lying down and then press up hard and fast straight onto your knees then when you get the hang of it try going from lying to standing straight up all in one go."

It didn't take long and Marco had had his first ride, and once he had, Jay could see it was going to be difficult to get him out of the water. He was hooked. And even though Antoinette and Jay couldn't have cared less if he had not got out of the water the whole day, eventually fatigue got the better of him and he paddled over to them and jumped off, floating the board next to him under one arm. "That was incredible man, I'm going to get one of these tomorrow," he said smiling. "Thanks so much for convincing me, shit that was amazing!" he reiterated. "My absolute pleasure," acknowledged Jay then turned towards Antoinette, "ok your chance now," he said. "I will, but not today," she replied. "Ah c'mon," said Marco, "you know you want to, let go of your inhibitions," he teased, smiling and winking at Jay. "Ok, pass the board over and I will ride it in then," she said 'bubblily' as only she could, accepting the challenge confidently and with no doubt in her mind that she would master the art.

Marco undid the leash off of his ankle and passed it on to Jay, who dove down and strapped it onto Antoinette's ankle and couldn't resist giving her bum a gentle squeeze on the way up to the surface. "That's one I owe you," she said smiling as his face appeared centimetres from hers, kissing her finger and planting it on his lips. Then as if she had done it her whole life she jumped up and lay on the board, paddling it around and taking it slightly deeper, no fear only total confidence as she turned as the next wave came through, paddling hard towards the beach until the swell acknowledged her presence, lifted her up and carried her forward in gentle, powerful effortlessness.

The board skated over the clean surface down the face and as it did so, Antoinette pushed up onto her knees, arms either side, her hands playing in the water. The wave broke just behind her and then the mass of bubbles fizzed and popped around her caressing her skin in delectable, feathery delight. As the board got to the beach and bumped on the sand below, she stood up, turning and looking at them both, raising her arms in triumph. "Wooohooo," she yelled out.

"That's Antoinette for you Jay my man, fearless, full of fun, determined and yes, full of shit too," he finished off smiling and laughing.

Jay body-surfed the next wave in, waded in up to Antoinette and gave her a huge hug, picking her up and spinning her in a circle around him. "Wow that was amazing. You're a natural." "So what's my reward then?" she asked still clasping her arms around his neck. "Hmmm you will have to wait and see," he said smiling and putting her back down again.

Marco came out of the water and joined them as they walked back up the beach. "So time for a bite to eat," he said, "gotta refuel the body after all of that." "Well, you can come past my place if you want, I've got a bit of salami and cheese, and I can pick up a couple fresh rolls on the way there," said Jay. "Hmmm, I was thinking more along the lines of a thick rump steak, egg, chips and salad," replied Marco licking his lips at the thought. "Well I have got an idea," said Antoinette, "you go have your feast Marco, and Jay and I will go have a normal sized lunch, then catch up with you later."

This caught Jay a bit by surprise, but in that instant he knew as awkward as the moment might be, he wasn't going to negatively influence the decision that he wanted from Marco, so he just sort of pretended he was not part of the conversation, threw the towel over his head and insinuated that his hair required a vigorous drying rub.

Then, when he as inconspicuously as possible peered through the towel, Marco was holding his chin, looking up at nothing, in self-thought, contemplation and deliberation. A small, almost unnoticeable smile appeared as he looked at Antoinette, "Good idea, I could do with a little time to myself anyway," then turning to Jay, "she's in your hands Jay, take very special care of her brother, or my life won't be worth living." And even though Marco still wore a slight smile, Jay recognised in Marco's eyes, that neither would his if anything did happen to, or happen to upset, Antoinette in anyway.

"That's settled then," said Antoinette, "you go have a bit of quality Marco time and we will see you later. Jay can give me a lift back home sometime this afternoon." Marco looked across at Jay. "Yeh, that's all good," confirmed Jay, trying to act as unemotionally unconcerned and normal as possible, when in reality, as the consequence of the thought of some real quality time alone with Antoinette had returned from his mind sending a rush of self-manufactured exotic drugs into his body, he could hardly breath never mind speak. But somewhere from within his kaleidoscopic haze, his mind partner made it through, "Calm down brother, you're going to have a heart attack or faint or something." The mechanism of 'self-internalisation' saved him, allowing Jay's mind to realise it had been caught unawares and half asleep, putting the brakes on the release of chemicals into his body, enabling the physical to settle down a bit.

Antoinette on the other hand couldn't contain her excitement and delight. She was such a free spirit she just didn't care, she knew what she wanted, what she had found, and couldn't care less if the whole world knew about it. "Yaaay, let's go then she said," picking up her stuff and grabbing Jay by the hand.

They walked back up to the car, Antoinette, swinging Jay's arm backwards and forwards as she literally skipped her way along. "We'll catch you later then Marco," said

Jay as they reached the car park. Antoinette let go of Jay's hand and hopped over to Marco, "Thank you so much big brother," she said kissing him on the cheek as Marco 'squinched' up the side of his face. "Yuuuk don't do that," he protested. So she promptly gave him another peck on the cheek, and then giggled. "See you later, don't get into any trouble." Marco grunted. "You take care and stay safe too," waved Antoinette.

# The Quality Time

Jay had tied the board onto the roof racks; they both got in and drove out towards his place. "Just gotta get some rolls from the bakery quick." he said. "I'm not that hungry," she replied, grabbing hold of his upper arm, leaning across and snuggling into it. "You fill me up with everything I need."

Alone together they were at and in perfect harmony. The world around them didn't matter. It was as though their spirits became intertwined, communicating with warmth and energies beyond the realm of physical existence and understanding. Neither of them had anticipated it, but they could definitely feel it.

Jay, now in warm perfection, managed to speak first. "You're crazy man, and you drive me crazy, what is it about you?" he asked. "I don't know," she replied, but when I'm with you I get this intense, beautiful, overwhelming happiness, incredible, childlike buzzing. It's like I want to dance with you all day and all night, with my arms in the air and your arms around my waist. I want to fall asleep and wake up in your arms and feel happy, safe and complete forever." Antoinette's words stirring some ancient, infinitive memories etched deep within Jay's mind as he instinctively pulled his arm in hugging her even closer and tighter. They didn't say another word for the rest of the way. There was no need to, they were unconsciously communicating through means they had yet to recognise, but at this point neither could even begin to understand or care.

How they eventually got to Jay's place, parked the car and went inside neither of them knew, but as the door closed behind them Antoinette turned Jay towards her and they kissed, slowly at first just touching each others lips, breathing in each other's breath. Jay held her shoulders gently squeezing them on impulse. Their hearts started to beat as one as they moved in together, her breasts pressing hard up against his chest. Her arms now tightly around his neck, their open mouths coming wantingly together, their tongues playing, dancing, teasing and tasting. Jay's hands moved up onto her face massaging her cheeks and cheekbones before caressing her chin and bottom lip with his fingers. Their bodies had become weightless, almost fused together by the energies flowing in around and through them, the brilliant blue and red hazes being emitted, turning a transparent, translucent purple mist as they dissolved into each other in the most gentle of whirlwinds.

They managed to part their bodies allowing their hands to explore. Jay put his hands flat up against her stomach, trying to hold as much of her as possible, then slowly caressed them around and onto her bum. Antoinette was holding her hands flat against his chest, every now and again gently squeezing his nipples, rolling them in her fingers turning his temperature up high.

With their mouths in everlasting exploration, Jay moved one hand back around to her front and like warm silk, folded it over her breast, and reciprocated by clasping tightly and playing with her nipple. There was no intention, preconception or other as his hand by pure love moved down to unbutton her pants. Antoinette tensed ever so slightly, and pulled back very gently to look him the eyes. "Nooo," she whispered, "not now." Jay smiled, "Wow, those are some dangerous looking eyes you got there," he said, moving both his hands back onto her bum. Antoinette smiled, "Well, those are some beautiful soft melting eyes you got there," she said closing her eyes again and gently fusing her being back into Jay's.

Neither knew how long they stood there just swaying in each other's arms, bathing in each other's warmth. "Hey, you have got a visitor," said Antoinette, not letting go of or lifting her face off of Jay's shoulder. "Oh, yeh?" replied Jay not even comprehending her statement. "Aaah, he's so cute," said Antoinette.

Now slightly more in tune Jay turned to see a little puppy dog staring at them through the ranch sliders, wagging his tail in appreciation of the movie he was watching. "Oh that's Pluto from next door; he pops around for a visit every now and again. Go let him in if you want, he's a real lovable pooch."

They let go of each other and Antoinette made her way over to let the puppy in. "Gosh man, he's sooo cute and so cuddly and soft," she said picking him up and snuggling him up close. The puppy overjoyed with the company and attention allowed Antoinette to give him all the attention he could get. "So what do you feel like to eat or drink?" Jay asked moving through to the kitchen. "I'm not that hungry, maybe just a cold drink would be good, thanks."

Jay poured two drinks and moved back through to the lounge. Antoinette was sitting on the floor cross-legged in front of the couch with the dog very comfortably being pampered on her lap. Jay put the drinks down next to them then stepped over and around Antoinette, sitting down behind her with her shoulders between his legs. "Ok here is your reward for catching your first wave," he said as his hands moved onto the muscles between her shoulders and neck.

Her head had no choice but to drop forward as his thumbs massaged her muscles. "Wow, you gotta loosen up a little, girl," he said feeling and working on breaking down the tight knots, "you are strung up bad man, you seem so care free and happy, but your muscles tell me a complete different story, what's that all about?" "Mmm," she groaned in pleasurable relief, "not now, I have so much I want to tell and share with you but pleeease, mmm, not now."

Jay moved his hands out towards her shoulders continuing to transfer his energies into her tired and tense muscles, then moved them back along her neck massaging her ears gently then spreading his fingers across her skull, drawing them in and out sending delicious shivers throughout her body. The purple mist spreading, wider, enveloping, as they lost themselves in and with each other.

His hands moved onto her cheek bones, lower jaw

and lips, squeezing, playing and plying them in the most naturally erotic way, then he moved back down her neck and out onto he shoulders. "Aaah . . . gosh . . . wow man, your hands are sooo soft and sooo warm," was all she managed to breathe out. Jay unconsciously slid the straps of her top and bikini top over and off of her shoulders. Antoinette's head fell backwards into his lap and Jay leaned slightly forward aiding her clothes in the direction they so desired.

The twin horizontal valleys formed between her shoulder and collar bones dropping off into a sheer cliff face over her upper chest then rising into two beautiful, magnificent ski slopes coming up until they converged and met with the perfectly rounded form reaching up towards them. Her nipples capping the pinnacles in a perfect, gentle pink, irresistible to his hands as they moulded around her breasts lifting, gently squeezing, then letting go, tickling her tummy, sides, armpits, breasts and nipples.

No part of her upper body was left untouched, and no part of either of their bodies were kept from vibrating as they tuned into and fed off of each others beings, feeding their spirits who returned the favour by commanding the brain to silently and continuously climax their bodies with the manufacture and release of extra sensory chemicals.

It was the movement of the puppy who had been fast asleep in heaven on Antoinette's lap taking a long, extended stretch and massive yawn as he was waking up that filtered in through Jay's physical, giving him a glimpse and reminder of his present and earthly state. "Shit look at the time," he said in a kinda soft shock, and then continued on, "shit, you take me to places so far

away, I forget where I am and how long I've been gone."
"Yuuum, I love taking you to those places," she said
opening her eyes pulling his head down towards her and
kissing him. "That was sooo beautiful, I love you so
much, mmm when can I get my next reward?" she asked,
lifting Pluto reluctantly back onto his feet and turning
around onto her knees to face Jay. She put her arms
around his neck, smiling and then pulling him in towards
her, kissing him long and hard. "Hmmm, well we will
just have to see," he said letting go and helping her tops
back up and over her shoulders, "maybe you will have
to stand up on the board next time." "No ways, that's
not fair, how long will I have to wait to go surfing again
never mind be able to stand up."

Jay laughed opening the door for Pluto who was
waiting expectantly to be able to be released for purposes
of relief. "Ok, let's just say no task required to be
achieved then. You want it, you got." "Whenever I want
it?" she questioned cheekily. "Hahaha yeh—whenever
you want," Jay said just loving being manipulated by
Antoinette and walking on through to the kitchen area.
"Feel like a toasted sandwich?" "Yeh that would be real
good, don't know why, but I'm a bit peckish right now,"
she replied walking in behind him. "What time do you
think Marco will expect you back?" "He won't really
have a time, I don't go out that much, so we can make it
anytime, how about tomorrow morning around twelve?"
she said walking up behind him and hugging him around
the waist like she never wanted to let go. Jay held her
hands tightly and they rocked their bodies to some silent
music playing in their heads. "Yeh well maybe one day
you will never have to go," said Jay without even caring
or comprehending what he was insinuating. "Yuuum,

can't wait," she replied.

They let go of each, Jay getting back to making the sandwiches while Antoinette jumped up and sat on the counter watching his every move. "But no seriously what time do you think you should be back? Bearing in mind we don't want to cause any undue concern and create a situation where Marco is not happy with letting you go again, which actually, come to think of it, sounds quite strange seeing as you are an adult," Jay said turning looking at Antoinette in a questioning smile. She looked down at the floor indicating to Jay that she had something to say, and wanted to say it, but seemed afraid to do so. "C'mon," said Jay turning back towards making the sandwiches to allow Antoinette the feeling that nothing could be that a bigger deal, "spit it out. I can see there is something you want to tell me." "Well ok, but I don't know how you are going to feel about me afterwards."

Jay stopped and turned; looking into Antoinette's eyes, her face for the first time had saddened and was full of doubt. "Hey," he said, "nothing can be that bad. C'mon man put a smile on the beautiful face of yours," he said walking over and holding her hands. "Ok," she said sitting up straight and regaining some composure, "you know those test rigs out at sea, and all the demonstrations they have been having up and down the coast?" "Yeh sort of, I haven't really been following it, but I've seen them out there on the horizon when we have been out to sea fishing, and seen a bit of the controversy and demonstrations on TV." "Well my dad is in charge of all of that, and I work for him," she blurted out in a hurry, as though it was burning inside of her and she wanted it out as quickly as possible.

Jay stared intently into her eyes, looking for the rest, but nothing more came out, he continued staring then breaking out into a smile, "Shit that's it," he asked laughing with some relief. "That's what you have been holding back from me?" Antoinette looked happily puzzled, "So you, loving the ocean and everything in it and making a living from it, aren't upset about that and the potential for off shore oilrigs in your backyard?" "Ok you want me to be honest?" he asked, "I actually believe it's a real good thing. Yeh must be done properly with the best engineering, health, safety and environmental systems blah, blah, blah in place. No shortcuts, no bullshit, but yeh why not? Let the whole region boom and benefit economically. And any 'mother' that argues against it better not be riding a petrol driven vehicle, or for that matter use any product that is produced from the by-products of hydrocarbons. Some of 'them' are just full of shit! Ok sure you gotta have people to make sure that rogue, 'fartass,' robbing, bastard business people are kept in check, because they are most probably even worse, but compromise, understanding, dialogue, networking, honesty, integrity and transparency, surely we can make it work to everyone's benefit?" "Wow you need to come and work with me," smiled Antoinette. "Do you want a job?"

Jay smiled, but wanted to know more. "So what's the story with Marco then? How come he sort of dictates where, what and how you can go?" Antoinette looked back down at the ground, this time because she really didn't want this conversation to go further. Not for any other reason other than the concern, almost fear that she might lose her Jay. She looked back up at him, her eyes watery, her voice quiet and quivering ever so slightly, "my dads an oil tycoon, a multi billionaire." Jay not letting go of her hands unintentionally took a step back. One sentence, causing instant confusion stunning him slightly as the past few days experiences flooded in and started answering questions he and been pondering subconsciously. Then his mind started to spin, questioning those answers with more questions. "See I knew I shouldn't have told you," she said jumping down off of the counter, turning and walking away. Jay reached out for her arm pulling her back around and in towards him. "No," he said, "of course you should have, I'm not upset or anything, just a bit dunno hey, shocked I guess, just give me a moment for all of this to sink in," he said hugging her in close for contact and confirmation.

They stood there in each other's arms for a bit, then Jay held her out by the shoulders at arms length, "and Marco?" "Marco is I suppose what you could say is my brother, it was never official, but my dad took him under his wing and sort of adopted him when he was still a kid. These days he's also my unofficial bodyguard. My dad insists that where I go, Marco goes, and he does not let me out of his sight. My dad has made it very clear that Marco is responsible for my welfare and will be held accountable to him if anything should ever happen to me." "Wow," said Jay, "don't quite know what to say." "Say you still love me," said Antoinette, smiling, free and relieved that she had told Jay everything there was to tell. "You're funny, he said, I love you even more now, can't believe you were so afraid to tell me all of that."

He gave Antoinette a gentle kiss and turned to take the toasted sandwiches out the machine. Antoinette jumped back up and sat on the counter. "So, I've answered all of your questions, now it's your chance."

Jay looked around at her over his shoulder and opened his eyes wide insinuating the words 'Oh shit here we go.' Antoinette continued, "So tell me what your day dream on the beach today was all about." "Hahaha funny, naah you will think I'm a little crazier than you actually already do and then you might genuinely run and hide." "No ways come on, that's not fair, I let go and told you everything, now you have got to too." "Ok, you want it you got it, but be prepared." "Yaaay, I'm prepared," she sort of squealed in delight, knowing that she just loved the stuff that came out of Jay's mind.

Jay walked over to the lounge with the sandwiches, "Follow me," he said smiling, "you might want to be sitting down on the couch when you hear all about it." Jay sat down, while Antoinette jumped excitedly and expectantly onto the couch next to him, legs crossed and facing him. Jay took a deep breath, then dropped his shoulders in kinda like a show of defeat, took another long, slow, deliberate breath, then dove straight into the deep end. "Dunno man, it's like sometimes I just kinda zone out and have these really, really, really vivid day dreams. It's like I'm living them, I feel them, I taste them and I can't get enough of them. I can't just switch them on or off . . . I wish I could, but no . . . it's just when I am really relaxed and in a really cool space, my body sort of switches off and my mind just takes over and allows me to travel to wherever I want to be and do whatever I want to do."

Jay paused looking for some kind of response acknowledgement or rejection. "That's amazing, wow that's like perfect meditation. So cool that you are able to do it and control it, you must teach me how you do it," Antoinette said. Jay laughed, "I would if I could, but like I say, I haven't quite worked it all out." "So what did you do in the last one? The one on the beach this morning." "I flew," said Jay pausing, wondering just how far he could go before Antoinette freaked out and decided that he might not actually be everything that she had perceived. "That's crazy," she said, "that's amazing; you have got to show me how you do it! You gotta teach me how and take me with you."

Jay smiled, "Well it takes a bit of practice, and it seems to work when you get it right. It's a long sort of story, which I won't bore you with, but it's like you've gotta get yourself into that space you are in just before falling into a deep sleep. You can kinda practice it at night when you are in bed, but the problem I found there, was that every time you got close to where you wanted to be meditation wise, then bang, you fell fast asleep, and the next thing you knew the alarm clock was waking you up or something. So you can practice it before going to sleep and then try it out when you are wide awake and in a perfect space with yourself and everything around you. But it's also quite weird . . . Like this morning, it's kinda like you don't even try to do anything. It just happens. Actually the more you think about it or try to 'get there,' the harder it is"

Antoinette didn't say anything as she sat there eating her sandwich unconsciously aware that she was. Jay stared back at her, their eyes loving each other, reaching in and communicating in ultimate silence. Nothing verbal needing to be said about their intense understanding. Silent in their connection, loving and wanting.

Jay leaned forward and touched his lips on hers. "It's like there is so much out there, so much natural beautiful, creative energy out there just waiting to be allowed in used and re-released. Like ok, you will just have to bare with me for a bit, but you will get where I'm going," Jay smiled reassuringly, "Think about it. How does stuff enter our bodies?" "I got it," Antoinette said throwing her arm up in the air as though indicating to a teacher that she had the answer, "through our mouths," she continued on gleefully. Jay laughed, "Yeh, you're right; we take food in, use all the energy we need from it then either store the rest as fat for some other time that we might need it in the future," he said tapping his six pack stomach and smiling in triumph, "and then let the rest go back to where it came from. But go a little beyond food how does other stuff enter our bodies?" he asked pressing Antoinette to think a little deeper.

Antoinette smiled naughtily, "No not like that," laughed Jay then continued, "well, just like food is energy and enters our body, all the other sights, sounds, smells, tastes and touches that enter our physical body through our senses are also energies that we can use, sometimes unconsciously, sometime consciously. Our senses through our ears, nose, eyes, tongue and skin can take in the myriad of energies readily available and just waiting to continue on their journey through you. What's so weird, is that they are always there, tons and tons of energies just waiting to be taken in, but a lot of the time we are sort of in such a hurry in and around our busy little selves and individual self important bubble worlds, we walk around with our senses half shut, and miss out on just so much that's available and just waiting to be used and shared."

Antoinette was intrigued, "Please don't stop she implored," reaching out and holding his shoulder. He looked up at her, smiling softly, raising his eyebrows and sort of shrugging his shoulders, cocking his head sideways, 'asking,' "Are you sure?" ensuring that she knew he was about to go even deeper.

Antoinette nodded her head. Jay took a deep breath, "so all of the stuff out there, the sights, the sounds, temperatures, touches, fragrances . . . The mind-blowing sunrises, exquisite sunsets, clear night skies all flooding into our eyes. The rustle of the leaves, the crash of the surf, the bubbles popping in their millions up and down the beach. The warmth on the breeze, the smell of the salt and seaweed. Everything, all of that stuff entering our bodies through our senses are actually all just energies in one form or another. It's weird, because they are 'invisible' as all energies are, and yet, ironically, you can see, taste, touch, smell and hear them. It's the same as electricity. So powerful it can heat the oven, light the streets, even kill the body, but electricity too, is invisible."

"Ok," Jay said pausing and taking a breath, "don't lose me now, so the senses of the body are able to harness these universal fuels, then they by design feed all those energies through to your brain, which is the mouth, the bodily portal to your mind, and your mind is like the brain of your soul, your mind and soul together being your spirit."

Antoinette clenched her teeth together and parted her lips indicating to Jay the he was starting to lose her a bit. "Don't think too much about it right now, just stay with me," he laughed, "but yeh, once you practice and learn how to recognise, realise, suck in and absorb all the beautiful energies available out there, filling your mind with them, then your mind, refuelled and ready to go, sort of takes over and sets your spirit free . . . And that's when you are able to daydream away," smiled Jay wanting to lighten the theory a bit.

"No, I get it," said Antoinette, "I really get it, and guess what?" she asked smiling from ear to ear and before he could respond answered her own question, "you are my favourite energy that I love to absorb into my mind and soul, and if I could I'd absorb your whole body into mine too." "You're funny," Jay said leaning across and kissing her. She threw her arms around his neck not letting him go and they got lost again in each other.

Jay drew his mouth off of hers and with their noses still touching whispered, "Well you must hear my theory along the same lines as the daydreams when two people's spirits come out and mix together with each other." "I can't wait," she whispered back and kissed him again.

Driving out towards Antoinette's place shortly after, both their bodies were still buzzing, vibrating, soaring to peaceful heights from their time together. The consequence of their spirits being released beyond the body to dance, play and make love, before having to return to direct the body to continue on fulfilling its earthly existence.

Antoinette reached out for Jay's hand, "so tell me more," she said, tell me what happens when two people's spirits meet." Jay's mind was a fluorescent feather. Free, alive, glowing and beyond content . . . and he spoke it as it was. "Well, it's like when two souls for some reason, fate, destiny, who knows, are drawn close together by the bodies they are in. Then it's like that same energy thing, when we, our bodies, are the actual energy. Like when we come together, our bodies 'wantingly' exuding our energies, our tastes, our heat, our touch, sound and smell, our look. And at the same time our bodies sucking as much of the other in as humanly possible, the energies as with the daydreams, setting the minds and souls, the spirits of the two alight, allowing them to permeate out and beyond their bodies, then they, just like the bodies are doing, become one, sharing loving and living each other. You know it's like when seconds become timeless and timeless becomes infinitive. Like can you actually remember the whole afternoon, or are parts of it just a day dream?" Jay asked smiling and turning briefly to note her reaction. "What afternoon?" she replied smiling and squeezing his hand, "gosh you have such amazing ways of describing and explaining stuff. That's exactly how I feel when I'm with you, everything is in slow, perfect motion and you put me in such a deliciously mystical space that, it all does seem like a bit of a blur and day dream. Like I was, but wasn't actually altogether here in my blatant bodily form. But I've just never thought about it that deeply or in that way before. I think it's incredible."

Again Jay wondered a bit how he had actually got there when he found himself pulling up Antoinette's drive way. Everything started becoming very raw and bright as they walked up to the front door, the reality of everyday life causing their flight to stall and start nose-diving back down to earth. It was like they were going to have to make an emergency landing, and their minds were working overtime, reading all the instruments available and directing the body accordingly to ensure that any potential disaster would be averted.

Antoinette opened the door, "Hey Marco we back," she shouted out. "Hey the princess and the prophet have returned safe and sound," he said walking through and smiling, shirt off, fully relaxed and beer in hand. Antoinette stopped for a second, eyes and mouth wide open. It looked as though Marco had, had just as much of an afternoon as they had, which was very unusual. He was normally just so stiff, so determined not to let go, to make a mistake, in fear of something that he could never seem to understand, but the 'afternoon off' seemed to have been the perfect medicine. He was literally a different person.

"Ha," said Antoinette putting her hands on her hips pretending to act like his mother "so what have you been up to this afternoon?" "Well just wouldn't you looove to know," he said back to Antoinette smiling and winking at Jay. Jay smiled back knowingly, "so how was the steak egg and chips?" "Bloody delicious man, pheeew they know how to grill them down here on the coast man, and the waitresses, mmm, they are even more delicious," he said laughing out loudly, proud and boasting before turning back towards the lounge.

Marco was on a high of note, "come through and sink a couple beers with me brother, he said calling Jay through with a big wave of his arm. Jay and Antoinette looked at each again wide-eyed, smiled and shrugged their shoulders. Antoinette grabbed Jay's hand and directed him through without question. "Go through my Jay," I'll get you guys a couple more."

"So how was your afternoon?" asked Marco as Antoinette came back through and handed them the beers before jumping on the couch and squashing up against Jay. "Mmm, too good," she replied, then very quickly added, "ok never too good, but as close as you are ever going to get," she said smiling. "Say no more," smiled Marco looking at Jay in a way that immediately instigated Jay into changing the direction of the conversation. "Don't really know where the time went, sort of like it's was quite weird, the whole afternoon seemed to be a bit of a blur with no beginning and no end." "Hahaha I wonder why?" laughed Marco, still bubbling over with the remnants of his afternoon's freedom and delights.

"It's times like these that make life on earth sooo good," continued Marco, stretching out all four limbs then relaxing back into the chair. "Since meeting you Jay I have for some weird reason," he said pulling as weird face as he could, "started thinking more and more about what it's all about and what we are doing down here, and the more I think about it, the more I realise I shouldn't take it so seriously. Life is too short to worry about all the shit that goes on. Like you said, 'live life and love living.' I think that's my new motto from now on in," he said taking a deep slug of beer and holding the can up to salute and cheer his new found attitude. "Too true," replied Jay, I'll drink to that," holding his can up high acknowledging Marco's cheer. "But remember life's not too short, it's actually very long," he said. "Hmmm how did I just know that there would be something I still didn't have quite right," frowned Marco friendlily. Jay smiled, "Well like I said, it's not too short, it's actually very long, buuut it's very fast. Think about it, to live for eighty odd years? Shit man that a looong time, but wow man it fly's by in a flash. So yeh it's understanding the difference between short and fast."

Jay paused taking a sip of his beer and noting Marco's expression, an interesting mix of confusion and understanding of what he had just heard. Jay started off again explaining by repeating himself first, "It's understanding the difference between short and fast, and I know that sounds weird and obvious, but I'm talking in the context of our lives down here on earth, because people sort of get the two a little confused, and it's quite important to understand the difference because there are consequences to it all." "And those are?" questioned Marco knowing he was going to get the answer anyway. "Well, firstly because it's so fast, you can make a bugger up very quickly and because it's so long the consequences of the bugger up can haunt you for more than a while, and vice versa of course, so yeh, enjoy life to the full, but be wary and don't get too clever," Jay smiled.

"Shit I just knew you would come up with something that made sense," laughed Marco, "and c'mon I know there's more." Jay smiled, "because life is so fast never give up an opportunity, don't sit around procrastinating for too long, it will pass you buy in a flash and you will sit around for a very long time pondering if only this and if only that."

Antoinette snuggled closer, implying that she was not going to miss out on any opportunity and future that involved Jay. Jay turned and smiled at her, knowing exactly what she was 'saying.' "You need to write a book and put all his stuff down man, said Marco you just gotta!" Jay looked back at him, his eyes glowing acknowledging the compliment.

"You also gotta remember though that there is at the end of the day no real rush." "Now you have got me," replied Marco. "Well to me there just has to be more than just this life on earth, you know it's like that word infinity." "Infinity? What the heck has that got to do with life on earth?" questioned Marco. "Well everything I suppose, it's like that age old unanswered, question. That never ending debate and dilemma. Where do we come from and where are we going? What's it all about? If God made us, then who made Him, and if on the other hand it did all start with a big bang, then what created the stuff to make the big bang in the first place? And at the end of the day, well I s'pose it's down to the inability of us down here on earth to cope with and understand infinity."

Jay took another sip of his beer and continued. "You know, for me anyway, there is no actual beginning and there is no actual end, so there is no actual rush." Marco raised his eyebrows in a sort of 'never thought about it like that before, tell me more' look, so Jay continued, "I suppose well that's kinda why we don't comprehend or even want to deliberate, or accept the concept. Most of us just find it way too frustrating to get a hold of. We are acclimatized and customised to, and understand how to start a certain project, and then enjoy seeing it through to the end. But no beginning and no end? What's the point? What's it all about?"

Jay paused for an answer but got none so just went on. "Hmmm dunno hey but what is intriguing, is that none of us ever seem to want our life on earth to end, so at the end of the day what's so frustrating about having no end? No end is after all what we want isn't it?"

"Ok well then how would you describe infinity then 'oh grand master'?" Antoinette asked, smiling and knowing Jay would have his answer. Jay mused. "I have thought about it often, and the best way I have almost been able to understand it is by using the example when JC split the basket of bread amongst the masses.

Everyone got some, it never ran out. So how could he have done it?" Again no answer, just Marco and Antoinette's eyes looking on with intrigue and expectation. "Well it's actually quite easy, he just kept on halving what he had left, giving half away and then again halving what He had left every time, and therefore never running out."

Marco let out a raucous laugh, "Hahaha, that is brilliant, but physically speaking, yeh right, it's obvious that eventually He would be halving a microscopic crumb which wouldn't fill a flea." "Well maybe, even if inadvertently," Jay smiled "you have just hit the nail on the head. Maybe infinity is more spiritual than physical, and just maybe that's why we just can't get our heads around it while we are down here on planet earth in this confined physical space and place. Maybe all the people He was feeding weren't starving for something to eat, but just starving for some spiritual enlightenment. The bread that was broken and shared was the bread of His mind and the soul, His spirit, given to feed, fulfil and enlighten theirs. Bread of and to feed the spirit and whoever wanted to be fulfilled in that way was able to feed from the basket held by or maybe even was itself JC. And the basket was never empty, no matter whom or how many took in their fill. There was an endless abundance, an infinitive amount of food to be shared."

Antoinette could not contain herself anymore, "Gosh, wow, man, that is amaaazing! I can actually picture and comprehend it now. It's like this void has been completely filled in my mind. It's recognising that knowledge, wisdom, spiritual enlightenment, the food and stuff of life will, can, never run out. It will always be there, waiting for whoever, whenever, however and whatever amount you or anyone else wants. That's infinity, there is no beginning and there is no end to it. That is so incredibly, beautifully amazing. I just love you!" she said and forgetting, not even caring that Marco was there, through her arms tightly around Jay pulling his face towards hers and melting her mouth onto his.

Marco 'un-phased' by it all now, got up, sighed, shook his head slowly from side to side in a cocktail of approval and acceptance with a dash of dismay, and walked through and got them another couple of beers.

"Hey no thanks," said Jay standing up as Marco returned and handed him another beer, "I gotta get going. I think I'll be out to sea tomorrow, so I want to be as 'fresh as' for my first day back out. Mike will be itching to catch some fish and make some money by now. He can get a bit agitated if he has to wait around for me when he's like that." "Naah that's all good," replied Marco, "most probably best if I slowed down a bit too. We also got a bit of a biggy out there tomorrow."

Jay looked across at Antoinette. "We have one of those 'all interested and affected parties' meetings in the town hall tomorrow, so yes, could get a bit, hmmm raucous, to say the least," she said. "Your beauty and Marco's brawn, you'll be fine," said Jay smiling and pulling her up to her feet. "Catch ya later, Marco. Thanks for the beers man," he said walking with Antoinette to the front door. "Take it easy out there Jay, catch you around sometime soon."

Jay and Antoinette looked at each other smiling, enjoying and slightly surprised by Marco's farewell comment to Jay. As they got to the door, they turned to face each other, instinctively wanting to top up with as much of each other's spirit that they could possibly get hold of. Their liquid kiss dissolving their bodies together into a weightless mass of perfect primal warmth and being. "I better go," he said from somewhere deep within without even speaking a word. "No, not yet, just a little while longer, pleeease," she echoed back kissing him even deeper. A mix of calm and butterflies fluttering throughout her person, remnants from a past passionate relationship. "You give my thoughts a voice, powerful and intimate, I love you so much," she conveyed across their one, time and space.

Eventually the purple mist dissipated back into its individual colours and they were able to comprehend earthly time once more. "Hey good luck for tomorrow hey." "You too my Jay, stay safe out in that big wide ocean, I love you so much!" "I love you too my Antoinette," Jay said smiling cheekily, and walking out towards his car, vibrating in perfect tune with the orchestral chemicals playing concerto deep within his body.

# The Wild Time

Jay woke up the next morning before the alarm went off. He was 'amped up,' fully charged and ready to go. Gliding at the perfect height, fully in control and loving it. "Shit can't wait to hear his excuses. Out whoring day and night, bloody disgusting," he said smiling and laughing to himself as he strode around towards Mike's place. As he got there, everything was as it was the last time he had popped around, curtains all still drawn, and no sign of life. "Fuck can you believe it, he's still not up," Jay said softly to himself, not thinking much of it. Then carried on as he would, jumping on board getting the boat prepared for the day.

He had done it so often it was like second nature, fuel, bait, rods, reels and radio. Loading and connecting it all up. There were no service stations, shops or first aid depots out there, and there was only one way to do it all before you headed out. And that was, the right way. The ocean in general took no prisoners and gave no second chances. Mike trusted and relied on Jay, and Jay respected and took pride in that trust.

With the boat locked, loaded and ready to go there was still no sign of Mike. "Hmmm must be stuck on the shitter," he thought, as he leaned up against the Landy and lit up a smoke. The early morning was perfect, Jay's whole body felt light and free as it took in what the day had to offer. The sky waking up unfolding into a perfect gentle blue as the sun rose higher and pulled back the pink and orange curtains. The one or two clouds that resisted being dissolved into the air were motionless as they floated above taking in the magnificent expanse of the earth. "Fuck I gotta give this shit up," Jay said to himself throwing the butt down and starting to get slightly frustrated with the waiting around.

"Hey morning Jay," came a pretty sullen voice from over the fence behind him. Jay turned around, startled as he realised that he was not alone in his immediate vicinity. "Hey morning Nigel, 'howzit' going?" Nigel looked at Jay searching, questioning and uncomfortably. Jay felt it immediately, he didn't know what it was, but his head shivered unintentionally and sent a wave of dry ice down through and shuddering his shoulders. "Not too good," replied Nigel breaking eye contact with Jay and looking up into the heavens, his eyes welling up. "Mike's not coming back Jay," he stammered. "What do you mean?" questioned Jay walking towards him. "Dunno man, evidently he had some really rare condition and it finally caught up with him and took him real quick." "What the fuck are you talking about man!" demanded Jay. "He's gone Jay, he passed on," Nigel said looking straight into Jay's eyes to ensure Jay knew and understood he was for real, tears flowing unashamedly down his cheeks.

Jay took a couple steps backwards to prevent himself from losing balance as the words hit him between the eyes like a baseball bat. He couldn't speak, he was numb from the toes up as the ice started to freeze his inner core.

"Sorry Jay, just didn't know how to tell you, there is no easy way." "No that's ok," whispered Jay, his mind in utter disarray as he staggered like a drunk to the edge of the boat, grabbing the rail for stability and comfort. His whole chest felt heavy as it started to take on the gravity of the news. He gulped and swallowed hard to prevent the tears that were being forced up from making there way out onto his face, but it was futile. As the ice melted so it poured out, and as it did so, he sobbed hard replacing the spent fluid with air.

He felt Nigel's arm come around his shoulders, and he turned and buried his wet face into his shoulder. Nigel just let him be, comforting Jay with his self and urging him on to get it all out. Jay pulled back slightly, "I'm ok thanks, Nigel," he said taking a deep breath, "just never saw it coming, just could never ever have expected it. Fuck man, why didn't he say something to me," he said exasperated then buried his head again and continued to sob. "No I'm ok," he said once more letting go of Nigel and walking around to the front of the boat. "Why the fuck didn't you say anything to me Mike?" he shouted out loud looking up to the sky and holding his hands up for an answer.

Nigel walked towards Jay. "Hey, Jay, it's ok man, he wasn't in any pain, and you know Mike, he was far too brave and proud to want anyone to worry or care for him." Jay turned and walked away as Nigel came closer as though the distance would somehow prevent any more of this nightmare from unfolding. "Fuck!" Jay said reaching for his smokes and lighting another one up. He took a deep drag then another then turned back towards Nigel. "Sorry man, I'm just a bit fucked up right now, this must be as hard for you as it is for me." "Come; let's go around to my place for a cup of coffee." "Thanks, Nigel, but I'll need to unpack the boat and stuff, then I just need to understand all of this. Most probably best if I just go back home for a while." "That's cool man, but please, take it easy and take it slow, and you know where I stay. If you want to just chat a bit more about all of this, just pop around anytime." "Thanks man, I'll be all good."

Jay's body now operating on instinct alone took control and started unloading the boat as his mind wandered aimlessly around in its own vacuum. Relying on habit his body walked back to his place, opened the door and got into the shower. The hot water massaging, caressing and comforting his skin, the steam penetrating deep within as he sobbed, breathed and gasped in lungful's of water vapour, slowly filling the vacuum, and resuscitating his mind. "Pheeew, rest in peace brother, rest in peace," he breathed out looking up at the ceiling. "Rest in peace," he repeated as he slowly started to temporarily manage the situation.

He climbed out the shower and started to dry off when he heard the knock on the door. The door opening before he had a chance to respond. "Hey Jay," said El walking in with Bee following close behind him. "We just heard the news. Fuck, man, we are so sorry. Are you ok?" Jay walked through with only a towel wrapped around his waist, his eyes and face still puffy, warm tears still leaking down his cheeks. His body only milliseconds away from shutting down as the relentless lack of instruction from his mind resulted in the brain not being able to concoct the chemicals required for its proper function. But he managed to squeak out an, "I'm ok thanks man," before he staggered into El sobbing uncontrollably.

El grabbed him hard under the arms, supporting and hugging him tightly. "It's ok brother, it's ok, get it all out. Don't worry man, he is at rest now, he will be fine," said El. Yeh, it's us that are left to mourn, it's our loss, but yes, I know he is at peace," replied Jay.

El walked Jay backwards and sat him down on the couch. Jay took a deep breath, "No I'm ok, I'm ok," he said reaching out for and swallowing the shot of whiskey being offered by Bee's outstretched arm. "Do you know where his body is right now?" asked Jay as the hot pungent rush of alcohol entered through his body into his mind, slapping it back into reality. "It's in the morgue up at the hospital. Joanne has been trying to get hold of you, something about instructions received from Mike's lawyer that you need to be made aware of." "Fuck my phone, where is it?" Jay asked, getting up almost frantically, but not really going anywhere. "Take it easy, Jay," reassured El, "everything is under control; we will go up and see them soon. Go freshen your face up a bit and get dressed, we will take ya up to the hospital."

None of the three of them said a word as they drove up towards the hospital. They didn't have to, they were all feeling the same way, comfortable in each other's presence as their individual spirits transcended their bodies, communicating and comforting each other in invisible and perfect silence.

"Hey cousins," said the security guard as they arrived at the entrance to car park of the hospital, his warm and genuine smile welcoming and reassuring, "I heard about Mike; you guys must be devastated," he continued on genuine concern, and then confidently lifted and reassured them, "but don't take it too hard. He's smiling down on you right now, he's happy and free." Then he leant over and peered through the window, "Hey Jay, you know Mike, he would not want you to be upset or mourn him for too long, he would want you to celebrate his life and remember the good times you had together," he said. "Yeh thanks Tim," replied Jay looking up towards him, his eyes welling up again from a mix of gratitude and realisation.

El finished filling in the security logbook, and handed it back to Tim before passing through the boom gate. "Thanks brother, your words are very kind, and so true too," he said winking and clasping Tim's hand in a show of gratitude. "Don't worry about going through reception, go around through the side door, then walk along to the back of the building on the ground floor, you'll find Joanne's office there, she'll be expecting you." "Thanks a million man, you are a star," replied El as he drove off.

The three of them walked according to the directions they had been given, Jay now sort of back in control of his functions leading the way, almost in a hurry. The white, spotless walls and polished floor feeding clinical messages into his mind, cleaning and sanitising it, allowing it to rejuvenate and regain control of its outputs into his body.

Jay knocked gently on the half open door, easing it

open. Joanne looked up in anticipation after having waited for and expecting their arrival. "Jay," she said hastily evacuating her seat, striding around and hugging him, then letting go and holding his face with both hands, giving him a loving and prolonged, comforting kiss. Then not letting go she pulled her face back slightly looking into his blurry eyes, massaging the top of his cheeks with her thumbs. "My beautiful Jay," she said, "are you ok?"

Jay reached up and held her wrists, squeezing them gently, thanking her by touch. "Yeh, still a bit shocked I s'pose, pwheeew it's all been so brutally hard and fast, but hmmm just sooo cool to have friends like I have," he said kissing her gently on the cheek and then turning towards El and Bee.

Joanne looked towards them, "Hi guys," she said giving them a wave with a couple finger, "thanks for taking care of and getting him up here," then tuned back towards Jay giving him another quick kiss and reluctantly letting him go, walked back around her desk. "Pull up a couple chairs and take a seat," she continued on, and with all three settled down picked up a piece of paper directly in front of her.

"Ok," she said looking up at Jay with a well-versed gentle, comforting smile, "I have the details of Mike's last wishes from his lawyer," she paused, "you do know he was a man of not many words and even less when it came to exhibiting any show of compassion, love or kindness?" she stated to, more than questioning Jay. He smiled, "Yep that would pretty much be Mike." "Well he doesn't say much, but wants you to take and distribute his ashes as you see fit."

Jay opened his eyes up wide in a show of surprise,

"What? Why me? Hasn't he got any family member that would want to do that?" "According to his lawyer, he does not have any other family, he was an only child, and his mom and dad passed on a long time ago." "What about cousins, uncles and aunts, all that kind of stuff, surely he must have some family." "Evidently his folks came across as migrant refugees when they were very young, something to do with the war and all that stuff. Anyways the story goes that his parents grew up together then eventually got married and had a son. That was Mike."

For the first time Jay started to realise how little he actually knew about Mike. Well, he knew him as a person like the back of his hand, but where he came from, his childhood and background, they had just never spoken about it. "Shit hey, when I think about it, I was so self-indulgent, so consumed in what I was all about I never actually got to know him. Shit I'm such an arsehole," said Jay despairingly annoyed with himself. "Easy tiger," said Joanne, "don't be so hard on yourself. As I said, he was a man of few words, but listen to what he did have to say."

Joanne picked up the paper again and started to read. "To Jay," she paused, "I know I was hard on you, always giving you crap about the way you conduct your life, but if the truth be told, you were my best friend, you were my inherited son, and I loved living my life through yours. You inspired me and gave my existence meaning. I am so sorry to have left you like this; I just never had the heart to tell that I was going. Thank you for being Jay. I love you."

Joanne paused and looked up at Jay, tears of grief streaming with relief down his cheeks. She continued reading on, "Ok, so that said and done, now it's time for you to harden up. I'm gone, whoop dee doo, big deal. I know you always act like this big, brave warrior, but I also know that deep down inside you are as soft as a marshmallow. So dry those eyes, pick yourself up and go and continue to live and love life like you always have. And your lady on the beach . . . something special about her Jay. Look after her."

Joanne stopped again and looked up at Jay. He was shaking his head smiling and crying at the same time, celebrating and grieving all at once, the circus of emotions that only the death of a loved one can bring on. "And then Jay," Joanne continued, "he finishes off with a request to you." She paused, "One last thing Jay, take my ashes and spread them as you wish, because that would be my wish too. Take care, Mike."

The noise of the circus had now reached its crescendo and Jay could not take it anymore, he got up and walked out into the passage, leaning up against the wall sobbing. Bee got up to follow, but Joanne stopped him, "just let him be for a while, just give him a bit of space, he'll be fine," she said reassuringly.

They sat waiting patiently until Jay came back in, "Sorry man, wheeew, just got a bit lost there for a while, sorry man, wheeew ok where were we?" "Well all the paper work has been done, we will be cremating the body this afternoon, then you can take the ashes and go and spread them to the winds and waters as you see fit," Joanne replied smiling, again reassuring Jay that this was just part of the circle of life of our bodies down here on earth.

"Yeh I think I will take a drive down South, hit the Wild Coast for a day or two, I know Mike loved it down there and yeh, may just let him go there." "That's a cool idea, said Bee, sitting up and paying more attention, "El and me will go get the camping gear, kayaks and stuff all ready, then we can head down later this arvo," he said looking at and getting a nod of confirmation from El. "Too true brothers, lets do it," replied El realising that this would be a way to celebrate Mike's death as he would wish it to be, and at the same time support and free Jay's spirit a bit.

The Wild Coast was a remote, rugged, rich and as the name suggested wild stretch of coastline. Just perfect to escape to, unwind, let go and regather. "Well that's settled then," said Joanne, walking up to Jay and putting her arm lovingly around his neck, "You will stay here with me while we get things all sorted, then they can come and fetch you later when we are all done."

Jay was now comfortably numb and quite happy to be chaperoned around at will by anyone that was willing to. And between Bee, El and Joanne, they were all more than willing.

"Ok what time should we be here?" asked El. "Around three would be good. If anything should change then I'll give you a call," replied Joanne. "Ok perfect then, we'll catch you later then," said El, standing and giving Jay a questioning raise of the eyebrows. "That would be good thanks El," replied Jay, "and thanks for the support. Shit man, I know I'm a mess, but it would have been so much worse without you guys." "All good," replied El dismissively. "Cheers Joanne, take good care of him," winked Bee with a smile. "Whatever Bee," she smiled back at him, knowing exactly what he was insinuating. "Get outta here."

Joanne waited just long enough for them to walk a

little way down the passage then turned to face Jay swinging her other arm around his neck to meet her first. "Ok now dry away those tears," she said letting go and wiping his face, "you heard what Mike said and wanted from you, to live and love life for him. Take a deep breath fill your blood with oxygen and let it flow and lighten that heavy heart." She paused looking at him lovingly, then kissed him even more so. "Ok, now you can take me for lunch and tell me all about this 'lady on the beach' of yours," she said happily with a hint of intrigue and loads of expectation.

Time stood still in mid supersonic flight for the rest of the day. So much had happened, so much mind and body bending emotion, a consequence of the relentless surging and bombardment, the toing and froing of the vast array of energies entering dissolving, precipitating, exuding and exploding in through in around out through and out again. And yet as Jay sat back down in El's 4X4, with the urn containing Mike's ashes between his legs, passing by Tim on the way out the hospital, it felt as though he had only been arriving at the hospital gate a minute before.

"Right cousins," said El restraining his excitement as best he could, "we're off, one last stop past your place hey Jay, load up your kayak and tent, couple of clothes and then hit the highway." "Yeh sweet," replied Jay. The day so far a never ending roller coaster ride had now seemingly come to the end, and as he climbed off of it, he couldn't quite work out what he had just been through but was consciously more than happy that it was all over.

"You guys bring any fishing rods?" questioned Jay as they turned into his drive way. "Hahaha," laughed Bee, "does a bear shit in the woods?" "True, hey, shit I gotta sharpen up a bit, pheeew sorry man I'll snap out of it soon," replied Jay. "Take your time brother, don't rush it, death isn't the be all and end all of life on earth," Bee said and then before he could finish stopped himself abruptly, squinting and thinking to himself about what he was saying before continuing, "oh shit well maybe that's not quite true," he said looking cautiously across at Jay who was smiling shaking his head in accepting dismay. "What I meant to say was, it's not the be all and end all, but it is very final and very weird for us to understand and accept, so take your time, time heals everything man." "Thanks Bee, that's really cool, I know hey, it's the finality of it all, but thanks man, I'll be all good," said Jay reaching out and grabbing Bee's hand in a high five type acknowledgment.

"Ok give me ten minutes and I'll throw some stuff together," said Jay as he got out the utility. "What about food and beers and stuff?" "Don't worry about a thing brother, we got it all," said Bee winking at El acknowledging that they had everything that they might want or need and indicating to Jay that they might have a bit more than what he could imagine or had bargained for.

Jay shook his head, smiling with a glint in his eye, "You fuckers, I can just imagine," he said unlocking the front door. "Hey open the garage door and we'll load your kayak and some fishing gear onto the trailer Jay," said El. "Sweet," he replied getting a bit of a bounce back into his step as the thoughts of the trip to come started permeating his mind, allowing it to react and direct his body to perform in order to accomplish its goal.

Jay, well versed in reacting to spontaneous ideas and

arrangements went around almost as though he was following a written procedure, ticking and talking off the boxes as he went along, "undies, shirts, board shorts, jacket, shoes, slops, toothbrush, toothpaste, soap, towel, sleeping bag, back pack, tent done," he said. Then stopping and thinking running through the list again in his head and looking around for anything else that would trigger him to remember something he might need.

He walked into the kitchen and picked up his pre packed picnic pack. It always came in handy, had a good range of stuff you need out in the bush, knives plates, can opener, torch. Some coffee, sugar, salt, pepper, small bottle of oil, powdered milk and stuff. He opened it up and threw a couple tins of food in for good measure and then the half jack of whiskey, a couple packets of smokes and one or two boxes of matches. "Right that's it?" he questioned himself. "Fuck my phone, still haven't found my phone," he breathed out irritably to himself.

He looked in all the obvious places and yes, sure enough, there it was down the side of the couch. Jay checked the screen, one missed call and three new messages. All from Antoinette.

"Shit!" he said out loud and then berated himself through his mind, "so lost in my own world again, I forget about others around me, fuck!" "Hey Jay, tried to call you, but you not picking up." "Hey Jay can you give me a call?" "Hey my Jay are you ok?" "Fuck!" repeated Jay out loud irritated with his daylong self indulgence, and dialling Antoinette's number.

"Hey my Jay," she said, without the phone even getting through its first ring, "I heard what happened to Mike, everyone at the meeting knew all about it. How are you?" she blurted out. "Much better now," he said

181

almost purring. His tone allowing Antoinette's anxiety to wane slightly. "No, seriously Jay, are you ok?" The energy of Antoinette's voice entering into his being calming and soothing. Slowing his rush down and returning some normality to his day. "I got sooo much to tell you hey," he replied, "wow gosh man, this must have been the craziest day of my life, well apart from the day I met you that is," he said laughing gently. "El and Bee have literally been taking care of me, and now we are off down to the Wild Coast for a few days," he said as though and even though it was the most perfectly normal thing to do. And that's because in his life, it was and always had been perfectly normal to just up and off for one or two days on a fancy and a whim.

"The Wild Coast," she 'confused.' "Oh, yeh, sorry, shit man, long story, looong story, but yeh we almost packed and ready to go," he replied.

Jay couldn't quite work out what the silence that followed was all about, but the longer it went on the clearer it became. "Hey Antoinette, sorry man, I actually don't know whether I'm coming or going right now." "Well can I come with then?" she asked as though it was more than obvious that she should.

Jay hadn't even thought about or considered it. To be true, he hadn't even thought about or considered Antoinette the whole day. Well, for a while when being interrogated by Joanne, but other than that, Mike's death had taken over his body, mind and soul for the entire day. But now that the consequence of her words had stated to vaporise his body, allowing his spirit to transcend outwards, nothing more seemed to be needed to be considered. Reality did though "Yeh, and Marco?" "I'll explain it all to Marco, he'll understand," she said confidently. "Anyways, I think he's discovered a new found freedom, since last time he was left alone to do his own thing," she said in a naughty voice. "Oh, yeh, what's her name?" laughed Jay. "Em," she replied. "No ways, seriously hey?" "Yep seriously, he's become a bit like a puppy dog lately, it's quite funny," she giggled. "Ok, if you think it's cool then all good. We will pop past your place in about twenty minutes; just throw some clothes and your toothbrush in a bag. We will only be gone for one or two days, and yep we will be roughing it so be prepared. And hey Antoinette," Jay continued on in a more serious and genuine tone of concern, "if there are any issues then just leave it and we can catch up when I get back." "No, there won't be any issues," she stated again with confidence and just a hint of determined authority. "Ok," said Jay, pausing then, "you're funny," he said exuding his happiness. "You're funny," she repeated, her voice exuding some mystical invisible juices that exploded in Jay's chest causing him to seemingly conquer the effect of gravity as his mind floated his body through to the cupboard to pick up another sleeping bag. "See ya in twenty minutes then." "Yaaay can't wait," she said excitedly, "love you my Jay" "Yeh love you too, see ya in a bit."

Jay walked out the house with his stuff, locked the front door and walked out to the trailer where Bee and El were finishing off tying everything down. "All sorted," Jay said and questioned at the same time. "Locked and loaded brother," replied Bee, then continued excitedly, "C'mon man let's get going now." "Sure you tightened those kayaks down nice and tight hey?" checked Jay. "Tight as a shark's arse at a thousand foot mate," replied El. "Hey can we stop by Antoinette's place? She's coming with us," stated Jay. El and Bee looked at each other smiling. Both with a cheeky, slightly envious glint in their eyes. This wasn't the first time that Jay had brought some 'comfort' with him on one of their trips, and as a matter of fact it would have been unusual if he hadn't. But Bee and El had just not even considered that he would this time around. But then again they had also realised that since Antoinette had been around, nothing Jay had done was predictable.

"Cool," replied Bee unashamedly excited at the prospect of once again having a female presence around and then followed on having a small dig at Jay, "Will be good to have someone to nurse you through the journey," he laughed. "Fuck off," replied Jay smiling and brushing Bee's comment off, and all three getting into the ute.

"Ok mate, where we headed then," asked El. "Bottlenose Dolphin Drive," answered Jay. "Sweet that's on the way out then. Waaahooo let's get the hell outta," exclaimed Bee, giving a rhythmic drum roll on the dashboard.

# The Wild Ride

The front door of the house was open wide when they pulled up on the pavement outside Antoinette's place. Jay had the ute door open and was exiting the ride before El had even shut it down.

"Hey give her a kiss and hug for me too," smiled Bee. Jay winked back at him as he tried his hardest to be as cool, calm and collected as he could, and not just sprint up to the front door like deep within was commanding him to do. The closer to the front door he got the more his heart pounded; he couldn't stop or control it. It was as though the shell that had been built around him maintaining the complete vacuum that had existed in his being throughout the day had now cracked. The external forces of expectation taking advantage of the weakness causing catastrophic failure as they exploded into his emptiness.

"Hey my Jay," she said running down towards him, leaping into his wanting arms, and burying her face in his neck. "Are you ok my Jay?" she asked, releasing her arms just enough to be able to look into his eyes. "Yeh, I'm all good thanks," he replied smiling sadly. "My Jay," she said and slowly pulled his lips onto hers, kissing him softly, long and warm. "I'm so sorry Jay, I'm so sorry." "No, I'm ok now," he said as they let go of each other for an instant before they grabbed tightly onto each other's hands, turning towards the front door where Marco was standing with Antoinette's bag. "Hey Jay, my condolences man. Wow, that was a real shock when I heard what happened." Thanks man, replied Jay, walking up, shaking hands and both of them giving each other a genuine and comforting hug. "Shit happens brother, shit happens, but, he lived a good life and I know he will be at peace right now. That's just Mike, nothing ever really phased him, took everything in his stride and yeh, he'll be all good in the world beyond this one," Jay said reassuring himself as the memories of Mike escaped from his mind unconsciously commanding his brain to release a spurt of sobbing chemicals into his body. Jay gulped and took a deep breath manipulating and directing them back out into the universe. "Yeh, I'll be all good," he said.

Jay glanced back at Bee and El waiting in the ute, confirming that they didn't seem to be in a hurry, then turned back and continued, "So you ok with Antoinette coming with us?" Marco lent up against the door post, crossing one leg over the other, folding his arms and looked up into the beyond, "more than happy brother, in between listening to all your wacky theories," he said looking at Jay and smiling, "and meeting, loving and living down here on the coast, I have sort of rediscovered myself. And yeh time to cool off a bit I think, let go, relax and live a little."

Antoinette had moved back onto Jay's arm, and squeezed it tightly, really pleased that Marco seemed so much more at peace. "Yaaay, my brand new beautiful, happy and free Marco," she said letting go of Jay and planting a kiss on Marco's cheek then giving him a huge, loving and happy hug. Marco responded giving her a tight hug back. "You guys take care; it's going to be an emotional one for you all, so please just take care," he said.

Antoinette looked up at him their eyes meeting and understanding that this was a new maturing phase in their lives, a turning point. A long overdue turning point that neither of them ever realised that they needed so badly or even saw coming. But now that it had, it was almost obvious that it was what they both so required and craved.

"You too Marco, stay safe and don't go overboard," she replied. Then thinking and smiling cheekily, "What the heck go overboard," she said. "Get out of here," he responded pushing her away gently. "And Antoinette," he continued in the more serious tone that Jay had known him for. They both stopped and turned. "Like we discussed, you do know that your dad will find out about this, and when he does, you know that he will hit the roof, so I'm not sure what you going to walk into when you get back."

The words in an instant causing a warm chill to open Jay's mouth slightly. He frowned and his eyes queried Antoinette. "Well it's time he matured and lived a little too," she replied with unadulterated confidence. Marco nodded his head in agreement. "I suppose so," he said with a tiny twinge of nervousness. "And don't forget to spoil Em, she's a beautiful girl and she loves you," Antoinette answered back reassuring Marco of his life ahead in the immediate future. "Yeh, whatever," he replied, squirming a bit being unconditioned in the art and practice of showing love or emotion.

Jay popped the door of the canopy open and threw Antoinette's bag in, then they both jumped into the back of the ute. "Hi guys," she said as she bounced and buzzed around in her own little heaven, spreading it and sharing it amongst them all. "Start this baby up and let's get going," she exuded excitedly turning and kissing Jay on the cheek. Bee just raised his hand staring and smiling at her, basically unable to speak as everything she emitted stunned him beautifully.

"Welcome aboard everyone," El sounded out in the voice of a jet pilot coming over the speakers just before take off, "please fasten your seatbelts, sit back, relax and enjoy the journey. We will be landing on the wild, Wild Coast in approximately three hours, the weather is windless and sunny and the sea is blue and warm. The crayfish are huge and delicious and the beer is locked and loaded in the chilli bin." "Yaaay, let's get there," shouted Antoinette exuberantly.

El drove out through the suburbs and onto the freeway. It was a pretty weird journey to get to the wondrous wild coast. One minute you are in suburbia just cruising along past the houses, dogs, kids and casualness. The next minute, scorching down a dual lane immaculately prepared highway with every make and model of car possible being passed or flashing by, all with a mission of intent. Then the highway comes to an abrupt, unfinished end after about one and a half hours, turning into a single lane rural main road. The long grass verging on intruding up and over the ragged edge of the tar seal. The pace of vehicle and person within slowing down to match the flavour of the laid back attitude of the environment around them. Sheep and cattle in their own peaceful world of open space. Farmers here and there on their machines idly tilling the earth or harvesting their labours.

Now adjusting to and cruising the rural road, all four of them were deep within their own minds, by nature discussing and debating the pros and cons of their visual time warp as their journey exposed them to wide and varying ways and forms of life and living. Antoinette starting to realise and piece together some of the stuff Jay had talked to her about, needed a bit more of a reminder, some more detail and understanding so she unintentionally broke the silence before she even realised it.

"Hey Jay have you ever told El and Bee your philosophy on the energies of this earth?" Jay looked across at her, a little startled by not only the sudden break in his subconscious deliberation, but also the question itself. He opened his eyes wide, opening his lips slightly to expose his clenched teeth in attempt to silently state, "No I haven't, what did you ask that question for? They will think I have gone mad."

But it was too late, Bee's curiosity had been pierced, and he was tired of the silence anyway, and wanted some 'action,' so he answered Antoinette on Jay's behalf, "No he hasn't," he said exaggeratingly indignantly. "What philosophy?" "Ah it's nothing man, it's not my philosophy anyway, just my point of view on some stuff," Jay replied trying to shrug off and bump the conversation into a different direction. "It's not nothing, it's beautiful and we could all learn something from it Jay," insisted Antoinette, punching him on the shoulder. "Yeh c'mon Jay, let it out man, are you not going to open up and share with some of your best mates?" Bee pressured Jay.

El's interest also now starting to bubble jumped in too, "What the heck, here you are keeping some good advice from your mates. What kind brother, c'mon share and share alike man," he said looking at Jay in his review mirror.

Jay looked at Antoinette, smiling and shaking his head in a show of mild despair, accepting defeat. She smiled and leaned forward giving him a kiss then sat back expectantly, eyes glowing with anticipation like a child waiting for her favourite bedtime story to start.

Jay pondered for a bit not quite knowing where to begin. The extended silence reaching a crescendo eventually drove the words forth. "Ok don't say I didn't warn you then," Jay blurted out, "but hmmm where do I start? It's kinda like we sort of exist in such a physical world down here on earth that we don't really look, understand or even try comprehending beyond the physical. Well sometimes we try, but then again because we don't quite know what to look for or recognise it when we find it, or if we do, then don' how to use it, we just let it go again. It's like it's too hard too difficult and sooo different, that yeh, it's just easier to forget about it all and remain entirely in the physical."

Jay paused. "And that's it?" frowned Bee. "No," said Antoinette, "that not even a piece of it all." "Oh cool, I thought I might have missed something," said Bee laughing, then looking at Jay realising that that would be one way for Jay to clam up, added quickly, "no sorry brother, I'm just being a dick, c'mon man, give the rest to us."

Jay looked at Antoinette's melting gaze and knew that he could not stop now. "So, I suppose what you must never forget is that us living down here in these bodies is all about the physical, so unless you get that right you are on a hiding to nothing in the first place. You know, eat well, sleep well, exercise, hygiene, the basics of looking after the body to keep it in tiptop condition to achieve whatever you want to achieve in your human life on earth. No matter whether it is work, sport, play or anything else for that matter, you gotta keep your physical in the best possible condition. But to me we got something much deeper than the physical going on too."

Jay looked across at Bee noting that he had turned to face him and was intrigued, listening hard and sucking in every word. He looked up in the review mirror to see El's eyes staring back at him. El giving him an instinctive nod to continue on as their eyes met.

"Well you know, everyone always says we have a soul? Well I know we do," said Jay expressively, ensuring that everyone knew that he meant and believed what he was saying. He paused then expressed further, "and every soul has a mind." Jay paused again confirming in Antoinette's eyes and expression that she had complete understanding to this point, she had after all heard it all before. Bee had a bit of a confused frown building. "Ok stay with me now, it will all make sense soon," he reassured Bee, then repeated what he had just said to get everyone back on track. "Ok so we all got a soul and every soul has to have a mind. The mind is like the brain of the soul, inseparable as is the human brain to the human body, and then, to me the mind and the soul together are what are called our spirit. So yeh our spirit for whatever reason is now taking the journey in the physical. In the human body. It's like our spirits needed to learn and understand something about being physically constrained. Well to an extent anyway. Dunno why, but it's just part of our spirits journey through time and space. Lessons in the physical to be learned to grow stronger and wiser, you know like patience, persistence, perseverance, all that kinda stuff that you need to endure being bound in the physical world. And then once learned you move on to some other dimension and experience, ultimately returning back to be part of the Creator of creation."

"Wooow" said Bee, "that's pretty darn heavy man." "Yeh, sorry got carried away a bit there and swam straight into the deep end, but I s'pose what I'm trying to say is that as much as you need to nurture and take care of your physical being, you need to be aware of the spiritual side of your person, because it can give you the edge in life on earth, it can help you in so many ways to accomplish, succeed, thrive and grow. It's like we all know that we need to eat to fuel our bodies. Food is the physical energy that fuels the physical body. And like I say this life on earth is all about the physical so fuel and look after it as best you can, but then, and I think this is what Antoinette was wanting me to mention in the first place," he said smiling, reaching for and squeezing her hand. "There are other energies out there, all around us, all the time, busting to get in and fuel our spirit."

Jay stopped and dwelled in the vacuum of silence filling the car. Waiting for a signal to direct him to continue. The longer the silence lasted, the greater the vacuum became urging him to continue. "So ok, that's all good, but what are these spiritual energies? How do they get in? And how do they or how can they benefit us down here in these human bodies of ours?" asked Jay.

"Shit brother, I do not have a clue, but you have started something now, so don't stop!" insisted Bee. Jay smiled, "Ok, so mother nature is giving off an abundance of the stuff all the time through sights, sounds, smells, touch and tastes it's like we are being beautifully bombarded with them all the time, the sunsets, the turquoise skies, the golden fiery sunsets, the emerald ocean, cool winds, the rustling of leaves, crashing of the waves, the cry of the fish eagle, crickets concertos, it's endless man endless. So once you recognise all of this as natures energies and start sucking as much of them up through your senses as possible, and then realise that your senses pass them through to your brain, your brain the gateway to the mind which feeds them into your soul, which digests and feeds off of them, transforming the energy into something more beautiful before sending it back out through the mind back into the brain, which in turn uses it to create specific juices that pleasurise and optimise your physical being and performance."

"Serious?" questioned Bee, "that's crazy shit man, shit I'm sure I could use that to direct me to win the Lotto man, that's incredible," he said excitedly picturing his ticket to fortune and success. "No, you bum head," laughed Jay, "Lotto is all about luck, this is different, it's nothing to do with luck, it's all about putting the final touch to the optimisation of your body, the optimisation of your physical state. Putting your body in the right place, the right space, to give it the edge to accomplish and succeed and exceed. But remember, most importantly, you need to master the optimisation of the physical first, like I say, eat, sleep, exercise and all that stuff then and only then master the optimisation of the spirit by understanding and using natures willing energies."

Jay was letting go, letting the whole day out, and he wasn't finished yet. "You can use the example of formula one motor racing to sort of see what I'm trying to say. It's like you can have two identical formula one cars, identical in every way, motors, bodies, tyres, fuels everything exactly the same, but then in one you add a special high performance additive to the fuel, which just gives it the edge, the advantage to win. But never forget the physical down here on earth, 'cause if the car with the additive has tyres that are slightly flat or too little oil in the engine, dirty wheel bearings or something like that, then it won't matter how much additive you give it, it's not going to make it to the end of the race never mind have a chance to win it."

"No ways!" said Bee, "that's flipping incredible, and you only come out with it now? What the heck brother, thank goodness Antoinette came along otherwise we would never get our share of you brain," he said winking and smiling at Antoinette.

"Well we do use all those energies all the time anyway, without even realising it," continued Jay, "like how good do you feel after a surf or walking alone in the bush or along the beach? It's because without even realising it you are just sponging up all of those energies through your senses feeding them all through to your spiritual core which returns the favour to the body, giving you that 'just oh so stoked' feeling and loving of life. And whatever and whenever you are trying to achieve, yeh it's not the silver bullet, but it does, like I say, give you the edge. And yeh, if for some reason you are down in the dumps, and for one reason or another have not been able to take care of and optimise the physical as you should, then use nature's stuff anyway, just to top you up with some stimulating juices. Pick you up and get you back on track."

Jay leaned back pushing his chest out and stretching his lower back. He took a deep breath, relieved that it was all over as he finished off with, "Anyway that's my spin on it, and it works for me."

Jay looked at Antoinette who just stared incredibly lovingly back at him. No one seemed to be able to move or say anything as they tried to digest all of what Jay had just said, then El spoke up, "Man, thanks for that Jay, real cool stuff to think about, makes real sense too, pheeew brother, knew you were a deep thinker, but wow man, that's some real cool stuff, thanks man."

Jay now understanding and acknowledging the impact he had made continued on a little longer, rounding it all off. "Yeh the more you recognise and practice it the more you understand and love it. Like I say, not just to optimise performance, but also just to give ya a bit of a lift when you are freaked out and frustrated. Just focus on the good sights, sounds and feelings, all the good energies around us all the time. And yeh learn to switch off your senses to negative stuff, walk out, turn around or just don't listen to it, 'cause all that stuff can and will have the opposite effect on your physical being and performance too. You can't worry too much about it all though and don't expect fireworks, it's very subtle, difficult to recognise or appreciate. We are just so used to the physical . . . 'I'm hungry, eat a hamburger, I'm full.' It's nothing like that, so don't expect that. And it's almost impossible to stay 'in the perfect zone' for long periods of time in our day to day life and existence. There is just so much being fired at us all the time, it all becomes a bit of a senseless noise distracting and confusing our minds. But it's good to be able to realise when we need a small squirt of the good stuff, and how to get it, just to keep us sane and on track. And when you do get the ultimate chance, like when we are down at the coast, just top up with as much as you can get, then amongst other, your memory will see you through the dry periods when you are stuck in an office in between four walls or something."

Jay paused, took a deep breath and let it out with the words, "Ok that's it, enough said, I'm done with all that stuff." "Shit brother, that was cool," said El, but I was concentrating so much I just hope I haven't missed the turn off." "No don't fuck around," said Bee as everyone in unison focused on their immediate surroundings and the road up ahead trying to re orientate themselves. "Naah don't worry," said El confidently, "check out that camel shaped hill up ahead, that's my first land mark, we hit a left onto the off road tracks when the first big hump lines up with the second, so yeh most probably about ten k's out before we get to the turn off."

"Are there no signs to the place we are going," questioned Antoinette tentatively. "Hahaha" laughed El, no there are no signs, that's 'cause in effect we are going into the middle of nowhere." Antoinette looked across at Jay who tilted his head to the side raising his eyebrows in a 'what do you want me to say' kinda way, then verbalising, "I did tell you we were going to be roughing it," he said. "But don't worry, you will looove it down there, I promise you."

"Yeh ok check out for an old abandoned tractor about two hundred meters in on the left somewhere, then the second track after that is the one we take," said El as he slowed a little focusing in on the land up ahead. "There she blows," exclaimed Bee proudly being the first to spot the tractor. "Aaah sweet as a coconut brother, good spotting man, complimented El and continuing on informing everyone on the journey ahead, "cool only about fifteen kilometres to go once we turn off from here, but be prepared, it will take about an hour doing it off road like we have to."

Right there's the first track aaand . . . there she is the second one," confirmed El, slowing right down and bumping off the road and onto the track. Then stopping the vehicle and engaging four wheel drive he continued on in relaxed excitement, "Right swing us a couple beers there Jay, the holiday has just begun." Jay slid open the inter leading window to the canopied bin of the ute and reached for a couple beers from the strategically well placed chilli bin. "You gonna have one?" asked Jay. "Of course I am," replied Antoinette, "I'm also on holiday you know." Her smile, her eyes, her face impossible for Jay to resist any longer as he leant towards her and they fused once more into soft, delicious oblivion.

"Ok boys and girls here we go," came the 'command' from El as he revved up the engine and stuck it into first gear. "Hold onto your horses, keep the beers wet and the seats dry," he said pulling off. "Aye, aye captain," responded Bee, holding his beer up in an acknowledgment of the command, "I will get the peace pipe going in case we encounter any hostile tribes along the way," he joked reaching toward the glove compartment and bringing out a huge stash of weed.

The journey once again took on a different feel and perspective as they wound their way along the track that was barely visible through the long grass. The grasslands carpeting the rolling hills for as far as the eye could see. An occasional rural hut could be seen here and there, and every now and again they came across a footpath that criss-crossed the track.

They drove on past a herd of cattle being driven along by a couple of young herds boys. The boys waved and smiled jubilantly at the sight of the ute, something a little out of their ordinary day and the prospect of a first world treat coming their way. El slowed the ute as the boys came running expectantly towards them. He reached into the bag beside him and took out a slab of chocolate. "Here you go cousins," he said as they approached his outstretched arm. "Thank you boss, thank you," the eldest of the boys said, taking the chocolate in a slow deliberate manner of respect and appreciation. "You got any work boss," he queried. El looked across at Bee then back at the boy, "You can clean fish?" he asked. "I can clean fish very well boss, me I can catch plenty crayfish for you too and get lots of fresh bait, everything you need for your fishing holiday boss," he proclaimed as his expectation rose. "Ok fifteen bucks a day, we here for two days so that's thirty bucks how's that," asked El. "Hey boss that's too kind, too kind, I will see you down there this evening boss," he said backing away excitedly already planning his marshalling of and instruction to the rest of the herd boys so that he could leave them to it and get going.

The rest of the boys had gathered around the eldest waiting patiently for him to divvy the chocolate up into equal pieces. There was no arguing, pushing or shoving, just an orderly unspoken hierarchal system of sharing the spoils of the day. "Wow that's amazing," said Antoinette raising her hand to wave the boys goodbye, "they look so rough, wild and free, and yet they are so well mannered." "Yeh out here hey have deep rooted tribal values that they practice," replied El, "they live a simple, healthy life out here and haven't yet been influenced by all the 'dog eat dog greed,' crime and corruption of the physical world of fast cars and other stuff that we are so reliant on in ours."

Nothing more was said as the four of them sat back contemplating the vast differences that existed between the two polar opposite worlds they had been part of in this one day. They couldn't help wondering which was better. In which you would be the happiest and learn the most? This was all part of the experience of visiting the Wild Coast; it was what drew a person back time and time again. Almost like a calling from the past, a wanting to go back and taste, remember and experience forgotten times.

The deeper they went into the grasslands the less evidence there was of humanity, and that fitted in perfectly with the peaceful silence that reigned within the vehicle. Bee had unconsciously taken out a small bit of dope and was busy rolling it into a joint. "Time to get a little higher, hey brother," asked El looking across and smiling at Bee. "What's that you said," asked Bee, a little surprised and then as his mind suddenly caught up to what his body was busy with answered slightly awkwardly, "oh the joint, yeh, hmmm yeh didn't quite realise it but yeh time to smoke a little." "Hahaha you're funny," laughed Antoinette, "you were miles away Bee." "Yeh sorry man, I was hey, this place just sends me into another world, almost like I'm not even here." Jay and Antoinette looked at each other smiling knowingly. Jay tilted his head then flicked his eyebrows upwards to 'say,' "Told ya it would be a wild ride." Antoinette leaned forward her kiss 'saying,' "I know you did."

"Ok time for a quick pit stop then," said El as he brought the ute slowly to a standstill and switched the engine off. "Two small rivers to cross, first one coming up just over that rise," he continued, getting out the vehicle and walking around the back to take a leak. The rest of them got out, all having a good stretch and walked to the front, Bee lit up the joint and took a deep drag, "Shit man I just love it out here. Pure freedom man, pure freedom. No cops, no politicians, no cell phone signal, nothing, just freedom," he said taking another deep pull on the joint proving and exaggerating just how free he was.

El now finished relieving his body of the remnants of his beer walked around to join them, Antoinette questioning him as he approached, "So tell me," she said, "how do you even know we are going in the right direction?" "Hahaha," laughed El proudly, "I've been travelling this track since I was in nappies. My dad used to bring us down two, sometimes three times a year. He loved escaping down here, and us kids obviously loved it too. And I dunno, you don't think about it too much as a youngster growing up. You just know with all your youthful confidence that you will easily find your way in, around and then back out. Doubt only seems to grow as our bodies grow, weird but kinda true," he said looking up to the sky prophetically. Then with the memories slowly seeping back up he continued, "It's like a challenge, a sort of badge of honour that you kinda silently get from your dad when you can direct the way all the way down to the beach for the first time. And now, well I know this track like the back of my hand," he said glowing and accepting the look of admiration he was getting from Antoinette.

Now with the memory gates wide open and his body being filled with vibrant juices, he clapped his hands together, "Ok let's get going," he said barely able to contain the building excitement of reaching their destination. They all reacted to his discharge and back in expectantly. El started, geared and throttled and they continued on towards the first river crossing. Coming up over the rise, El looked down towards the running water. It was flowing about a foot deep and needed to be crossed with care, but the rising thrill and anticipation of the journey's end had overdosed El's body with mild adrenalin, distorting his common sense. "Waaahooo," he shouted out as he powered the ute down towards the river, surging through the water sending a massive wave of white water way up above the windows on either side of the vehicle. The liquid grabbing hold of everything it could as the vehicle passed through, slowing it abruptly.

"Woaw, take it easy brother," said Bee, we wanna get there in one piece hey," "Yeh sorry guys, got a bit carried away there," apologised El as he worked the subdued vehicle up and out the other side of the river. The ute chocked, coughed and spluttered as it tried to rid its lungs of the unexpected deluge. El pushed the clutch in and revved her a little harder heating her up a bit to try and assist and coax her into bringing it all back out again.

Then she shuddered and died for an instant, before backfiring defiantly into life again as El kept pumping on the gas pedal.

El revved her up high again, the steam pouring out the engine bay as she shook and shuddered to get rid of it all. The three of them sitting there silently, willing her to make it through as they watched El practice his well-versed and experienced resuscitation technique. Slowly, bit by bit she regained full consciousness and composure as El nursed her back to health. "Fawk, that was close," he breathed relieving and reassuring everyone that they were back on track. Then he eased the ute slowly back into gear and drove up and over the rise on the other side of the river.

"Right one more river to go, then we left with about three or four k's and we are there cousins," he said regaining his composure. "Shit man give us another beer there Jay. Fuck my mouths gone dry man." "Hahaha, not surprised you dumb ass," replied Jay laughing and reaching for another couple beers.

They drove on towards the next crossing, the relief causing Jay and Antoinette to start a game of tickle as they touched, laughed and bounced around, filling up on each others excessive energies.

"Ok here we go again," said El as they got to the top of the rise looking down into the small stream. This one was hardly even flowing and the only way you could recognise it as a river of any kind was because of the small valley type terrain it was sitting in, and the wet rocky bed at the bottom of the valley. But even so, El was taking no chances this time around and stopped the ute on the top of the rise to have a good look before going down. Everyone was peering over to have a look when El, very, very slowly let out the clutch with the minimum amount of accelerator applied, now overdoing and exaggerating the care that was required to pass this hurdle. Then, as could be expected, he stalled the engine. "Hahaha laughed Bee, full stick or fuck all hey brother, hahaha." Jay and Antoinette laughed out loud too, Jay slapping El on the shoulder, "You go brother, you go hahaha," he said.

El sat there and took the ridiculing, he knew it was deserved and that he couldn't argue or defend it. And even though he had driven responsibly and immaculately up until he had lost contact with earth at the first river, he was now a little embarrassed and very aware of his actions, and so by instinct he went back to the basics. He pulled the hand break up hard, put the vehicle in first gear, pushed in the clutch and fired up the ignition. But nothing, not a whimper.

In that instant that he turned the key and got, zero engine response, in that microsecond, the inaction shot in, through and out again sending the blood draining from his face into his stomach to attempt to fill instantaneous hollow it was feeling.

He flicked the key back off then on again, nothing, not even a light up on the dash. His fingers reacted in desperation for a third and fourth time, but still, nothing. Dead as a doornail. "Oh fuck," he said. The slightly panicky tone in his voice reaching into all of them, causing Jay and Antoinette to lean forward to have a look at what he was talking about, and Bee to vocalise, "What the fuck now, brother?" "Looks like the battery is flat," replied El and exhibiting to everyone what he was talking about by leaning back out the line of site and flicking the key on and off a good couple of times more.

"Water must have got into the electrics somehow and stuffed the battery." "No ways," said Bee flopping back into his seat in despair.

"Hey pop the boot," said Jay exiting the vehicle, "might just be a loose wire or something." El pulled the catch and Jay lifted the bonnet. "Hmmm can't see anything obvious here, you got a long screwdriver or something handy like that, I can flick it across the terminals and see if there is any spark there, or maybe it's something else." "Here you go, you can use these jumper leads," said El walking up to the front of the vehicle with Jay. "Hmmm flat as a pancake," confirmed Jay as he repeatedly flicked the one lead across both terminals of the dead battery.

"Oh fuck!" exclaimed El, talk about being stuck out in the middle of nowhere." "Well we could try push staring her?" suggested Jay. "Yeh might as well have a go," said El, "but hmmm don't hold out much hope with a battery that flat, but definitely worth a shot." "Ok you jump in, and we'll all push ya over the ridge."

El, Jay and Antoinette all went around to the back. "Ok ya ready?" asked Jay as they all took up the strain. "Yeh all good," responded El. "You got the ignition switched on?" "Yeh all good to go, lets do it!" commanded El. "Ok lets go, all together one two, three," came the instruction from Jay as they all heaved in unison to get the back wheels of the ute over the rise and let gravity take its effect. El let the vehicle maximise her speed before dropping the clutch and pumping the gas. The ute burbled her way down the rise and came to a sudden shuddering rest in the river bed as the friction of the unfired pumping pistons overcame the forces of momentum.

Dejection starting to set in, El folded his arms across the wheel, leaning on it for support. Antoinette, Bee and Jay wandered down and joined him. "What now?" asked Antoinette. She had never ever been in a seemingly impossible situation as this. She had been involved in multi million dollar dealings and projects, solving and resolving all kinds of disruptions, disputes and breakdowns but never stuck out in the middle of nowhere. "Ah this is nothing," reassured Jay, "we'll sort something out, not a 'biggy.' And guess what?" "What?" she asked looking at him expectantly. "I don't care anyway." "What do you mean?" As long as I'm close to you I don't care," he said putting his arm around her shoulder and squeezing her in close. "Mmm," she responded snuggling in even closer.

"Hey sorry guys, this is my entire fault," acknowledged El as they got to the ute. "No it isn't," said Antoinette, this whole trip was your idea and I'm loving it, no matter what happens along the way, it's all just part of the journey and it's all fun," she said smiling broadly at him, melting away the guilt he was feeling. "S'pose you right, even if we have to camp here for a night and then make a plan and move on out tomorrow, it'll all be good." "Yeh I don't mind said El reaching in for another beer, I just love the freedom man I just love the freedom, we will get down to the coast tomorrow."

Then literally out of the blue came a voice from the top of the rise "Hey boss, what you doin' down there?" It was the older herd boy. El didn't answer him, and the boy didn't wait for an answer as he jogged his way down towards them and then repeated the question inquisitively, "what you doin' down here, boss?" "We stuck cousin, flat battery," El responded. "Oh shit," the boy said holding his hand to his mouth in concern, then followed on excitedly, "but don't worry boss, another man came this way last weekend, he hasn't come back out yet so he will still be down there, I will go fetch him for you boss."

The boy didn't wait for a response; he was already jogging up and out the river towards the coast, beaming with pride knowing that he was going to be the hero of their day. That he was the one that was going to save them, and he was not going to give anyone the opportunity to stop him. "He reached the top of the rise and turned briefly, "I will fetch him for you boss, you don't worry, you don't go anywhere, I will fetch him," he said, and he was gone. "How's that for a bit of luck then," stated Bee, reaching into the ute and rubbing up some more weed preparing another joint "That is incredible," said Antoinette, "that is truly incredible, what a lovely natured boy."

It was all quite surreal as they all sat there, doors open, relaxing and taking in the sights and sounds that encapsulated them in the valley. The soft gentle energies filling them up with a kind of content peace and perfection that one can only get when you are isolated from the rigorous relenting bombardment of modern day life. Nothing was said for a long while as they, without ant effort or idea, soaked it all up and got lost as they drifted around together in the day dream.

Bee's mind somehow realising the 'trip' it was on from something Jay had said earlier, was still not quite able to understand it all, so it eventually directed him to speak. "So ok, so we are spirits from another time and place, and we have been planted in these bodies of ours? So just remind me then 'Oh Great One,'" he said taking a long deep drag on the joint and then slowly puffing it out in a deliberate long stream of blue smoke, "what the heck for? All your theories on energies and stuff that's all cool man, but shit man, what the heck are we actually doing down here?"

Jay's body twitched as the sudden unexpectedness of Bee's words made it through and snapped him back into being one. He relaxed back into the seat, not thinking too much and not wanting to entirely abandon the flight he was on. "Dunno hey, who knows?" he replied squeezing Antoinette's hand and smiling straight back at her soft child like expectant eyes. She grabbed his hand with both of hers, pulling it in between her breasts, Bee's questions had aligned with some of hers, and if nothing else, she just wanted to hear Jay speak a bit more. She wanted to hear, taste, feel and experience everything that he had from deep within his being, so she intuitively took the opportunity and urged him on. "No come on Jay, you must know," she insisted, knowing that Jay would have thought about it all. "Come on Jay," she persisted, squeezing his hand even harder into her. "Yeh c'mon Jay," said El, "shit man share your stuff with your brothers man, what kind?" he continued on reaching out towards Bee for the joint.

Bee handed it over and then turned towards Jay in an attempt to encourage him even more, "C'mon man Jay, looks like we gonna be here in the river for a while and this is a bit of a spiritual journey we are on anyway you know, so let it out brother, share that mind of yours," he said, in genuinely deep request, as the effect of the marijuana obliterated the illogical human rat race that everyone lived their lives in. Time becoming comfortably inconsequential.

Bee not even getting the slightest reaction from Jay turned back, then glancing at El and nodding his head backwards let El know without saying anything that them two back there are at it again. Jay hadn't taken his eyes off of Antoinette's, neither of them could, they were living in each other's perfection. Their physical connection, their touch, sight, and sounds entering each other's deepest spaces, igniting and exciting their spirits to permeate beyond and assimilate, fuse, dance, smile, love and play. Their spirits wanting more spun around and around, dancing together in perfect electric fusion, the whirlwind drawing their lips together sharing, tasting and losing themselves in the eye of the perfect soulful storm. As the winds got lost in brilliant harmony, they opened their arms spreading wider and wider, reaching out, wanting to share with everything they touched. And as they spread, they dissipated slowly, gently and relaxed back into Mother Nature's expanse.

Antoinette and Jay opened their eyes simultaneously, and with their lips still touching, smiled at each other. "Mmm," was all that could escape from Antoinette. "Mmm," came the response back.

Bee waiting patiently for his answer from Jay took the opportunity and got a word in while he could, "You two don't mind us, no you just carry on back there while we just keep ourselves company," he said with a hint of envy. El jumped in while he could too, "Ok now that you two have regained some form of control could we get back to what we were talking about in the first place?" he asked.

Still gazing into each other's souls, Antoinette whispered, "Love you," as they both moved back from each other just enough to satisfy Bee and El's presence.

Jay was gliding at perfect height and it seemed to him that he was speaking without even having to, "Ok, again, just my thoughts, but for what they are worth," he said, "and yeh just remember you asked hey?" he confirmed. "Yeh, we asked," reiterated Bee almost impatiently reassuring Jay that they really wanted to hear what he had to say.

Jay looked out into the distant, delectable horizon and continued on. "Well it's like a bit of a oxymoron kinda thing, before we, as you previously put so eloquently, were planted in these bodies of ours, well we must have been just like, I dunno hey, like these amazing free spirits. Our minds and souls travelling free on the winds of the universe. Time and space inconsequential, just think about it and you were there. No physical boundaries or constraints, no friction, no oxygen required. Growing and learning with and from the energies of the Creator. Growing, meeting, learning, living and loving with similar minded souls of the Creator. Ok don't want to get to deep on the if, what, how, why and when about all of that stuff 'cause I haven't quite got it all myself, but hmmm, not sure if by choice or design, but whatever or however, we were obviously meant, as part of the journey to experience the physical."

El and Bee hadn't moved a muscle, they were listening intently, their minds tuning their hearing to receive every word, tuning their brains to accept, and send it all through to be digested.

Jay continued, "So that's why I say it's a bit of a oxymoron kinda thing. Because one minute we are free as a bumblebee in a paddock of jasmine, then the next we are kinda like stuck in these bodies of ours, unable to fly as we always have. And now that we are constrained within our bodies, we don't want to leave them. Like we all seem to be so scared of death and dying. Weird, but maybe that's why we have come down here to earth and are in our bodies. To be able to really appreciate the pure freedom of unrestrained flight. How would our free and wondrous spirits ever know, understand or master the beauties, desires, wants, needs and constraints of the physical if they didn't experience it all?"

"Well haven't they got a university up there or something, couldn't we just have been taught it all," questioned Bee slightly seriously. "Hahaha," laughed El, "that's funny; it's like you sort of thinking that you don't actually want to have had the experience down here on the blue planet." "Shit man, listening to Jay I'm just thinking about what I left behind, and now it's like true what he says, you sort of like don't wanna let this all go . . . weird man, really weird," said Bee with a frown forming on his forehead. "Well I did warn you before I started," said Jay smiling, "but yeh don't take it all too seriously. To me, just know and understand that you are down here to learn and grow," Antoinette sneaking in "And love" as Jay took a breath, "Yeh and love," he said desiring with incredible, delicious warmth back at her. "So yeh just understand and enjoy the roller coaster ride. Live, learn and love the physical but try remember, feel and understand the spiritual too, then you can work and have fun with both while you have got your time on this beautiful earth."

Jay relaxed back into the seat, allowing it to take over the mild stress his body had been put under as it had been on duty during his presentation on his perception. No one spoke for a while as they asked and answered their own questions that had been created in their minds. Bee opened up his stash and started crushing another bit of dope in the palm of his hand, before rolling it into a joint. "Hey grab us another beer there, Jay," he said exiting the vehicle at the same time and lighting up.

Jay got four beers out the back and then got out of the vehicle too, with El and Antoinette following suit. They all walked up out the stream and sat on top of the bank looking towards the direction of the ocean and where the local herd boy had run off to look for the camper that had come past a couple of days ago.

"Hey give me a 'tug' of that thing," Jay said reaching out towards Bee. Bee took a drag then passed the joint over to Jay. Antoinette had a naughty glint in her eye as she watched Jay take a good couple solid drags, holding each one in to maximise effect.

"Ever smoked a joint?" he asked noting her curiosity. "Yeh, of course," she said in the most obvious of lies, and at the same time reaching for the joint and taking a tiny puff of it, half chocking as her crystal pure lungs battled with the smoke. Then before letting it go had another couple puffs in between sips of beer before passing it back to Jay.

Then they all just sat there, happy, and at peace with each other and their seemingly isolated and tranquil island of perfection that surrounded them. The sun over their shoulders just beginning to fade behind the hills setting the evening sky alight, turning the expanse a pale blue. The couple of wispy white clouds slowly being painted the whitest of pinks.

"Hey, why don't we bury a stake in the ground then winch ourselves to the top here and try another push start down the hill?" said Bee out of nowhere. "Because the battery is flat and the winch won't work," answered El. " Oh fuck, yeh, that's right, that's so funny, let's winch ourselves out hahaha," laughed Bee, with everyone following suit. "I'm gonna get us another beer, fuck lets winch ourselves out hahaha," he repeated and got up to walk back down to the ute.

Antoinette stood up and stretched then stopped looking intently at the horizon, "Hey look there," she said pointing into the distance. Bee turned and looked in the direction she was pointing, the combination of marijuana, beer and the shadowed land making long distance viewing and interpretation precarious to say the least. "No fuckin' ways, don't shit me man," he said uncontrollably, "it can't be man, no it is, it's a vehicle and it's coming this way."

Jay and El were already up, Bee's dubious determination of the 'vision,' coupled with the doubt that had been growing with time that anyone would by coincidence ever be in the vicinity of this part of the planet needed to be verified one way or the other. "No ways, it is too, no ways, waaahooo we're on our way again," exclaimed Jay throwing his arms around Antoinette's waist picking her up and twirling her around in celebration and victory. El just stood there staring in a delicious daze of disbelief, it was to him the most surreal of visual spectacles. Endless long and wide open lands, with only a speckle of mankind here and there, then this mirage type blur of a vehicle drifting over the lands in its own dust cloud and the dwindling light. "Shit I can't believe it! I can't believe it man!" he uttered in relief.

# The Wild Coast

It was getting dark as the track opened up into the clearing under the trees overlooking the lagoon. The river's waters relaxing and spreading out to lie down as they reached over the white beach sands. Their long, arduous rush down and across the lands all worth while as they folded into and were comforted by the warm welcoming arms of the ocean.

"Waoooh," exclaimed Antoinette as they all jumped out of the vehicle, "this is amaaazing, waooow," she repeated as she walked in front of Jay and pulled his wanting arms around her in excited, loving appreciation. "You ain't seen anything yet," said Jay smiling and hugging her, then kissing her on the back of the neck, causing her being to vibrate and bubble out in electric goose bumps as his touch entered to deep within her.

"Hey, we better get our tents set up before we run out

of light," said El, his words, directing everyone to focus on the practical realities of the physical before getting lost in their own bubbles of dreamy paradise.

"Boss, you made it," came the boy's words as he appeared from a small clearing, beaming from ear to ear. "Heeey cousin," said El striding towards him, his hand out stretched. He grabbed the boy's hand shaking it with vigorous appreciation and then pulled him in giving him a breath squashing bear hug. "Shit man, you are a star cousin, your wage just went up to twenty five a day man."

The boy looked up at him, his eyes glowing from the recognition that he had just received. "Thanks boss, you too kind," he said continuing to shake El's hand as though this was now a bond of infinitive brotherhood, then continued on excitedly, "I chose the best spot for you boss, you follow me boss, I will show you," he said walking back towards the tunnel like clearing he had just come out of.

All four of them followed him expectantly, bending and walking under the branches and then on along a short pathway which opened up onto a flat plateau. The view was incredible! To the right you could see for miles up the long winding river, then to the left, endless wondrous views of the beach and ocean. The moon, still making its way around teased its grand arrival as it shared some of the suns energy it had received with the earth, sending out and caressing the oceans horizon in a magnificent pure white blue crystal sheen. The sight entering their eyes, stopping them all in their tracks, as their inner most directed their bodies to soak up as much of it as they could. The flat grassy patch glowed a turquoise green as the moon peeped up and over the rim of the earth.

It was obvious that the boy had spent some time clearing the flat ground of leaves, small branches and other bits and pieces of debris. "You camp here," the boy said, breaking the silence of the distant waves. El looked across at him shaking his head in true gratitude. The boy smiled and started walking back towards where the ute was parked.

El, Bee and Jay were well versed in sorting their camp site out, and pretty much had it comfortably set up within half an hour or so. "Anyone feel hungry?" asked El as he walked in with the last of the chilli bins. "Shit, dunno why man, but I'm starving," said Bee. "Hahaha, you got the munchies there brother," laughed Jay. "The "munchies," shit I got the 'starvies' man, think I might start a fire and cook a steak or something."

El looked across at the boy, "How about you cousin, you keen on a steak?" The boys eyes lit up, "Me I'm always keen on a steak boss, I'll get the fire going," he said, reaching into his pocket for a box of matches and walking towards the fire place that he had already prepared, obliterating any second questioning or guessing about whether they should or shouldn't be having something to eat.

"How about you guys," asked El turning towards Jay and Antoinette. They looked at each other agreeing in their eyes that neither of them were hungry, and with the erratic remnants of the day's chaotic ride flickering backwards and forwards across his mind as it started directing the body towards sleep, and not taking his eyes off of Antoinette Jay answered El, "Think we'll just turn in for the night hey. Pheeeweee man, it's been a looong day, and I think it's all starting to catch up with me a bit," he said. And then remembering a bit more he turned towards Bee and El, "Hey thanks so much for supporting me brothers," he continued. "No worries, brother," they replied in unintentional perfect unison. El continued on, "Shit you have had a big one, brother and I know you would be there for any of us so, stay strong brother and remember he is in a good place right now." "Thanks man, you too. Sleep well; we'll catch ya in the morning then." And then with El noting the mild confusion the conversation seemed to have had on the boy as the vibe within the campsite slowed suddenly, continued on, "His uncle passed on cousin, we come down here to let him go," he explained in as brief a manner as he could so that the boy would understand. "Sorry, boss, sorry," the boy said towards Jay dropping his head in a show of respect. Jay smiled back at him, "Thank you cousin, I'm ok and my uncle too, yeh he's travelling light, free and happy right now," he said looking up towards the sky, warm tears rolling uncontrollably down his face as his loss boiled up and out of him once more.

Jay took a deep breath to cool the boil off a bit, then wiped away the tears, his weariness shutting down his emotional receptors allowing him to regain his composure, "Catch ya guys in the morning then," he said turning with Antoinette in his arm towards their tent. "Sleep tight," said Antoinette turning back toward the three standing around the fire, "and thank you so much for allowing me to join you and share this trip. It's only been a few hours and gosh it's been beautiful." "You sleep tight too," said Bee, "don't let the bugs bite, and don't let Jay either, and yeh it's been an absolute pleasure having you with, but next time leave Jay behind," he said smiling broadly at his own parting comment.

Antoinette blew him a kiss and smiled before they climbed into the tent. And with the exhaustive day filling them both to the brim, their bodies gratefully succumbed to the gravitational force of the earth as they lay down in each other's arms. Their noses touching as they breathed each other in before their open gasping mouths moulded into each other, the liquid touch of their lips causing intoxicating chemicals to be released, putting their bodies to sleep as their spirits left them for the night to make love in the moonlight.

The sumptuous heat of the early morning sun slowly filled the tent, evaporating what was left of the fuel that had allowed him to fly away with Antoinette for the night, and as his spirit returned to its capsule, he opened his eyes and looked straight into Antoinette's. "Morning," she said kissing him before he had time to answer. "Gosh wow man, that was freaky," she said, "it was as though I was with you the whole night," she continued on excitedly. "Well hello, you were," he answered back smiling ever so sarcastically.

She sat up and punched him on the arm, "Funny," she said, "you know what I mean, it was as though we never slept, I can't quite remember it all, but we were just sort of . . . I don't know . . . sort of like just everywhere, together, I don't know, it was sooo clear when I first woke up and now I can only remember bits and pieces."

Jay looked at her smiling knowingly; he didn't say anything, just waited a bit longer so that Antoinette could sort it out for herself. "That was crazy," she said and then smiling naughtily, "mmm crazy and sooo delicious too," she continued licking her lips. "I know," answered Jay, "I was there too you know," he said sitting up on his knees, stretching his arms as wide as they would go and pushing his chest out, before throwing himself in rugby tackle style onto Antoinette and hugging her tightly.

They lay there for a while comprehending and understanding something. Neither of them quite knew what it was, but they were both feeling and understanding it a little better the longer they thought and questioned themselves about it. Then after a time, Jay sat up again, his body reacting to the fresh crackling of the fire outside, "Hey come," he said, "it's time for some delicious campfire coffee, and I tell you what, Bee can cook a five star breakfast out here in the bush. Come," he said pulling Antoinette up and out of the tent.

Bee, El and the boy were already standing around the fire. Bee with a ginormous 'Bob Marley' hanging from his mouth as he arranged and stoked the fire to achieve his desired temperatures in the different zones. Small flames for beneath the kettle, with hot coals for under the two frying pans.

"So early in the morning Bee?" questioned Antoinette genuinely surprised at the sight of the early morning joint. "Hey, you know what they say," he said smiling, "when in Rome."

The mood was a bit of a strange one as they all stood around with aimless patience and contentment. The fire brilliantly mesmerising, the sunrise over the ocean welcomingly, warm and spectacular, the lagoon liquid and alive with the early morning feeding frenzies as the game fish erupted through the shoals of baitfish which were trying to take cover in the shallows. Bee had lined up the coffee mugs and being already loaded with the delectable granules, the aroma just added flavour to their early morning 'Wild Coast bubble' as the boiling water was poured in.

"Mmm, that is sooo good," said Antoinette taking her first sip. "Gosh I know I have said it before, but this place is incredible, it is a wonderland." "It's funny," said Jay, "another one of those human 'freak outs' that we never seem to get right. We work our whole lives in the towns and cities of this world just to be able to kinda like retire in some island style environment just like this, but then when we finally make it to our own piece of paradise we want all the mod cons to go with it, decent roads, running water, hot water, electricity, fridges stoves, tv's and then poof, you look again and your island paradise is just another town." "Live and let live a little brother," said El, "just enjoy what you have got while you have got it, you can't stop the sands of time brother, you can't stop the sands of time." "Too true, man, too true," said Bee taking in and blowing out a huge plume of blue smoke.

El's words were as Bee said, very true. It was no use arguing or fighting against the transfer of energies that came with the passing of time, and they all somehow acknowledged that by there accepting silence.

With the bacon crisping up nicely, Bee added in the tomatoes, then started on frying the eggs. The herd boy was almost drooling as he ferreted feverishly around Bee. He was the perfect apprentice, reading what Bee would require next before he even asked for it, a bit of extra wood fed into he corner of the fire, egg flip, salt, pepper, plates, it was almost as if he could read Bee's mind. And then, with the meal plated and ready to go, they all tucked in, and it was as Jay had promised, delicious, absolutely delicious. There was something about breakfast being cooked over an open fire in the bush that could never be replicated in any restaurant. And if you knew what you were doing, as Bee did, then the experience was taken to an even higher level of wonder and satisfaction.

With their bodies filled and fuelled and now more able to deliberate mentally, the conversation moved on to the somewhat reluctantly anticipated. "Ok brothers, and sister," El started, "what's the plan of action?" "Well I know where Mike would want his ashes to be let go," answered Jay looking out into the middle of the ocean." "Yeh me too," said Bee, "out in the middle of the deep and beautiful blue." "Yeh, well that's settled then, might as well get the kayaks and stuff down to the beach and we can move out from there," said El. "I'll come give you a hand, boss, then I'll come back and clean up for you," said the boy. El winked and gave him a thumbs up, then they all moved out back to the ute to unload the kayaks.

It was quite a trek to get down to the beach, the boulder laden track was as 'unmaintained' as one could get and it was a bit of a mission to get down just by yourself, never mind carrying a couple of kayaks along for the ride.

With the paddles strapped to the kayaks, El and Bee took the two singles, El holding the front of each one of them, with Bee at the back of them. Jay and the boy followed handling the double, with Antoinette taking up the rear taking charge of getting Mike's urn down in one piece. They stopped when they reached the bottom of the decent and laid the kayaks down next to the lagoon, it was still about a kilometre before you got to the ocean, but it was more than obvious that it would be a lot easier and more fun to paddle down to the ocean's edge than walk the rest of the way.

"Ok, thanks cousin," said El giving the boy a high five, "we'll see you back at the camp later then." "No boss," replied the boy, "I will be watching for you, then I will come down and help you back up again." "Hey cousin, you too good man, I think I will have to take you back home with me," he said jokingly.

The boy looked shyly down at his feet, in a way wishing that El could and would fulfil his suggestion. Then he looked back up at El, "Does the boss want some crayfish and mussels for tonight?" he asked. "Shit yeh," answered Bee on El's behalf. "All good boss I will catch them for you then."

The boy turned towards Jay, "Hey Jay stay strong," he said pumping his heart with his fist. The soft words of sincerity warming and comforting Jay. "Thanks so much cousin," he replied turning and winking at the boy. "Hey cousin," Jay continued, "what's your name?"

Bee and El looked up expectantly, realising that it was a question they had never asked. Antoinette too waited for the answer. "I'm Kaya," he said happy and proud, as though he had been bursting for someone to ask. "Hey Kaya, you a good man," said Jay, "you have helped us too much; you are a special kinda person. Not many like you left on this earth. You will go far, you have much to teach many," he said almost prophetically. But then again, it was not rocket science, it was more a kind of spiritual science, it was as though Kaya had always been with them, grown up together as like the younger brother kind of thing, and all the energy he emitted just felt so natural, so familiar, so good and so real.

Kaya 'bubbled' and smiled, "You too Jay, I have seen it and I can feel it in me, you too are a teacher," he said implying without a trace of vanity that he knew and understood what Jay had been saying to him. "I will see you all later," he said turning and jogging, almost bouncing off along the lagoon edge towards where the rocks walled in the ocean in the distance.

"Rrright," said Jay, "you ever been on a kayak before?" he asked Antoinette. "Uuum hmmm not really, but I can surf," she said, smiling. "Hahaha," funny said Jay, "ok you jump in the front and just get a bit of a rhythm going with the paddle, it is as easy as, and we do have some nice flat water to practice in till we get to the ocean."

Antoinette moved eagerly towards Jay handing him the urn and untying the paddles. Jay packed the urn securely in his backpack and nosed the kayak towards and into the water. Antoinette sat down in the kayak and wobbled around a bit until she got her balancing bearings sorted. Bee and El were sort of transfixed watching her every move. Apart from her being beautiful to watch anyway, they were subconsciously deliberating between themselves as to whether this was such a good idea or not. The ocean in all it glory and magnificence, did not discriminate, and if you got it wrong, there would be consequences. But by the time they reached the ocean, following close behind Jay and Antoinette, their concerns had waned to an extent. It wasn't just the mesmerising tranquillity and beauty of the place that entered their core enticing their spirits to transcend and be set free out and beyond the body, but also, Antoinette as with her first and only surf was a bit of a natural on the water. She had natural, abundant, but measured confidence and belief, and with that came the abundant ability.

The tide was coming in filling the lagoon, and with it came the playful aftermath of the surf. Lines of small waves barrelling their way up the lagoon, getting bigger and bigger the closer they got to the mouth. "Waaaoooh, this is fun," shrieked Antoinette as their ride got more and more imaginative. "Yeh, just get the feel of it all," said Jay, "you can multiply this by ten or more when we go out through the surf. So yeh, just listen to my instructions, and if you can," he said splashing her with a large paddle full of water, "do exactly as I say, then it will all be sweet." "Aye aye captain," she said stopping paddling and saluting him cheekily.

The lagoon swung in a long deep searching curve to the right before it sniffed the salt water and eagerly cut back left to make it back home. Inexperience would have sent Jay and Antoinette following the lagoon all the way to the ocean, where they would have been spat out literally into deep and turbulent water. Jay knew this, and how to avoid it.

"We'll paddle up on to the bank in front of us and pull the kayak up onto the dune, then have had a good look at the conditions before we go for it," he said directing the craft straight ahead. Their kayak came to a gentle bump as it caressed the sand and Jay stabilised the craft with his feet either side while Antoinette stood up in the warm, ankle deep water.

Bee and El beached their craft and did the same, and then together, they picked up the kayaks and walked up the small dune, put them down and stood looking out to sea. No one spoke as they took in the sights, sounds and smells, the energies of the universe in front of them, flooding in and filling their innermost, which then fed them back out into their bodies, exhilarating, calming and wonderising them into a meditative kinda state. Taking them out into the ocean before they had even got there.

Bee filled to overflowing was forced to speak, "Wooow, check out that 'right' peeling through man," he expressed as a four foot, glassy, transparent mass of liquid turquoise stood up on the outside, then, defied by gravity, folded at its peak grabbing in as much air as it could before tumbling back crashing in bubbly delight, chasing itself down and along the clean face surfing its own self to the beach.

Outside the surf zone, it was like a mirror. Perfectly calm with an occasional patch of rippled water where the feint breeze touched down to kiss the ocean surface. But the ocean also held the juices of distant storms and passed them on and out towards the beach in powerful, mobile lines of surf.

"Hmmm, are you sure you want to do this hey Antoinette," questioned El. "Do what?" replied Antoinette still in wonderland and without even actually considering the question. El looked towards Jay for the answer. Jay flicked his eyes upwards and smiled, acknowledging to El that Antoinette did not even realise the consequence of failure. "We'll be right," Jay said, "there are long breaks between the sets, so it'll be all good."

El shrugged his shoulders in acceptance. He knew that Jay was as good as you could get with reading the ocean conditions and handling a craft through the surf. "Ok most probably best if you guys go first then," said El as he directed them all back to the reality in front of them. "Yeh, good idea," agreed Jay, moving back behind Antoinette and putting his arms around her.

They literally melted into each other as she responded by holding his arms tightly into and around her. Jay kissed her on the neck, the touch of his lips exchanging warmth, comfort and deliciousness, causing his mind to instruct him not to remove them for as long as possible. Bee and El looked at each other in subtle, but obvious envy, before Bee could not contain himself anymore.

"Ok love birds that's enough," he said jokingly serious. His words opening Jay's eyes, "Rrright, you see the sand bank out there," he said softly but assertively into Antoinette's ear, and at the same time pointing out to where the white water remnants of the backline were surging across the shallow bank. Antoinette nodded. "Ok so inside the bank, it's just the shore break at the edge of the beach we gotta tackle otherwise it's pretty calm. So we will walk through the 'shorey' and then jump on. Tell me when you feel ok with your balance and all that and then we will paddle up to the bank. I will be watching for the break and when I say go; ya gotta paddle your butt off. Don't stop, don't think, just paddle ok?" he said raising the tempo in his voice as it progressed through the planned paddle out.

Antoinette nodded again, not saying much as the reality of the expedition ahead started to sink in. "Still keen?" questioned Jay. "Funny," she replied smiling excitedly, "you are not going to leave me on the beach, I can't wait to get out there," she confirmed. "Ok lets do it then," said Jay giving her one last squeeze before letting go and moving to the back of the kayak.

Antoinette picked up the front, and with Bee and El picking up the other two kayaks they all moved down the dune to the ocean edge. The energies of the ocean starting to engulf them as they got closer. The sound of the crushing surf out back and rushing water in front delectably deafening as it surged into them, the warm water surging around their ankles as they stepped into it.

Jay didn't speak, he was in tune with Antoinette and conducted their speed of entry into the water and over the shore break by nudging the kayak forward or holding it back, communicating through invisibility. Walking in to knee deep water they laid the kayak down. The ocean instantaneously loving, licking and splashing at the bottom of it, expectant as she waited to play with and delight them all with her power and beauty.

"Ok wait for it now, you see this one coming in now, go over the top of it then jump on," instructed Jay. Antoinette did exactly as directed and Jay held the back of the kayak for as long a time as he dared so she could stabilise herself, before he jumped aboard. "Ok start paddling gently now, just get the feel of the craft and the water, become and move as one with the ocean."

Jay paddled in time with Antoinette's stroke rate and they made their way out to the bank. "Feeling all good?" he questioned. "Loving it my Jay, loving it," she replied. "Wow this is brilliant," she exclaimed, "I just feel so beautifully alive, wow I love it!"

With the sand bank approaching, the wash coming off of it took a bit of a stronger hold of the kayak, slowing her down and surging around her. "Yow those waves coming in seem a looot bigger when you are down here," she said. "Wanna go back in?" he questioned giving Antoinette her last chance before committing to the wild and wonders of the ocean. "No waaays, are you mad," she reaffirmed. "Ok, just keep paddling slowly then, we won't be going anywhere with the water ripping over the bank towards us, but just keep padding to keep us up here. Then when I say go, then just go hey, don't dilly dally, paddle your heart out."

Antoinette acknowledged his instruction with a vigorous nod, her senses overloaded with the incoming energies not allowing her to speak. Jay waited for two sets of waves to go through just to make sure he was reading it as it came, then after the second set, and as the ocean predictably lay down to take another breath, he commanded Antoinette into action, "Right, lets go, Antoinette, paddle hard and don't stop till we are out there."

Antoinette's stroke rate doubled and Jay powered in behind her. The kayak conquering the grip of the surge slid forward in defiance and victory and moved onto the wash, bubbles and opposing water force surging over the sand bank. Jay could see the humps of the next set forming menacingly in the distance. If they faltered now, it would be all over, and self preservation afforded him to encourage, "That's brilliant Antoinette, just keep it up, whatever you do don't stop now!" he stated over the sensory rush carrying on around them. His words caused Antoinette to power the strokes deeper and harder, her determination feeding off of the ocean's power and brilliance.

As they got over the sandbank the flat water greased the bottom of the kayak doubling their speed across the water. The first of the distant humps eagerly moving towards them, now making its presence felt, squeezed Antoinette to speak, "Yiiikes, that's huge," she said.

Jay hadn't taken his eyes off of it, subconsciously measuring their progress out in relation to the humps progress in. Time accelerated to extinction as the hump reached and 'mountained' up in front of them. "Woooaaaw!" exclaimed Antoinette, as it came upon them and lifted them up effortlessly towards its summit. Jay stroked hard up the mighty, magnificent face then slowed as they reached the top. The kayak shot over, freefalling in a tornado of silence and slow motion onto the receiving water below. "Waaahooo," she exclaimed as she released some of the exhilaration back into the universe. Jay smiled, loving it, but knew it wasn't over yet, they were still very much in and around the impact zone "Pick your paddling up again," he reiterated, "there is more coming, we are not out yet."

The next even larger mountain was already upon them, up and over, then the next, and another, before they were deep enough to just ease over the juveniles still maturing and making their way in.

"Well that's it," he said "your first successful launch." "That was incredible," she replied. "Wow, now I am really starting to understand why you love this ocean of yours so much. "Wow it's like a tonic, Jay. Wow! That was crazy beautiful, I just feel so, I don't know, so full of love, life and wonder. It's amazing!"

Jay laughed, "Come here," he said gently pulling on her shoulders until she was lying back between his legs, then leaning over her and kissing her on the forehead. He pulled back slightly and they kissed each other with their eyes as they stared into each other's souls. "Gosh Jay I love you sooo much," she said from somewhere deep within. Jay smiled, "Love ya too my Antoinette."

"Aaah not again," came the cocky voice of Bee as he paddled up next to them, with El not far behind. "Gees you two need to get a room," he said laughing and splashing Jay with water. "Pheeewee," whistled Bee, "some mean sets coming through hey, how was it for you Antoinette? Scary?" "No ways, I loooved it," she replied. "You did well, hey," congratulated El, "hmmm you didn't leave much of a margin for error with that first one, Jay?" "Naaah but I had faith in my co-pilot's power and ability," he replied, "and yeh I had Mike with me too," he said smiling and reaching around to his backpack and tapping the urn. El smiled, "So how do want to do this, Jay?"

The mood wasn't sullen or sad, almost the contrary. It was like they were celebrating returning Mike's ashes to where they came from. To where he would want them to be.

"Well I know Mike would not want any fanfare, just quiet and peaceful. I think I have said all I wanted to say about Mike to you guys, and yep, thank you guys again for all your support, it's been incredible. Don't quite know how I would have handled it all without you guys. But, no," he stumbled, taking his back pack off, opening it, reaching for the urn and removing the lid, "is there anything you guys want to say?"

Bee straightened up, his eyes noticeably watery, then he looked up into the sky and spoke, "Hey Mike you ol' bastard," he said then took a deep breath, "I wish I had got to know you a bit better, but it was real cool knowing and sharing the time that we did have. Catching up and talking shit every now and again on the beach was really cool man, really cool. Enjoy the ride Mike and rest in peace," he finished off tears now unashamedly streaming down his face.

Antoinette was looking at him wide eyed, "Gosh that was beautiful Bee, that was beautiful," she said. "Thanks, man," he replied. Jay looked across at El. "Yeh, well I just wanted to say, that yeh, hey, Mike, I'm going to miss seeing you around and like Bee, now that you are gone, I too wish I could have got to know you a bit better. But I also know that you will never leave us completely. You will always be in our minds and are literally part of us, so, yep, take it easy out there Mike, we will miss you down here." "Wow that was also so beautiful El," said Antoinette. "Thanks," said Jay, "those were some amazing words, and like I said, I think I have said everything I want to and you guys have just put the topping on so yeh," he said holding up the urn to the gentle breeze. "Hey Mike, travel safe, travel free, travel wild, thank you for everything you taught, showed to, and shared with me." Jay paused looking up to the sky, then slowly tipped the urn towards the sea. Mike's ashes flowed out into the breeze, drifting out to the horizon, ever so gently sprinkling down into the water that he lived and loved so much.

They all sat there on top of the ocean, mesmerised in their own space, and as Mike's ashes dissipated back into infinity so did their grief. Jay smiled, his being tranquil and at peace with his loss. "So what you guys gonna do with the rest of the day?" he asked. "Shit man I think I'm gonna go back and ride some of those beauties we just came through," replied Bee. "Yeh I think I'll join you hey," said El, and you guys," he questioned knowing that it would be a bit ambitious for Jay and Antoinette to go and play in and out of the surf. "I was thinking of taking a paddle along the coast," replied Jay, "go show Antoinette the cove, then catch a walk back along the track to the camp site."

Bee and El looked across at each other smiling

relieved that they would not just be 'dumping' Jay and Antoinette, but also knowingly. They knew that a visit to the cove wouldn't just be a show and tell.

"Well that's if you're keen to go have a look hey, Antoinette," Jay said not wanting to dictate what they were going to do next. "I'd love to go have a look," she replied unable to hide here anticipation and expectation, knowing and wanting just to be able to spend some time alone with Jay. "Cool, that's all sorted then," Jay said barely able to speak in a controlled manner or tone. "Sweet we'll see you back at the camp later then," said Bee turning his kayak towards the shore and paddling hard towards the surf as though it was going to run out. "Catch ya guys later, take care out there," said El, turning and following Bee in, also not wanting to miss out on any waves. "Catch ya later, said Jay, "enjoy the surf."

Then in a seeming instant they were alone, in a universal bubble of perfect perfection. Their bodies set alight and buzzing, they were one again, their warmth, their heat, were one. Their spirits evaporating outwards beyond their bodies, dancing, playing and assimilating into each other, were one. Jay, vibrating, leaned forward, reached out for and gently massaged Antoinette's shoulders, then let go with one hand pointing to the rocky outcrop in the distance, "See over there," he said, that's where we are headed for." "Mmm, I'm ready when you are," she purred.

They didn't speak a word as they paddled for the next half hour or so towards the cove. They didn't have to or want to, there was something so deep, some connection so beyond the physical, it would have been futile to communicate verbally. Then as the point got closer and closer, so the form of the cove became visible, and so did the realisation that they had to now get back through the surf onto the beach.

"Hey beautiful, you ready for this?" Jay asked as he steered the kayak closer in towards the backline, the humps starting to make their presence felt the closer they got. "I have complete faith in my captain," she replied turning and smiling sending the butterflies in his core wild again. "Hahaha," he laughed, "well you can reward me when I get us in safe and sound," he said, "but we will do the same as when we came out, but in reverse, just wait for the big ones to go through and then catch a bit of a smaller one in." "Aaah come on," she replied, "don't let me down now, why can't we catch a big one in?" "Hmmm ok, if that's what you want, but be prepared, the 'take off' can be a bit scary, and if we get it wrong you will have a long swim back to the beach." "Life's for living, my Jay, and I don't mind a swim if that's what it comes to."

Jay had been by instinct planning their route in for some time, almost like coming in on a glide path when landing a jet airliner. The angle of approach in relation to the wave direction. The distance in from the beach so that you were not caught in the impact zone with nowhere to go. The sequence of the sets of waves, all taken into subconscious consideration, and then without any warning, he spoke with intent, ensuring that Antoinette would respond accordingly, "Ok here we go, don't look back now, but paddle hard," he said turning and watching the mountain erupt out the ocean behind him. He wasn't paddling hard just yet, just getting Antoinette's routine and power going. Timing the input of his paddle power to harmonise with being in exactly the right place at the right time on the steep slope was critical.

They needed the perfect ride down the face to gain enough velocity to stay just ahead of the mighty, wanting avalanche that was sure to follow. But if he left his paddle too late, the summit would slip by underneath them dragging them into the impact zone of the one to follow. Too much paddle, and they would be too deep into the zone and would be catapulted over 'the falls' and freefall off of a near vertical cliff face.

Neither scenario was an option; he had to get it right. Jay started picking up his pace as the fluid giant approached, billowing upwards in mighty volumes of mass and power. The foot of the mountain reached the back of the kayak, grabbing hold of and pulling it effortlessly backwards and up the face.

"Waaaoooh," gasped Antoinette as the power fed through her core. "Don't stop now!" commanded Jay as he drove his paddle into the slope, urging the kayak to relent to force of gravity and break free of the liquid glue. Up they went, dragged back in slow motion, the slope, leaning forward, approaching the point of no vertical return, then one, two, three, determined and forceful strokes, broke the bond and the kayak started slowly but deliberately dropping down.

The kayak in an instant recognising its ride to come picked up momentum, jubilantly surfing free then triumphantly racing down the face. The speed, the rush, the power, the freedom was incredible. "Waaahooo," they shouted out in tandem, Antoinette holding her paddle up high with Jay using his to control the direction of the kayak and prevent it from being pushed side on. Momentum took over shooting them down and out in front of the marching wall of water as it transformed into a mighty beast, stood up high on its hind legs before charging down behind them with wild, bone crunching determination. Hissing, spitting and letting out a mighty primal shuddering roar, chasing them down and eager to show off and prove its power.

The beast was tireless, relentless, and caught up with them effortlessly. Then, showed off by engulfing them in a giant mouth of powerful, soft, salty, warm, eager bubbles before blowing them out, rocketing them towards the beach, before relenting and lying down behind them, dissolving back into the ocean. They paddled with the white water over the bank, then as suddenly as it had started; it ended as they crossed over into the channel.

"So how was that," asked Jay. Antoinette could not put words to it, and just sat there shaking her head, and then managed, "That was, I don't know, how would you describe it? There are no words" "In surfing, it's what we called stoked,' said Jay, 'it's just kinda like how you feel after you have been out in the surf sharing Mother Nature's bounty. You can't quite find the words to describe it to anyone." "Wow, well I am so stoked then," she said turning and smiling.

Antoinette sat with the paddle across her legs, in awe and digesting natures abundant wonders, while Jay waited for a good looking shore break to come up so he could surf it up onto the beach. Taking his pick, he took off on one and it willingly took them for a ride, then as it realised its limit, the water slid back down the sand into the ocean, leaving them high and dry. Their liquid fluidity and rush abruptly replaced with a surreal and unexpected serene solidity. The transformation of energies keeping Antoinette sitting, contemplating and playing catch up with her time and space.

Jay stood up and took her paddle, then reached for her hand. She grabbed hold of his and stood up, threw her arms around him and gave him an endless salty kiss. The world laughing, loving and spinning timelessly around them. Then the ocean nudged the kayak up against them, allowing them to part mouths and look, take in and appreciate the splendour that they were captured in.

"Gosh Jay, this really is paradise," she said, as she took his hand with both of hers. Jay reached down and took the front of the kayak, and they walked up towards the coastal fringe, where he secured it to a small tree trunk, then they both sat down, Antoinette between his legs, Jay with his arms wrapped tightly around her. Neither knew how long they sat there for, and neither of them cared. Their minds dictating to their bodies not to move, but just to stay within each other so that their beings could be together as one. Antoinette moved slightly to the left and lent backwards, Jay came forward and they again got lost in each other's mouths. Their spirits not wanting their time together to end gave instruction to their brains to fill their bodies with beautifully warmed and intoxicating chemicals. The purple haze spread out and beyond their bodies, almost free to travel, but not quite able to just yet. Not quite experienced in or understanding the consequence of leaving their bodies behind.

Drifting in and out of the real world, they tried as hard as they could to resist. There was so much to talk about, so much to discuss, question and debate, but it was futile, their spiritual beings would not allow them to reason in the physical. They were together now and wanted it to stay that way. They stood up together and drifted along the beach towards the cove entrance. Jay had clasped her hand so tightly it was as though it was in a vice, but not of cold steel, rather of soft, firm warm flesh. It felt sooo good to her, to be wanted and protected, to be so loved. It felt incredibly natural, like it had always been, and always would be. Like it was meant to be.

Her right hand came around and grabbed his right arm tightly just above the elbow, and she buried her head deep into his neck. The cove came and went on into an endless expanse of beach as they walked on in oblivion, loving and living off of each other's energy and life forces being emitted. Their spirits in perfect tune and in perfect love. Neither of them knew where they were going or for how long they had been walking, and it wasn't because they didn't care, it was as though they were in a meditative state, in a state of purity and tranquillity. They were literally in another world, where time and space had become irrelevant.

They wandered on up and down the dunes, until the sun had started its descent for the day and the birds were gathering in the dune forest fringes after a frantic days flight, play and feeding. The energies being released through their chirping and chatter becoming a crescendo in Antoinette and Jay's ears. The world around them, a crystal clear blur.

Stopping without stopping, their beings embraced. There bodies, minds, and souls were now intertwined, inseparable and desperately in love. The sustained transfer of energies was electric. A delicious 'insatisfiable' buzz throughout their bodies, the consequence. Their souls fusing together in an explosion of the most brilliant and gentle warmth, like two clouds becoming one, dissolving into each other, sharing all they are, all they have, their time their space, their water vapour and lightning within. Sharing, and loving sharing their very being.

Their minds, as they connected by default, now in solution together, working in unison giving their bodies instruction to ensure a closer and prolonged contact of of all three, their bodies, minds and souls, their physical and spiritual beings. They had become one, and wanted to stay forever as one.

The magnetic rush surging around their bodies overpowered any hope they had of remaining touch free. This was as natural as one could get. Jay reached down and gently lifted her skirt. He held and massaged her bum before moving his hands around to her front, running his fingers from the point up along either side of her V until he reached her tummy. He repeated this over and over again just feeding off of everything she was letting go. Her breath delicious, her warmth, an orange fiery glow, her soft, wet tongue tantalising, playful and irresistible.

His hand moved onto her and even though she only emitted the most gentle of groans as he did so, it was as though she had just injected him with an overdose of some kind of exotic, unrelenting adrenalin. Jay dropped to his knees and fed off of her, clasping her with both hands at the same time, knowing exactly where and how to hold and massage her.

Antoinette, couldn't understand what he was doing to her, she didn't care or want to either, this was her man, taking from and giving to her, sharing their energies and pleasures in a place were they were destined to be and belong. He kept on giving more and more of his energies while soaking up all she was emitting until she reached a point where she felt like she was about to explode. Antoinette let go of his head and reached out to hold onto the palm trees on either side of her. Her eyes tightly shut as she clenched onto the vegetation, and as she began to climax, her head drew back involuntarily, her eyes opened wide and her body convulsed as the waves of warmth and pleasure erupted both from her feet and head at the same time. The waves moving towards each other and exploding as they collided and surged around in her middle, releasing the energies absorbed in a flood back to the universe.

Antoinette's legs gave way in slow motion as she sank down onto her haunches taking in and releasing large quantities of air in slow deliberate breaths. Her eyes reached and made love to his in a steamy, delectable, blurry gaze, before their lips melted together again and they drank from each other for an eternity.

Antoinette gently forced him to let go and leant him backwards. She grabbed him hard then she leant over kissing his stomach as though it was about to run out and she wouldn't be able to get any more. Then he too succumbed and let go, his whole body stiffening as the electricity exploded from within searching for the earth that it was destined to return to.

Jay opened his eyes, trying to focus on the world around him. He tried to move back up, but she pushed him down again, intent on getting her fill of all she could from him. Gasping in, and then slowly releasing, a huge lung full of air he tried again, her mouth let go of his stomach and she looked up at him, her eyes glowing luminescent and she beamed a huge smile, before sinking her lips back onto his. They held each other in a melting, everlasting embrace as their tongues married and played, not wanting to leave or stop for anyone or anything.

Neither of them had any cognisance of time, and Jay wasn't sure what it was that made him open his eyes, but when he did it was already going dark. Reality seemed to smack him on the forehead and he pulled back and kissed her on the lips saying, "Hey we need to start getting back." "Do we have to?" she replied, "lets just spend the rest of our lives here," she smiled. "Hmmm should we?" he said smiling back, and again they launched each other mouths together and were, once again, lost to time and space.

It must have been the birds going quiet that finally forced them both to recognise that it was now definitely time to let go of perfection. They stood up together, Jay put his arm around her and pulled her in close, their beings did not want to separate until they had no other option, and absolutely had to. "Hmmm hope I can remember the way back to the track," Jay said teasingly. "Well I hope you can't," she replied cheekily.

Jay found the track and they started out on the way back to the camp "Phew there is so much more I wanted to speak to you about, so much more I wanted to say ask and find out," Jay said, realising that they hadn't said two words to each other the whole way back. Subconsciously they hadn't wanted to, all it would have done would have been to create more questions than answers, more frustrations of the reality that surrounded and enveloped them. Antoinette's dad's persistence in managing her life. What would he say? When would she have to go back? Where would back be?

Jay continued on, "I know that in reality we hardly even know each other, but it's like, I dunno hey, just like we actually do, and are supposed to be together. But there just seems to be so many kinda like, I dunno, hurdles to jump." "I know replied Antoinette, but be patient, the universe works in her own special and mysterious way."

Jay looked down, a little embarrassed by his sudden outpouring and impatience, "Yeh I know," he said. "It's funny, but I always wonder when we have been together. Should I just be grateful for those very special moments and opportunities we have been allowed, or should I be freaked out because I can't have more?"

Antoinette didn't have the answer, and didn't want to let him know that she continually asked herself the same questions. Well, not right now anyway. She could sense that he needed her reassurance rather than doubt, so she turned and smiled to him and just answered with, "Don't even think about it, my Jay, just be and walk with me, when and while we can, 'cause these times are too special and too perfect to waste on doubt and deliberation."

Jay laughed out loud and with a huge grin replied, "Doubt and deliberation!" he laughed out loud again. "Funny! Where did you get that from?" "I don't know, just popped into my head," she said smiling and dropping her head in a show of humility. Jay bumped her gently with his shoulder, "You're funny, hey," he said smiling and then repeated, "doubt and deliberation hahaha!"

They were nearing the car park and even though Jay had reached the stage where he didn't really care anymore, logic prevailed and he allowed himself to be put back into real world mode. And with the realities of life on earth now melting back into them Jay realised that he actually hadn't even asked how she was going in her day to day life. It had been a bit of a whirlwind time for him, but now it just seemed to have been so brutally all about him.

Realisation, triggering slight embarrassment and frustration in allowing himself to be so self contained and centred he blurted out to Antoinette, "Hey, so tell me, how did your meeting with everyone go the other day?" Antoinette looked at him and smiled, "Well funny, but Mike's sudden and unexpected parting seemed to have taken centre stage. Everyone was a lot more subdued andaccepting about the exploration we propose to do out to sea. A lot more than I would have ever expected," she repeated emphasising her point.

"It was as though everyone there all of a sudden seemed to understand that there was much more serious and real issues in life to deal with than just posing and making comment and noise for purely political and petty reasons. I suppose the finality of death has that kind of impact on people? So yes everyone just listened to our proposal, they asked a couple of pertinent questions on their health, safety and environmental concerns, and of course the economic benefit to the region. So yes, all in all it was pretty good. Seemed to be another step in the right direction for us and our relationship with the local community too." "Wow, that's amazing," replied Jay, as they made their way into the light of the fire.

"Heeey, they have returned," beamed Bee genuinely happy and relieved to see them back. "Gees you guys were making us worried. Shit man, don't you know what time it is?" he asked bordering on the tone of an anxious mother.

Antoinette walked up to him and gave him a hug, "Aaah Bee, you were worried about us," she said, loving the unexpected concern. Bee melted and hugged her back, "Yeh well not really worried," he said trying to avoid any embarrassing label being applied to him some time in the future, "just didn't want your dinner to spoil," he said rather awkwardly pointing towards the fish and crayfish grilling on the fire.

"Wow! Those are beauties," said Jay walking up and slapping Kaya on the back. Kaya beamed, "Plenty more where those came from Jay," he said, "but these ones I caught specially for you guys, specially for you guys to feast and celebrate Mike passing on into his next life," he continued looking straight into Jay's eyes with conviction and total belief.

"Hey Kaya, like I told you before, you are a good and wise man," Jay said extending his hand and then taking Kaya's pulling him in and hugging him like the family member he seemed to be. "Thank you brother, thank you so much," said Jay.

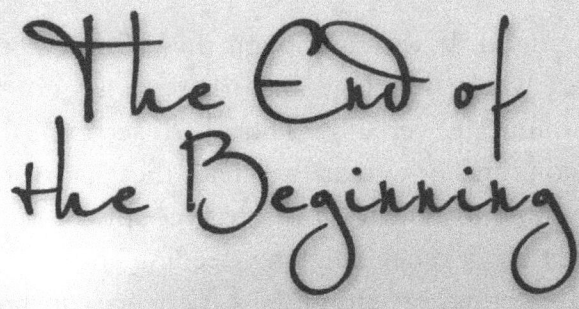

# The End of the Beginning

They left as late as possible the next day, balancing the irresistible magnetism of the remote island type fantasy, with the reality of getting back along the track back to civilisation in one piece. But it was already dark when El drove out off the track and onto the rural main road.

"Ok one for the road," Bee said relaxing back in his seat putting his feet up on the dash and lighting up another monster joint. The remnants of the place still drifting around in his blood, refusing to allow him back into reality. Not that he was in any rush to return back into it anyway.

Antoinette lay down on Jay's lap and faded into dream world as her body succumbed, rested and set her spirit free. No one spoke much on the way back, the odd comment about something that passed by, but nothing meaningful. It was as though they all knew what each other were thinking and there was no need to communicate verbally. They had accomplished their mission, and now that they had, they had for the first time, time to reflect on the past couple of days. It had been a crazy time. Thinking, feeding and acting on the hoof. Acting on impulse, experience, instinct, who knows? Spontaneous action and interaction, working towards a common understanding, wanting and outcome.

And as the entrance onto the freeway came into distant view the sight caused El to unintentionally break the silence as he spoke his mind, "Pheeew! So, brother, the journey takes another turn," he said and then immediately wished he hadn't, but it was too late.

"Yeh, fuck," said Jay softly! Then took a deep breath letting it out in a long sigh, "Dunno hey, dunno what I'm gonna do now. Might have to let go of the ocean and go get a real job," he paused. "Funny but that's what Mike said to me the last time we went fishing. Shit! He knew he was gonna go hey, just didn't want to tell anyone. Just didn't want anyone to show any concern or care. Shit, he was a hard ol' bastard you know." "Hey maybe you can get a job with Antoinette's ol' man," said Bee excitedly. "Hahaha yeh right," laughed Jay, "I think the only thing I'll get from Antoinette's dad is his boot up my arse."

Bee and El laughed and then El obliged to reassure Jay after starting the thought line in the first place continued, "Things have a way of sorting themselves out. It's like ol' Brian once told me one day, in life you can't connect the dots going forward, but when you look back as to how they have connected, everything will all make sense."

The three of them went quiet as they thought about what El had just said, subconsciously thinking and looking back at their 'dot line' to date. "That's so true hey," blurted out Bee, "if Mike hadn't died, we wouldn't have all gone down to the Wild Coast." El looked across at Bee, smiled and shook his head in disbelief. "Yeh, something like that Bee," he said continuing to shake his head. "Hmmm, more like if I hadn't been commercial fishing I wouldn't have met Antoinette," smiled Jay "Aaah no, what have I started now," exasperated El. "Shit, let's just all forget about the dots for now," he said still smiling and shaking his head.

"There she is," said El as their turn off from the freeway came upon them, "home sweet home." Jay stopped massaging Antoinette head and turned her face ever so gently toward him, caressing her cheek bones as he did so. "Mmm," she said as her spirit returned back in to direct her body. She opened her eyes and looked straight up into Jay's. "Mmm, I want to wake up like this every time," she said reaching up and pulling his lips onto hers. She let him go just far enough for her to be able to whisper, "My Jay, I love you sooo much." Then she pulled him back down kissing him, feeding off of their time together.

"Ok boys and girls," said Bee in his best microphone sounding voice he could muster, "this is your co pilot speaking. On behalf of captain El and the flight crew, I would like to thank you for flying with us today, we are starting our decent now, so if you can put your tongues back in your mouths and sit upright in your own seats without touching each other till further notice that would be good," he said turning and smiling at them. Antoinette put her hand on his head shaking it from side to side, "Ok co pilot Bee," she said smiling back, "and yes I looved the flight, the journey and the flight crew. You guys were amazing, thank you so much for letting me share that time with you."

Bee pulled up the drive of Antoinette's place and they all got out, the four of them stretching in unison. Antoinette walked up to El and gave him a big hug then did the same with Bee. "Gosh thanks again, hey guys, that was incredible," she said "Hey it was real good having you down with us, and yeh impressed with your ability on the kayak," said Bee nodding in sincerity. "Thanks for joining us," said El, "it was a real pleasure having you along, and yeh, you are just what Jay needed," he paused, "and still needs," he continued. "Well the feeling is mutual," she replied smiling reassuringly.

Jay had got her bag out the back of the ute, and walked towards them. "I'll just see Antoinette to the door, won't be five minutes," he said, taking her hand and walking up towards the house. "Take your time brother, no rush," said El as Bee and he leant up against the ute, "more than happy to take a break and stand a while after sitting through the journey.

The outside light was on lighting up the front door, and it opened as they approached. Marco's frame, flanked by Em, almost miniaturised under his arm, taking up the whole space. "Hey Marco, how's it going?" bubbled Antoinette, happy to see him so relaxed. "Hi Em," she continued, "looks like you have been taking real good care of my big brother," she said smiling and striding up to Marco throwing her arms around him and giving him a big hug.

"Hey sis," he replied and then giving a thumbs up to Jay, "how's it going there brother? You guys have a good time?" "It was amazing replied," Antoinette before Jay had time to even open his mouth. "Marco, we have got to take you there one day. It is the most beautiful place on earth," she continued on excitedly. "And you guys what did you get up to while we were away?"

Marco and Em looked at each other smiling knowingly. "Well we didn't kinda get out much, just cooled off at home," he said not taking his eyes off of Em's and pulling her in close. Antoinette and Jay looked at each other and simultaneously opened their eyes wide. "Hmmm, maybe I should just leave my questioning there then," said Antoinette smiling and turning back towards Marco.

"Hey did you get my voicemail," Marco asked. "Voicemail, I haven't even had my phone on, there is no signal down where we were and you just sort of relax into this space where you just want to leave it all behind for a while. So, to answer your question," she smiled, "no I didn't, not urgent or anything hey?" she queried now slightly concerned as her whole being started filling with the energies of the 'real world' surrounding her.

"Well I wouldn't say urgent," replied Marco, "but like I said before you left, you do know that your dad would find out about your trip and may not be too impressed by it all." "Yeh," she said relaxing a bit, thankful that that was all it was about. "Well yeh, not too impressed might have been an understatement. He hit the roof."

Jay just stood there in the blur and haze, trying to take it all in as it was being delivered. "Seriously!" exclaimed

Antoinette, "well it's time he grew up," she said, slightly annoyed, and a little embarrassed that Jay and Em were obviously realising just how controlling her dad was.

"Well, he wants you to give him a call as soon as possible. I said I would make sure you do as soon as you arrive." "Gosh he makes me so cross sometimes," she said. "Well please, just make sure you call him tonight, maybe best when you cool off a bit but you must call him, he's obviously quite freaked out at me too, so please Antoinette," Marco said trying to instil some sanity, peace and tranquillity into what he could see could turn into a bit of a family feud.

Jay feeling a little awkward, butted in, "Hey Antoinette, I better get going, El and Bee will be getting restless and wanting to get home." "Yes ok my Jay," she said softly, her mood changing instantly on hearing his words indicating his departure from her presence. She turned and threw her arms around his neck and pulled him in close, "Thank you so much for taking me with you," she whispered, "I love you so much." "Me too," said Jay pulling back slightly and giving her a gentle kiss. Then reluctantly letting go and starting to walk back towards the car, Jay turned and said, "I will call you tomorrow sometime. Don't know what I will be doing or what's going to happen next, but call me when you get a chance, let me know how it goes with your dad. Catch ya later Marco, cheers Em, see you guys around sometime." Em waved goodbye, Marco calling out after him, "Take care brother, see you around soon."

Jay got to the car and all three of them jumped in "Oh shit said Jay, her ol'man has evidently flipped." "What the fuck for?" queried Bee. "Ah long story hey, Antoinette's his only blood child and he sort of molly coddles her a bit, seems he is a bit paranoid about letting her have too much freedom. Don't know why, not sure hey, maybe he is scared of losing her or maybe he is scared of some kind of harm coming to her." "Who would ever want to harm her?" Bee questioned. "I dunno, but he is like this big wig oil tycoon dude, so maybe he is worried the 'greenies' will kidnap her or something, or maybe some other arsehole wanting money. I don't know, but whatever it is, that is why he's got Marco lurking in the background the whole time. Sort of like her permanent bodyguard."

"Seriously," said Bee genuinely surprised that this kind of thing was happening right in his simple backyard. "Yeh, seriously," replied Jay. "Anyway, the shit has now well and truly hit the fan. One he knows she is messing around with some local fisherman. Two she went away for the weekend with him and his mates right into the back of beyond into the middle of nowhere, and three . . . her bodyguard let her go and was not with her, So yeh, we will wait and see."

El taking it all in piped up, "Surely he can't be that freaked out, shit she is a grown, educated women. Shit, what planet is he on? If anything this will do him a world of good and maybe get him back down to real earth." "I just hope you are right El, I just hope you are right," said Jay.

El pulled up Jay's driveway and switched the engine off. "Back home safe and sound," he said, bringing Jay back to the here and now. "Hey thanks man," Jay replied climbing out, "that was real good. And I know I have said it over and over again, but gees man, you two guys saved me. Fuck, seriously, don't know how I would have got through all of that if I had, had to do it alone."

El got out and took a long exaggerated, acknowledging stretch, "You would do exactly the same for us Jay, so yeh no worries brother and just glad you got out the other side all in one piece."

"Hey I'll open up the garage and then go get a couple of cold ones if you guys are keen," said Jay. "Sounds like a plan," replied Bee getting out and moving towards untying Jay's Kayak.

The three of them sat on the front deck, relaxing into the mission accomplished. Bee couldn't resist it any longer, wanting to get deeper into the zone and started rolling a large joint. He lit it up taking a coupe of deep drags before passing it along. Nothing was said, just the sounds of the crickets, the blue blackness of the night sky speckled with the fluorescent light of the stars. The warm, salty air, all permeating delectably through their senses, calming and soothing their spirits.

Then the empty beer tin caused Jay to get up and go and fetch another couple from the fridge. On the way back out, habit forced him to open up his backpack and reach in for his cell phone. Handing El and Bee another beer he sat back down again and switched on his phone. One, two, three messages came beeping through. "Shit brother you're a wanted man," said Bee.

Jay checked his phone, a couple of missed calls, a voicemail and two messages. He checked the messages, "Good day Jay, Bill here Mike's solicitor, give me a call when you get this message." "Good day Jay, Bill again, I need to speak with you, left you a voice mail."

El and Bee were both looking at Jay expectantly. "Dunno what that's all about," said Jay dialling into his voicemail, "Mike's solicitor wanting to talk with me." "Good day Jay," said the voicemail, "I need to speak with you quite urgently, please call me when you get this message." El and Bee were all ears, eager to hear what it was all about "Hmmm just wants me to call him urgently," he said, "weird." "Well give him a call then," said Bee sitting up, "It's a bit too late in the day now, I'll ring him in the morning."

They finished their beers and then El piped up, "Well, Bee, time to rock and roll," he said standing up not giving Bee, who was getting more and more comfortable, any option. "Yeh s'pose so," replied Bee reluctantly standing up. Jay got up too, tired and worn out, the beer and marijuana the cherry on the top, draining the last bit of resilience from his body.

They walked through and Jay stood at the door to see them off. The ute drove out and Jay waited watching the red glow of the tail lights take the corner at the end of the road. His mind was a million miles away deliberating with itself and so instinct took charge of his body, sending it back inside and into a steamy hot shower, then collapsing it face down on his bed.

His mind returned in the morning with a bang, opening his eyes wide, "Ok brother, time to sort your life out again," it said, subduing his body in place ensuring that he could focus on doing just that. "Fuck where do I start," he said out loud, "Antoinette, shit, wonder if she's phoned her dad, and the voicemail, shit I need to phone Mike's solicitor."

And then a bolt of liquid ice ran through his veins as he was reminded of the reality of his situation by his mind partner, "And don't forget that you need to find yourself a job too, time is ticking and the bills don't stop coming." "Oh fuck," he replied," the ice now reaching his extremities causing him to jump out of bed.

"Easy brother, it's not the end of the world, just prioritise, you know you can always climb onto another boat, so it's not a train smash." "True hey, ok what's the time," he thought looking at his phone. "Seven thirty, ok I'll make something to eat then give the solicitor a call, check out what he wants, then call Antoinette. When all that's sorted, hmmm, spend the rest of the day plotting the way forward with getting another job. And yeh maybe go down to the ski boat base and see if I can get a ride on another boat until I know where I'm headed." "Sweet," his mind partner said with a hint of sarcastic naivety, knowing that it wasn't going to be that simple, but happy to have some kind of direction.

"Ok so on this earth, it's body first," he said to himself, taking a packet of bacon out the freezer and putting it into the microwave to defrost. Then, after frying up the bacon, some tomatoes, mushrooms, and eggs, a couple slices of toast all washed down with a strong coffee, he was ready to get started. He picked up the phone and dialled out. "Bill Forbes and associates, Jill speaking how may I help you?" came the answer. "Good morning Jill, it's Jay here, Mike's crew. I have got a couple messages from Bill asking me to get hold of him." "Oh yes. Good morning Jay, Bill has been expecting your call, may I please make an appointment for you to come in and see him?" "Yeh sure. Do you know what it's all about?" "I'm not really at liberty to talk about it, but I know Bill would like to see you sooner rather than later." "Well, I will have some time on my hands over the next couple of days," Jay joked, "so it won't be an issue, whatever time suits you guys and I'll come over." "That's great, how about nine thirty this morning?" "Yeh no worries, replied Jay I will see you then." "Thank you Jay, that's great, we will see you at nine thirty then Bye for now." "Yeh see you later," Jay said, putting the phone down, and wondering what it was all about.

"Ok next," he thought, following on with his plan of action, "Antoinette," the word itself warming his body, then the reality hit, "shit wonder what her dad had to say" cooling it off a bit. Jay dialled her number and got no reply. He let out a sigh of disappointment, "Ok, then, best get tidied up and head on down town."

As with any small town, everyone sort of knew where everything was, even if you had never used it before, and so Jay knew where the solicitor's office was situated. He parked his car, and full of bacon and eggs bounded up to the first floor and into the reception.

"Hi, Jill," he questioned as the receptionist beamed a welcoming smile as he walked in. "Good morning Jay," she replied, as though she had known him her whole life, "thanks for coming in on such short notice. And my condolences too," she said, "gosh you have been through a bit of a tough time lately." "Yeh, thanks," he replied, "it's been a bit of a wild ride, but luckily I have had a huge amount of support from my friends, so made it through with not too much drama." "That's all good then. If you would like to take a seat, I will let Bill know you are here," she said smiling and picking up the phone.

Jay had hardly sat down when Bill came marching through, arm extended, "Jay, good to see you and thank you for coming in," he said grabbing Jay's hand and shaking it in earnest. "My condolences Jay, I know Mike and you were very close," and without giving Jay a chance to respond, continued, "come through, we have a bit to discuss," motioning Jay to walk ahead of him into his office.

"Hold any calls there, please, Jill," he said then turned and followed Jay in. "Take a seat Jay, I think you are going to need to be sitting for this." Jay sat down, Bill's words creating more questions than answers, straightening Jay's back and opening his ears wide. Bill locked both his hands behind his head and stretched backwards looking at the ceiling, and then keeping his hands together moved them to in front of him on the desk, he took a deep breath. "Ok," he said breathing out, "where do I start? Ok, so here in front of me I have Mike's last will and testament." Bill paused looking for a reaction from Jay, but there was none, so he continued. "You my friend are the sole beneficiary of all of Mike's assets."

Jay tilted his head and looked to the side, trying to comprehend what had just been said to him. He looked back at Bill waiting for more, some more explanation of what the lightning bolt he had just received meant. Bill read Jay's face and so gave more detail. "He had no other family Jay. He was a war baby, orphaned and adopted. No siblings that he knew of and both his adoptive parents passed on years ago."

Jay stood up, confusion and frustration evolving into mild anger. The inheritance had not even registered, the unknown life story, the unasked and untold story of Mike coming down on him like a brick wall as he realised once again just how little he had bothered to ask Mike about himself.

"Sit down Jay," said Bill, "I know what you are thinking, don't be too hard on yourself, I knew Mike very well, he was like a clam. Shut tight and wouldn't let anyone in. Sit down and I will read you something that

Mike wanted you to hear."

Jay sat down, his mind unable to deliberate with itself. Bill started to read, "Jay, my son," and like a cloudburst, the three words flooded into Jay's spirit and started pouring out through his eyes, streaming down his cheeks. "Now that I'm gone, and you can't take the piss, I just wanted you to know, that as hard as I was on you, you meant the absolute world to me. You were the son that I never had. Or should I say, you were my son. The times that we spent together were some of the best times of my life. You gave me back my youth, you allowed me to remember what love, laughter, fun and life were all about. You allowed me to live life and love living it. Thank you Jay, thank you."

Bill stopped and passed Jay the box of tissues. "And yes you need to get a real job, and so hopefully you will accept the one I'm about to offer you. I want you to become the skipper of our boat. The ocean, I know, is your favourite playground Jay, so go and play. Don't stop playing Jay, don't change, stay Jay. So if you will, I want you to inherit my estate, it's not huge by any standard, but please, I want you to have it, to treasure it and to grow it."

Bill could see that Jay was not taking this all in so stopped and gave him time to catch up and compose himself. But the amount of energy that the information had piled into Jay's spirit had 'maxed out' and it needed some time and space to digest it all so it directed Jay to speak. "Can you excuse me for a moment please Bill, this is all too much, I just need to get out for a bit," he said.

Bill stood up, "I understand Jay, please take your time, but please, I need to get a couple of the legal issues sorted out as soon as possible, so if you can, when you have digested it all, come back in so that we can finalise everything." "Yeh thanks I will," replied Jay through his mind partner who was trying to keep him in one piece." Jay got up shook hands with Bill and walked out the office. Jill looked up at his watery face and smiled sympathetically, "Take care Jay, these things take time," she said, "we will see you soon." "Yeh thanks," replied Jay, "thank you. I'll see you guys in a bit, just gotta get my head together, hmmm as I'm sure you can see," he said smiling embarrassingly.

Jay knew what he had to do, get to the ocean as soon as possible. Take a long walk along the beach. He parked his car and then his mind commanded his body to jog down the grass banks down onto the sand, in an attempt to avoid any more contact with anyone. He needed to be alone with his mind and soul, alone with his mind and soul in the restaurant of the spirit, to feed off of and fill up with Mother Nature's best. Mother natures calming, rejuvenating juices of invisible and ancient, exotic dimension.

He was miles down the beach when he stopped and sat down on the rocky outcrop, his body now light, warm and beautiful. He looked up at the magnificent blue expanse above, "thank You," he said, and then repeated with the utmost appreciative relief "thank You!" He took out a smoke and lit it up, took a deep drag then his mind partner now back in some control spoke, "Well that's the job part of the plan sorted brother." Jay answered, speaking out aloud, "That's no lie hey. Shit, I never saw that coming." "You can say that again." "That's no lie hey. Shit, I never saw that coming." Jay said again out loud, smiling at the same time as his mind partner cringed. "Hmmm that is so weak hey, so weak."

Jay, now having made his own peace, got up and started walking back towards the main beach and the closer he got, the more the reality of the here and now filtered through. "Ok, one thing left for ya to do today hey," came the message. "Shit, I must give Antoinette a call," he responded, reaching for his phone and then remembering that he had purposely left it behind in his vehicle. The whole self deliberation instinctively causing him to look up to where he had parked his car. He was still some distance away, but he could see that, even though most of the car park was empty, there was a vehicle parked right next to his. Two people standing out in front of it, leaning up against the bonnet. "Hmmm wonder who that is, he thought, picking up his pace, knowing that they must be there to speak to him.

As he got closer, the two frames became distinguishable, Jay's heart leapt in delight as his eyes received and sent through the visual waves of light. It was Antoinette, well Antoinette and Marco, but Antoinette was all Jay cared about right now. Another rush of deliciousness was released into his body as she waved down at him, causing him to break into a bit of a trot and then bound up the grass bank towards them. She came down to meet him as he got near the top and they met in a huge bear hugging embrace. Jay picking her up and twirling her around before placing her down and kissing her with every ounce of love he had. But Jay could sense that something was different as Antoinette buried her face deep into his neck. He couldn't quite work out what it was, but confirmation came through when Antoinette started sobbing. Gently at first, the mild convulsions becoming stronger and stronger as they reverberated through his body.

Jay pulled back a bit, holding her firmly by her shoulders. He looked into her eyes that were looking straight back at his in desperate watery redness. The sadness and frustration blatant. Antoinette hadn't spoken a word, but Jay's soul sank and withdrew as it deciphered the message coming through to it. But not wanting to believe it, his soul demanded he ask the question, "Hey my Antoinette, what's wrong?"

She looked down, sinking her face back into his neck and pulling him in close, unable to speak, as she continued to sob. Jay looked up over her towards Marco for an answer. He hadn't moved a muscle and was still sitting up against the bonnet of the car. He noted Jay's desperate questioning look, unfolded his arms opening them up in an 'I dunno brother' kind of motion, then stood up turned and walked in a circle, letting Jay know that a lot of shit had hit the fan hard and he did not have the answer.

Jay again took hold of Antoinette's shoulders, "Hey what's wrong," he asked again wiping the running makeup from her cheeks, and this time noting that she was immaculately dressed. "I have got to go back home," she said tears streaming down her face. "Hey calm down," whispered Jay, lifting her chin up so that she was looking at him. "What do you mean you gotta go back home?" "My dad was furious, he wants me to come back home," she blurted out between sobs.

Jay was listening but not registering, as he tried to calm her down. "Hey that's ok," he said. "No it's not ok, he doesn't understand or see any reason," she replied pulling away from Jay, "I want to be with you." "You will be with me," he reassured her.

"No, you don't know my dad . . . he doesn't want me to be with anyone, it's like he just does not want me to have my own life, it's like he is scared of losing me or something."

Jay looked back up at Marco, who tilted his head sideways in hopeless acknowledgement of the pain that was being unleashed. Jay grabbed hold of Antoinette's hand and walked her back up towards the car park. "Hey brother, said Marco, how's it going?" "Hey," said Jay, "shit has hit the fan big time hey?"

Marco didn't answer; he didn't have to, but then reiterated the dilemma, "Sis, we have to get going. We need to be at the airport sort of like right now," he said looking at his watch. His words drove hard into Jay's mind stunning it into confusion causing him to lose his breath. "I'm not going," said Antoinette, "he can't dictate to me like this." "No c'mon sis, he'll calm down. Go home, sit and speak with him, he'll be ok. He will understand and then you can come back down again." "No, I'm not going," she replied.

Marco looked across at Jay, willing him to make her see sense. Jay held her face gently, regaining his composure, "Hey my Antoinette," he said, "I'm not going anywhere, I'll be here for you. Just go sort it all out with your dad." She looked into his eyes searching for the belief that it would all turn out that way. She threw her arms around his neck and pulled his lips onto hers, pressing her body hard up against him in an attempt to melt into him and become one.

"We have to go now," urged Marco softly but with intent. Antoinette refused to let go and so Jay gently undid her arms and walked her around to the passenger door. "I gotta sort a few things out this side anyway," said Jay, "you go sort your side out and I'll prepare mine for you," he said smiling.

Antoinette climbed in, bent forward hiding her face in her hands, still sobbing uncontrollably. Marco walked around and shook Jay's hand tightly. "I'll catch you around brother." "You don't have to go back too?" "Yeh I will fly back with her, but then climb on the next plane back with another colleague to continue the business we started. I'll still be here for the next few months, so we will meet up for a few brews when I get back."

Jay nodded, the numbness continuing to ravage and deaden his body as Marco went around to the driver's side, jumped in, started up and reversed out. Antoinette looked up towards Jay as they started to pull away, but couldn't bare to see what she was leaving behind and buried her face back into her hands. Then, they were gone and Jay was left there standing in a pool of confusion and despair. His spirit in disarray leaving his body frozen and incapacitated in a bubble of slow motion. His senses numbed and unresponsive to everything around him.

When Jay got back home, he slumped down on the couch, his body tired, worn out. His mind out of control as it plummeted into the depths of despair. A thousand unanswered questions battering away as his mind partner sat silently contemplating how he was going to pull Jay out of his uncontrollable dive. "Don't worry brother, remember Gee? You went through a similar thing back then when she left, you'll pull through. You just have to give it some time." "No, this is different; I've never connected with anyone like this before. It's like she was part of me and now that part has been ripped away." His mind partner was strangely sympathetic, "Ah c'mon, man, you can do it, let it go, just let it go." "Fuck I don't want to let it go, I don't want to let Antoinette go, this is bullshit man." "You gotta do it brother, you're gonna make yourself sick."

Jay's mind in a state of frustrated confusion as disarray sucked all the sustenance it could from his body. For hours deliberating with itself, searching for the answers to find, lift and free his spirit which seemed to have withdrawn to deep within, lost, forlorn, smashed. The consequential erratic manufacture and presence of volatile chemicals in his body predictable. The pit of his stomach felt like cement, heavy, stuck and congested. Waves of unpleasant prickly heat spread in slow, deliberate spasms across his chest to underneath his armpits, grinding their way along his inner biceps. His cheeks prickled uncomfortably, his lower butt dull, stiff and sore, almost as if it was paralysed; his legs were heavy and unresponsive. He felt drained of all good energy, his whole body devastatingly tired and nauseous.

"How can her father demand to have her back? What an arsehole!" "Hey easy man, you are creating worry and shit for yourself for nothing. You know it . . . worry and doubt are the biggest waste of time and energy. If it's meant to be, then she'll be back and you would have wasted all this time and energy for nothing. And if it's not meant to be, well then she won't be back and you will still have wasted all this time and energy. Stop digging yourself a hole and just harden the fuck up," Jay's mind partner responded now starting to get a little more frustrated with him.

"Ah what the fuck," said Jay out loud and getting up, walked through to the kitchen and reached for the Tequila bottle. He flicked the top off, squashed it and threw it up against the wall, taking a deep slug swallowing it down and then taking a second.

He had had plenty of experience with alcohol and knew that this was one way he could temporarily shut his body down and off from the incessant and persistent questioning of his mind. Jay was not used to this brand of despair however. He was normally so confident, so at peace and in love with life. So used to being able to suck in and live off of nature's pleasures, to feed off of and meditate with her abundant energies. And now, it was as though everything had gone into rewind, and he was being siphoned dry.

"Ok brother, time to cool off and get back into the golden zone man," his mind partner coaxed gently as the initial effects of the alcohol started to fog the brain filtering the effect of his mind. "Go get a breath of fresh air and soak up the sunset."

Jay half smiled to himself, shaking his head slowly as he walked towards the ranch slider. "Yeh, whatever," he said trying to reassure himself, "what will be will be, it is what it is," his smile disappearing as his own words hit home. "It is what it is," he repeated despondently, "shit that just sounds so fruitless and so final," he breathed out and then took another deep glug from the bottle.

He lay down on the deck flat on his back, looking up at the sky, the hard wood comforting the myriad of aches and dull pains playing havoc along the length of his body. "Yeh I'll get over it," he thought as he watched the clouds play. Dancing, mixing, mingling and sharing their time and space with each other. The wind and departing rays of the evening sun, not wanting to miss out, joining in, creating a mystical world above. The mobile, melting pinks, whites, golds and blues entering through Jay's eyes into his mind and soul, his spirit. The ocean brought in on the breeze into his ears, the smell of the salt air and the feint chill of the evening on his skin, all doing the same.

Jay's body shuddered and erupted in goose bumps as his spirit reacted and expanded like a sponge to the sudden wash of universal fuels pouring in. "Mmm, thank you," he said softly knowing and believing that whoever had been responsible could hear his words of gratitude. Jay closed his eyes in an attempt to trap anything that had entered from leaving. He was, for the time being, in an induced peace and he wanted to stay there. His spirit now unwound, permeated outwards caressing the whole of his body as it did so warming it and allowing it to glow. His mind accepting and marginalizing the circumstances as it set the body up to glide on autopilot in semi sleep mode.

Jay loved being there, hovering in and around his body, letting go to travel into the spiritual dimensions then, just before he was too far gone, returning back with a bit of a nervous jolt, then try to recollect it all in detail before doing it all again. He would hold his being in this pre subconscious state for as long as he possibly could, before the luxury of letting go completely was overwhelming, and his body gave in to his spirit and shut down to sleep.

The chaos that ensued over the next couple of weeks was a relieving distraction to Jay. There was all the legal paperwork and stuff that had to be sorted out at the lawyer's office, the move into Mike's house, the rearranging, and the getting used to it all. Bee had decided that fishing was going to be a much better career choice for him and that he would now crew for Jay, then just top up his income with the odd electrical job. So he was at Jay's place just about every day, and if they didn't go out to sea they just worked on getting the boat and tackle ready. Or just went down to surf or to dive for crayfish. Marco came around regularly to sink a few cold ones and to keep Jay informed with what was going on back home with Antoinette keep him on an even keel.

It was around three weeks since Antoinette had gone back home, Bee and Jay had just finished packing the boat away after a solid day out to sea and walked upstairs and out onto the baloney. Jay strolled wearily across to the strategically positioned bar fridge and took out a couple of beers handing one over to Bee. "Shit man, life is so good hey," said Bee flopping down into the outside couch. "Just think about it, out to sea working hard," he stopped and smiled, "busting my arse to catch fish," he smiled again, "then back to this, my buddy's own pad, couple ice cold frosties, watch the sun go down. Shit man, this must be as close to perfection as you can get."

Jay smiled back, but didn't say anything. "Aaah, c'mon man, don't tell me you still pining for your cherry," continued Bee after noting Jay's limited response. "Yeh, I miss her like crazy." "When's she coming back?" asked Bee. "Dunno if she is, I get a text every day, but nothing to indicate that her dad has cooled off in anyway." "Hmmm I better not, aaah what the heck I'll say it anyway," said Bee, "What a fuckin' arsehole! Shit what is he? Some kind of dictator or something?" "Not sure what it's all about," replied Jay, "so, don't really wanna pass judgement or comment." "Fuckin' arsehole," muttered Bee as he got up to get another couple beers.

Bee was just on his way back to the couch when the doorbell rang. "Maybe that's her now," he said smiling. "Naah, that will be Macro hey," replied Jay, "he said he was going to pop in this evening." "Come on in!" shouted Bee down the stairwell. "Up here," he said as the door opened and Em and Marco came through. "Hey, Bee how's it going cousin?" said Macro, "All good brother, c'mon up."

Bee already had a few more beers ready to hand to them as they walked out onto the deck. Marco was beaming, almost glowing as he walked up to Jay and gave him a hug. "Hey brother, you are not going to believe it hey." Jay's eyes lit up from Marco's glow, expectant, and willing Marco to continue on. "She's flying back in." "No don't fuck with me," said Jay. "Seriously brother, not sure exactly when, but she's coming back down." "What the heck why didn't she tell me?" "Well," said Marco rather sheepishly, "she asked me not to say anything, kinda like, one, she wasn't quite sure if it was even going to happen right now and two, she said she wanted to surprise you." "Well how do you know it is going to happen then?" questioned Jay not wanting to get excited about potential only.

It was all Marco needed, he was busting to speak and tell Jay all his news "Well the ol'man phoned me to get my side of the story. Evidently Antoinette and he had a huge row in which she threatened to leave and never speak to him again. She's not eating, not working, and he is seriously worried about her. And he also seems to have now realised she is her own women and not his little girl anymore."

Marco took a deliberately long, slow glug of his beer to give Jay a chance to respond. And he did, "So yeah, don't stop there, what else, what did ya tell him about me, and what did he say about Antoinette coming back?" Marco now had Jay on a string and decided to play with him for a while, his demeanour changed, as he became more serious, "Well sorry man I had to tell him like it is, I told him you were a bit of an arsehole and if I had anything to do with it I wouldn't let Antoinette anywhere near you."

Bee and Jay looked at each other then back at Marco. Noting how well he had played them, he burst out laughing, picked up Em and twirled her around effortlessly. "No dumbass, I told him you are a real cool guy with amazing intentions, and that you have got a dream lifestyle to match. Man he was shocked, I think he had been grinding away, picking up bits and pieces of information then constructing this monstrosity of a vision of a delinquent commercial fishermen and his friend's beach bumbing on the coast somewhere in some hick town in the middle of nowhere. Looking back, I actually think Antoinette going back and having it out with him was the best thing that could have happened for everyone, especially him. I think his imagination had started to run a bit wild and was beginning to drive him around the bend. So," he said taking another deep gulp of beer and then holding it up high in celebration, "Antoinette is coming back down."

"Fuck this, I'm rolling a joint," said Bee. "Paaarty, talk about connecting the dots," he shouted out giving Jay a high five. "Hey Jay," said Marco, "please brother, don't tell her I told you, or not until she's down here anyway." Jay looked across at Marco and realising the strings were now in his hands, played them accordingly, "How much money you got?" he questioned threateningly, beaming from ear to ear.

Over the days that followed, knowing but not knowing when, was driving Jay to distraction. His entire being was on crazy fire, and he could not sit still for a minute. He knew it was going to happen, because of the subtle but noticeably more excited tone in Antoinette's texts. He could feel her bubbling over with excitement and anticipation, and that just turned the intensity of the heat up.

Bee had taken a couple of days off to catch up on an electrical job he had committed himself to, but that did not deter Jay from going out to sea. It was the one place that would keep him sane, patient and at relative peace until Antoinette got back. Bee had promised he would come down and give Jay a hand to launch and then come back down to help him load up again. He was, as always, true to his word. Besides which, anything was a good excuse for him to escape the binds of working on a building site so as he could get a sniff of the beach in the morning and afternoon.

"Shit you nailed it today," said Bee peering into the fish hatch which held about two hundred kilos of good sized reds. "Not bad, hey," replied Jay smiling and locking his fingers behind his head, stretching back and puffing his chest out in 'satisfactive' pride. "Sheeet, man, what the heck?" commiserated Bee, "that's my two days' work on site sitting in that hatch." "Snooze you lose boy," replied Jay smiling, "but don't worry brother, plenty more where those came from. When ya finishing up?" "Friday I'll be finished." "Oh well, on the bright side, you won't be missing out on any fishing over the next couple of days," said Jay. "The weather is moving up the coast tonight and looks like it will stick around until the weekend. So, your timing wasn't that bad after all. Well, excluding today that is," he winked. "That does give me a bit more peace of mind then," said Bee, genuinely distraught at missing the days' fishing and feeling kinda hard done by.

"Ah well I better get back on the job and make the most of it then," he said turning towards his van. "Hey Bee," shouted Jay out after him, "thanks a million for coming down to help me load up again brother. Much appreciated." "No worries," said Bee smiling back with a thumbs up. "Good catch man, good catch. Good on you," he said as he started up and drove off.

The fish buyers appeared as Bee's van drove up and off the access road to the slipway, almost as though they had been waiting for him to leave. They haggled with Jay for a bit, but soon gave in when they could see that he didn't really care about their game right now. They couldn't work it out, but he seemed to be in a different time and space to them lately. Their usual and predicted 'threats' of a flooded fish market dropping the price, of the broken freezers unable to hold fish, and the sudden unexplained lack of demand of a certain species that happened to have been caught that day, all which usually frustrated the skippers of boats to no end, just had zero effect on Jay. So they ended up huffing and puffing, but paying market price for the fish, loading them up and then knowing that they wanted more, reluctantly had to let their guard down and thank Jay for the fish. This ensured that he knew that they really appreciated being the first buyer to be called, but also insinuated that he was a hard man to deal with and that he didn't leave them with much of a margin to make a living out of.

Jay responded by thanking them for their business and then, with a knowing smile remarked to them on how great he thought their brand new 4x4 was. He winked, the buyers smiled, acknowledging defeat and also accepting Jay's veiled acknowledgment of their business prowess and achievements. Driving off they gave a loud toot and wave of appreciation on the way up the slipway access road.

When Jay got home he was tired and weary but had a strange yet very recognisable buzz of light, airy, bubbly anticipation deep inside his core. Although his wariness took centre stage the bubbles lifted his spirit and it permeated outwards, inquisitive and searching for the time to come. Searching for the energy it could taste and smell but couldn't yet see.

Jay parked and unloaded the boat then floated upstairs and into the shower, into his own very private time and space. Into the golden, misty zone where he could daydream about the times gone by, times to come. The where, what and why we are down here on earth. Without knowing or understanding how, he was able to take himself to places he wanted to be, travel beyond the body as he wondered, discussed and debated with himself and the Creator.

He didn't know what was going on in everyone else's head, but he knew within himself there was so much more to 'being' than just the body he was in right now. There had to be! So much unanswered mystic, myth and magic. Many, many, many generations had come and gone. But still no one actually knew what we were doing down here. He knew and could feel deep within that this wasn't the be all and end all. It excited him to know that there was still the most incredible discovery. The most incredible awaking to come.

Jay drifted out the shower, got a beer out the fridge and strolled out onto the wooden balcony. With still a couple of hours before sunset, he gazed out into the ocean that reflected a tranquil, fluid array of greens, blues, pinks and oranges pouring from the evening sky. His senses now in complete tune, capturing the energies surging towards him, soaking them up, and allowing them to flood his innermost spaces to overflowing, creating a channel for a consistent stream in, through and out. This allowed his mind to feed off of the food of the universe, and stay in a place where he could continue the journey and discussion. Ask the questions and receive the answers.

Dragging his eyes off of the distance, he watched as beachgoers walked to and fro, enjoying the late afternoon sunlight and the thrill of the weekend to come. Two dogs had met up and were bounding along together in a bliss and oblivion that could only be matched by that of a child. A fisherman stood watching the tip of his rod for any sign of life. It was one of those evenings when Jay just felt at one with life, not wanting or wishing for anything. But there was something, something that he just couldn't figure out. His shoulders were strangely warm, the warmth extending up into the base of his neck. Where was it coming from? Something was feeding in from a distance and he was experienced enough to know to expect the consequence. This excited him, the realisation and anticipation catching him off guard as his breath was taken away for an instant. He took a long gulp of the crisp beer, leaned on the rail, took a deep breath in to get a taste of the ocean air and thanked the Creator for this perfection and existence.

He was smiling from the inside and it came out into its physical form on his face, exuding everything that he had just taken in, when his cell phone alerted him to an incoming message. Jay got a sudden rush of goose bumps. A delicious rush starting in his thighs and passing up, into and along his arms. Intentionally slowing his whole body down, he kept the rush going for as long as he possibly could. Savouring it like a block of chocolate gently melting away in the mouth. The longer he held it, the more his heart rate picked up, his body becoming weightless. His self-deliberation continued on, "Crazy how an invisible sound can enter the physical body, pass into the mind, which then dictates back to the physical, instructing it to release a surge of delicious celestial chemicals" he thought, and thanked the Creator again for this ability and wonder. "Wonder what it is? How does it all work? Shit man, wish I could understand it a bit better and bring it in on demand."

Jay subconsciously started moving towards the table where he had left his phone, picked it up, and flipped it open. "1 new message from Antoinette." This time the energy entering through his eyes into his mind and back out into his body, forcing him to gasp a breath of the fresh, salt-filled air. He lingered again soaking up the heat and pleasure before reading the message.

Hey my Jay I'm back! ☺

"Shit," he said without even thinking. Went to pick up his beer, put it down again without taking a sip, walked inside then came back out, picked up the beer again and took a deep slug. "How the heck does she do this to me?" he whispered to himself. Picked up his phone and replied

*Wow gosh man don't do that to me! ☺ Where are you?*

The main beach car park, forgotten which place is yours since you moved.

His heart was beating so fast and hard now that he thought that if he was ever going to have a heart attack, this would surely be the time. It felt like it had swelled right up into his throat and even his ears were starting to beat to the rhythm.

*"Walk down towards the south for about three hundred meters. I'll be waiting in front for you.*

Ok see ya soon. Love ya!!! ☺

The adrenalin, now sending his heart rate through the roof and his breathing into some erratic drowning mode, Jay tried to calm himself down. He was well practiced at it, so had sort of regulated his essential bodily functions by the time he felt the sea sand between his toes, even though he couldn't quite remember his journey down from the balcony, through the house, out into the garden and over the sand dunes. "Shit I must have teleported down here," he thought and smiled as he said out loud, "seriously I must have teleported down here. Wish I could bring that in on demand!"

With his eyes glowing with anticipation and desire, he looked north trying to discern between the other figures on the beach and his most beautiful. Nothing! Minutes dragged. He walked back up to the top of the dune to get a better view, back down, then up again. Nothing! "What the heck?" he mumbled anxiously, then his phone went off again.

Just locking the car, be there in five ☺

*Cool I'm down on the beach waiting for you.*

Jay sat down on top of the dune and with his eyes still focused north, picked up a handful of sand, clasped it and then let it run slowly out, forming a tiny little mound between his legs. After about the third mound, he saw the beautiful bounce and sway that he so yearned for. She was still a silhouette in the distance, but he knew it was her. Jay swallowed hard and took an uncontrollably deep breath. He stood up and gave a long, slow, high deliberate wave of his arm. Antoinette responded immediately, she knew exactly what he was feeling, she had felt it all.

Although they couldn't quite work it all out, they had known for sometime that they were connected. From that first time on the beach when he had come off the water from fishing and they saw each other, the peace, tranquillity and pleasure of them being in each other's presence was frighteningly evident to them both. Frightening because they were, in human terms, complete strangers, yet wanted to immediately experience each other's wholeness and being.

Then there were those times when she had walked onto the beach full of people. Jay knew she has arrived without even seeing her. And without even looking she knew he was there. And when they came towards each other, and they looked into each other's eyes, the energies entering each of their bodies quashed the myriad of activity taking place around them into a misty blur of silence, as the most delicious warmth overcame their entire bodies.

Jay instinctively started walking down the dune in

Antoinette's direction. Her body automatically breaking
into a trot, then she started to walk again when reality
kicked in as she wondered what anyone watching her
might be thinking, but then dispatched that thought to
the winds and started to jog towards Jay again. He had
continued to walk towards her, rather than waiting for
her to 'arrive' he couldn't help it, the force of attraction
was immense and instinctive.

"Hey," he said and his whole body smiled. Antoinette
buzzed, her body literally vibrating. "Hi ya," she beamed.
"Woaw you back," he said as she leapt into his arms and
threw hers around him in a vice-like grip. Jay put her
down and held her face so that he could look at her, and
believe that this was all actually happening, and he hadn't
just lost himself in the shower somewhere.

"My Antoinette," he said, his eyes blurring as the tears
welled up. Tears were pouring down her face as their lips
came together, their spirits igniting in purple heat as they
fused in perfect dance. The whirlwind not allowing their
bodies to part until they were satisfied that this was all
real and that the universe had finally created time and
space for them to be together.

As they idled shoulder-to-shoulder back up the sand
dune towards the house, Jay was the first to speak, "Why
didn't you tell me you were coming," he asked. "Well I
knew I was coming back, but didn't know exactly when,
until yesterday. And I wanted to surprise you," she
bubbled in a way only she could, pulling him close. They
looked at each other, bumped shoulders and continued
the walk back to the house in the perfect silence of
footsteps, heartbeats, breath and ocean.

Jay opened the door and they walked in. He closed
the door, and they turned and faced one another. They

both knew what was about to come, but were vibrating so high on the desire alone, they wanted it to last for as long as possible. So they just stood, there kissing each other with their eyes.

Jay's hands held her hips. Antoinette had her arms around his neck. The waves of energy surrounding them, causing their bodies to sway gently in perfect motion. It was as though they wanted their inner most energies to exude outwards and assimilate, taste and feel each other and become one. They gazed at each for ages, loving and living the moment, their groins uncontrollably pressed hard together.

"Mmm I missed ya so much," Jay said in a low, gentle, almost growl. Antoinette closed her eyes, pulling him towards her. Their lips met, mouths both just open enough for their lips to clasp each other's in perfect, gentle deliciousness. Their mouths and tongues becoming ever more eager and uncontrollable as they slipped into the dimension they so yearned for. They were now holding each other so close and so hard they had literally became one. Their hands exploring each other's upper bodies, demanding and determined not to allow any skin to go untouched or unloved. Their bodies were each other's bodies and they wanted to feel them, caress and own them.

Jay moved both hands back down to her hips then slowly up towards underneath her armpits. His thumbs reaching over onto her bra. Antoinette moved her shoulders back a bit to allow his hands to go further. Jay caressed his right hand over the left cup of her bra and into the second. His hand filled with her firm, silky soft breast and he gently rolled his fingers over her nipple, causing her to exude a deep hum. They opened their eyes, parted lips and smiled together as though in a ballet. "Gosh, you're beautiful," said Jay quietly.

They continued staring at each other smiling and swaying together for who knows how long until on some perfect and distant understanding their eyes closed and their mouths came together again searching deep, feeling, grasping and tasting.    Antoinette had unconsciously allowed herself to be pressed up against the wall, both their pants were now undone and open, as their hands got more ambitious and even more explorative. Jay sank down to his knees and very slowly and gently, slid her pants down around her ankles, making love to her belly button with his tongue, while his hands loved her legs and bum.

His hands firm but soft, warm and gentle knew exactly what the parts of her body wanted and needed. Neither of them even knew what they were doing anymore, they had both gone to where they wanted to spend the rest of their lives. Together in an unidentified explosion of brilliant and timeless emptiness. The physical was just the part of being human on this earth, and came so naturally to them that they knew it was meant to be. But this was so much more than just the physical connecting, there was an understanding, a fusion, a bonding so beautiful and beyond the human it could never be restrained. It was from an ancient time and space. They just hadn't figured it all out yet.

Antoinette was grasping Jay's head as he moved down towards her pleasure zone. He transferred everything he had through his hands, fingers, mouth and tongue to deep within. She groaned and gasped for air and her eyes opened and closed involuntarily as their body's minds and souls worked in perfect unison and harmony. A kaleidoscope of juices rushing through her body, the ice-cold heat, lighting up every hair on her body and when she couldn't resist it any longer, it culminated in an explosion and release of celestial energies as she climaxed. Her eyes shut tight seeing deep into space and then opened wide seeing nothing as her whole body shook with uncontrollable pleasure and satisfaction.

Jay experienced every bit of it, they were one, connected in every way, and he wanted more, he wanted never to be disconnected again. If he could swallow her whole right then and there he would have.

"Come here," gasped Antoinette between breaths, as she grabbed his head and guided him back up towards her mouth. She kissed him long and hard, searching with her tongue, wanting to lock their mouths together forever. She pulled him in close and held him tight. His hands couldn't stop, and he was in the perfect nowhere land, when he felt the wall against his back. Antoinette had swung him around at will, parted mouths and was on her way down before Jay even came back to earth. "Ooouch," he whimpered in pleasure as he massaged her sweet head as he was sent into oblivion. When he couldn't take it anymore, he fell to his knees; Antoinette straddled him, giggled and then took him in. They both held on tight and sank their mouths into each other again.

This was as close and connected their minds, bodies and souls could get on this earth. Unknowingly they were achieving what they subconsciously craved all day and every day since birth. This wasn't just making love; this was the consequence of the complete assimilation and ubiquitous state of two ancient spirits. Born together in time and space unknown, separated by travelling different journeys, then born on earth to learn grow, search and find each other again.

Jay tore his mouth away, reached out backwards, leaned on his hands and thrust his hips upwards as his body called time and erupted. Every muscle filled with blood and pumped up like rock as his eyes were forced closed and he went into erotic paradise. As with Jay, Antoinette felt every bit of what he had, she watched him quivering all over, and thrusting herself downwards to take as much of him as possible they reached their desired pinnacle together.

Jay lay down on his back and Antoinette followed down on top of him, burying the side of her face perfectly into the hollow between his shoulder and chest. He opened his eyes and stared into a haze of blue, red, pink and purple. He didn't even think about what it was, or if it was even real. He actually couldn't even think right now, even if he wanted to. He held her by the shoulders and gently pushed her upwards. She looked into his misty blue eyes and he saw that hers were filling with tears, "I missed you like crazy, my Jay, and gosh, I love you so much," she said wriggling free of his grip and burying her face back into his chest.

Neither of them were sure if they had slept or not, but it was dark when Antoinette whispered in his ear, "Hey Jay, do you think you could take me flying with you?" Jay hugged her and asked, "Where do you want to go?" "I don't care, I just want to fly away with you and be with you forever." Jay gently rolled her off of him and stood up, pulling her up with him. "Come," he said, let's go have a shower first."

The fine spray and steam warmed their bodies as they soaked up the waters juices and fed them through to massage and soothe their souls. Holding each other, swaying to the invisible perfection, Jay soaped her down, caressing every inch of her perfect silky skin and then she did the same to him. They climbed out the shower and Antoinette turned her back to Jay as he dried her off before he guided her through to his bedroom and dressed her in one of his T shirts, then laid her down.

Now in the most brilliant trance, she smiled at him, pulling him down next to her. They lay there on their backs, mesmerising each other with their heat, body fragrance, breath and delectable touch. Hands clasped, Jay breathed, "Ok close your eyes and believe," he said, "don't think, just let go, come with me, transcend and we will fly up and kiss the moon."

Their bodies were of the most comfortable warmth, beating as one, as they drifted into the ultimate numbness, into the perfect golden silence, weightless and free. Both of them shuddered with magnificent delight as their spirits started to move from the hanger, the transparent glimmer of the now purple moonlight lighting up the runway, delighted in showing off their spirits as they silently caressed their way outwards in the most unique brilliance of cosmic colour. And then, they were gone.

Bee was already loading the boat the next morning when Marco came to a screeching halt on the grass next to him, "Hey Bee thank fuck, man. Shit I've been going crazy man, have you seen Jay or Antoinette?" "Hey Marco," he replied in his usual 'no worries' kinda way, "no, not yet, but I'm sure he'll be down in the next few minutes, most probably double checking on the ocean and weather conditions or something." "And Antoinette, have you seen Antoinette?" questioned Marco none the less frantically. Bee somehow recognised Marco's intensity and stopped what he was doing. "No brother, didn't even know that she had landed this side again." Marco continued on blurting out in semi panic, "She flew in late yesterday afternoon, I was expecting a call from her, but didn't worry because I knew exactly where she would be headed. I waited up for her then fell asleep on the couch. When I woke this morning, still nothing man."

Bee was still not phased about it all; he was not used to this kind of worry and concern amongst adults, and would not give it a second thought if it were him. He knew what Jay and Antoinette would be up to and so, what the heck, live, love and let live and love man. So he just continued listening to Marco rant on. "Just been to the airport man, she hired a car, I checked it all out and then went to the beach and there it was, just parked there. I waited and waited. I texted both Antoinette and Jay, I tried phoning them, but nothing man, nothing. What the heck is going on? Shit I'm beginning to panic a bit man."

Bee hopped down off the boat. "Easy brother, you worried about shit man, slow down, you gonna have a heart attack or something man. Come, let's go check up inside. But be prepared, he said smiling, don't know what we gonna find."

Bee's calmness made its way into Marco's space and he smiled back, accepting Bee's energy and relaxing into it a bit. Marco's smile broadened and he shook his head putting his guerrilla sized arm around Bee,s shoulder, "Yeh, sorry man, old habits die hard. I have got to learn to let go hey. I have got to learn to let go."

Bee walked up to the door and tried it. It was as usual unlocked, so he walked in and then knowing Jay, he thought it best to make his presence known, just in case. "Hey, Jay, you coming fishing man? Shit! The day's nearly over. What's up?" He paused thinking about what he had just said and then broke out in a huge grin, "Hmmm, what's up, maybe that's a poor choice of words," he said to Marco beaming from ear to ear.

But no response from Jay, nothing. Bee shrugged his shoulders, still unconcerned, "Oh well, you leave me no option then," he said bounding upstairs with as much intentional noise he could possibly make, Marco in hot pursuit.

Bee pointed to the pile of clothes at the entrance to the bedroom, "Told you," he said proudly to Marco, emphasising how Marco had worried himself for absolutely no reason. "Hey Jay, time to rock and roll brother, I know how warm you all are on that nest of yours but we gotta earn a livin' hey," he said nosing his way cautiously into the bedroom as they both peeped around the doorway, nervous as to what they might be walking into.

The vacuum of whisper quiet stillness drew them deeper into the room and to the edge of the bed, where they both peered down at Jay and Antoinette. The beautiful peace of the both of them lying there filtering up to deep within Bee and Marco, mesmerising them into a tranquil, trancelike state. As they continued to stare, Bee was able to speak first, "Are they sleeping?" he whispered. "I don't know, they must be," said Marco in his lowest voice possible. Bee moved in slow motion bending over to put his ear close to their faces. He stood back up in even slower motion. "They're definitely breathing," he whispered, his mouth staying open in awe at the sight of their unconscious beauty. "Must have been a good night," he said. "Do you think we should wake them?" asked Marco. "Naah," replied Bee, "leave them be, they are miles away, let's go grab a cup of coffee and wait for them to come back down to earth."

Marco smiled, and again put his huge arm around Bee, this time pulling him in and giving him a lung squashing bear hug. Then they tiptoed out and into the kitchen and put the jug on the boil. "Thanks Bee, thanks so much. Shit you saved me man. Tell you what though, I just can't wait for them to get back hey, I'm missing them already man." Bee smiled, "Me too man, me too."

The End

www.ingramcontent.com/pod-product-compliance
Lightning Source LLC
Chambersburg PA
CBHW062136170626
46813CB00002B/722